THE TIME ELEMENT
and Other Stories

JOHN O'HARA

THE
TIME
ELEMENT

AND OTHER STORIES

RANDOM HOUSE · NEW YORK

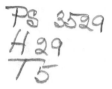
Library of Congress Cataloging in Publication Data
O'Hara, John, 1905–1970.
The time element, and other stories.
I. Title.
PZ3.03677Ti   813'.5'2   72–5133
ISBN 0–394–48211–5

Manufactured in the United States of America
by The Book Press, Brattleboro, Vt.
98765432
First Edition

FOREWORD

This is the first of several projected volumes of O'Hara stories comprising work that either was not published in any form during the author's lifetime, or was published in periodicals but not collected by him for a book. He left an impressive number of both, in addition to many unfinished stories and the beginnings of novels that he had put aside but kept, with the apparent intention of returning to and completing them.

The stories presented here all seem to have been written during the 1940s, most of them in the second half of that period. Sixteen were published within the decade, and four subsequently. Nearly all of the unpublished stories can be approximately dated by the author's return addresses on the typescripts; "The Favor" can also be so dated, even though *The Princeton Tiger* did not publish it until 1952, and likewise "At the Cothurnos Club" and "All I've Tried to Be," which *Esquire* bought in typescript in 1972. The reason for placing "That First Husband" (*Saturday Evening Post,* 1959) with these stories is the author's statement in his Foreword to *Assembly* (1961) that he had written no short stories for eleven years before he began again in 1960.

Though future information might date the stories more precisely, they appear to belong together, and to belong with *Pipe Night* (1945) and *Hellbox* (1947). And if the author had not abruptly stopped writing short stories in 1949, he almost certainly would have collected a new volume in the early fifties that would have included most if not all of these stories.

The abandonment of short-story writing coincides in time with, and may in part have been the result of, O'Hara's break with *The New Yorker* after twenty-one years of continuous and astonishingly frequent appearance in its pages. The break was caused by an extremely negative *New Yorker* review (August 20, 1949) of *A Rage to Live* and probably explains his failure to collect and publish the stories in this volume, fifteen of which appeared in that magazine in the three years between November 1946 and November 1949. When amicable relations were restored nearly eleven years later, and he embarked on his second and final great period of story writing, he did not need, perhaps did not even remember, the earlier work for the six big collections he published in the sixties.

In the forties O'Hara was already producing more stories than the periodicals hospitable to him could absorb; of the fifty-seven stories in *Pipe Night* and *Hellbox,* twelve had not had magazine publication. In the sixties, when some of the markets had disappeared and many of his stories were much longer than the earlier ones, the ratio shifted to such a degree that he seemed to be writing for books primarily, with magazines a secondary interest: seventy stories, or slightly more than half of those included in the six collections, had not appeared in magazines, and there are many others from that period that are still unpublished.

Not all of the stories eligible by date of composition, in both the published and the unpublished categories, have been included in this collection, and their exclusion rests only on editorial judgment that they are below the level or lack the special interest of those that are included. There are several stories here, published and unpublished, that are less good than the majority and about which it can be said that "they do not enhance the author's reputation." His reputation does not need enhancing nor can it suffer from the exposure of work below the level of his best, and I believe that even the least story in this volume has something about it that the many admirers of his total work will be happy to have the opportunity to read along with others that are among his best. There is one not very characteristic story about which the comments of readers and reviewers are especially interesting to look forward to, because after many readings of it, I am as much baffled as intrigued: "The War," which is not dateable by the methods cited. I think I know what its intention is, though I cannot say that it succeeds or explain it to myself or to those to whom I have shown it; but I wouldn't dream of leaving it out.

Albert Erskine

CONTENTS

CONTENTS

THE TIME ELEMENT
and Other Stories

ENCOUNTER: 1943

Allen was standing near the curb, waiting with the other people to cross Forty-sixth. He was glad he wore his muffler and he wished he knew where his gloves were. The last cheating taxi whizzed past and the cops' whistles blew and Allen was ready to move when he got the little punch in the ribs. It wasn't a hard punch, feeling it, but it must have started as a pretty hard punch to feel as much of it as he did through his overcoat, and without looking he knew who it was all right.

"Hey," she said, and he looked down and around, and it was Mildred all right. She was grinning.

"Hyuh," he said.

"Didn't they get you yet?" she said.

"Didn't who?" he asked, then, "Oh. No, I'm too smart for them."

"Yeah, I'll bet," she said. Somebody bumped her. "Which way you going, I'll walk along with you."

"Just uptown," he said. "I'm not headed anywhere in particular."

"Well! Then we could go some place and have a beer or something. I'd like to *talk* to you."

They were walking slowly uptown. "What about?"

"What about?" she said. "Anything. Mutual acquaintances. Or maybe you do' wanna sit and talk and have a drink with me."

"I do' wanna sit and have a *fight* with you," he said.

"Why do we *have* to fight? We don't have to fight if you control your temper and so forth. Let's go down the street to Eddie Spellman's."

"All right," he said. They turned at Forty-seventh.

"Now *don't* do me any *favors*," she said. "If you rather not go, say so now but don't act disagreeable when we get there."

"They'll think I'm Victor Mature," he said.

"Yeah? *They* will, but *I* won't. Oh, you mean *polite*. Victor Mature isn't polite. He's a blabber-mouth."

"I jist mentioned the first name of an actor that came into my head," he said.

"Well pick one that's polite if that's what you mean. Herbert Marshall. Ronnie Colman. But don't pick Victor Mature if you're picking a person for their politeness. My God! Victor Mature polite! Anybody as dumb as you I'm surprised you had the sense enough to wear an overcoat if you're that dumb. You'd be more typical if you came out in a bathing suit."

"All right," he said. They turned in at Spellman's and went straight back to a booth. A bald-headed Irishman came to them before they had sat down.

"Well, here's a couple of strangers for you," he said.

"Hello, Eddie," they said.

"But don't go start getting ideas," said Mildred.

"Now I wasn't getting no ideas, Mrs. Allen. I only made the statement that it was a pleasure to see a couple of old customers."

"That's all right, Eddie," said Allen. To her: "A rye?"

"No," she said. "Why do I have to have a rye? Because it's cheaper? I think I'll have a Ballantine's and soda and with some lemon peel in it."

"I'll have a rye," said Allen.

"Right," said Eddie, and went away.

"That Mick will have us in bed by five o'clock," said Mildred.

"You never liked him," said Allen.

"He never liked me, so why should I like *him?*"

"You're crazy. Eddie likes everybody," said Allen.

"All right, he likes everybody, then I don't want to be everybody and be liked by Mr. Spellman."

"Well, only—you suggested going here," said Allen.

"Because I assure you only because I ran into you. I assure you I didn't give him or his lousy joint a thought since the last time we were here together two years ago, and I never would of given it another thought for another two years if it wasn't that I ran into you."

"How are conditions at the 21 and the El Morocco?" said Allen.

"If that was intended for sarcasm it just shows how wrong you are. I was at Elmer's twice last week if you want some information."

"Who said anything about Elmer's?"

"See? That's how much you and your sarcasm. Elmer's is what they call the El Morocco."

"Don't get me wrong. I believe you go to them places. Once in a while I read the papers."

"When somebody leaves them on a subway train," she said.

"When somebody leaves them on a table at the Automat," he said. A waiter, not Eddie, served their drinks. They drank. She drank about half of hers and looked at him, at his face, his hair, his tie, both shoulders.

"Did I ever sleep with you? I can't believe it," she said.

"No, it was two other fellows," he said. "Or twenty."

"I'll hit you right across the mouth with this bag, you talk like that to me. You started it, you with that little bum off the streets from Harrisburg."

"All right, I apologize. Only I don't know what you expect me to do. Sit here and take it while you look at me like I was a ghost and then come out with 'Did I ever sleep with you?' "

"I shouldn't allow myself to even get mad at you."

"Then why do you?"

"Oh, it isn't because I'm still in love with you. Don't think that, for God's sake. I *don't* even get mad at you. I get mad at myself. My God, seventeen years old . . . Say, I *voted.*"

"Yeah? Who for?"

"None of your business. I don't have to tell who I voted for. I didn't tell—anybody else. A lot of people asked me to vote for certain people because they knew it was my first vote and they all said to get started right, then when 1944 came along I'd know which way."

"I get it," he said.

"You get what?"

"It's easy. The gang I see your name in the paper with, they were all for Dewey."

"Very clever, aren't you? Well, I'm not admitting anything, see? Oh, what about you?"

"Who did I vote for? Al Smith. That's the last person I voted for."

"I didn't mean that. I mean, where are you in the draft?"

"Where do *you* think?" he said, sipping his drink.

"I don't *know*. You could put your mother down for a dependent, and are you all right again?"

"Go on," he said.

"That's right," she said. "I guess you're over age too."

"I'm surprised I didn't see you in some Waac uniform or something."

"Is that a crack?"

"No. You mean a corny crack about wacky? Give me credit for better than that."

"Well, I never can tell with you," she said. "Do you think I have time for another drink?"

He laughed. "How should I know?"

"My date," she said. "Oh, that's right, I didn't tell you what time I had the date for." She looked at the bar clock. "No, I guess not. I'm going to a cocktail party but I have to meet some-body before I go."

"You're right up there, aren't you?" he said.

"What do you mean?"

"Cocktail parties. Elmer's. All that big stuff."

"Well, why not?"

"Sure. Why not? You're young, and you're a dish."

"You think so, Harry?"

"I still got eyes," he said.

"Well, thanks for the compliment," she said. "I apologize for what I said when we came in. About rye being cheap. You were always all right with money when we had it. It wasn't money that was your trouble—*our* trouble."

"Thanks, kid," he said. "I guess you better blow now or you'll be late."

"Don't you want me to stay for another? We aren't fighting now."

"No, but maybe in two minutes we would be," he said.

"Maybe you're right," she said. She stood up. "Well, I guess I better say goodbye. I'd like to see you sometime, Harry."

"Why?"

"Didn't we get along all right just now? We had a little scrap but we ended up all right. Here—" She reached in her purse and tore the back off a pack of matches. "That's where I live. Give me a call."

"All right," he said.

"Don't forget," she said. "G'bye." She smiled and left.

From his corner of the booth Allen called out to Eddie, who came back and stood at the table. "Yes, Harry," he said.

"Could you let me have a quart?"

Eddie rubbed his hand over his smooth bald head. "I don't know, Harry. That tab is gettin' pretty big and you oughtn'ta be drinking so's it is." He turned his head, looked in the direction in which the girl had gone, then he looked at his diamond ring. "All right, Harry. I'll wrap it for you."

CONVERSATION AT LUNCH

We were lunching—Harmon Gray and I—at the Cothurnos Club when I happened to look up at the moment Norbert Abbott was passing our table. He kept on going, joining another actor at the opposite end of the dining room.

"Did you see who that was?" I asked Harmon Gray.

"I saw him," said Harmon.

"But I guess he didn't see you."

"No, I guess not," said Harmon.

I myself never had met Norbert Abbott. All I knew about him was what everyone knew: that he had made a spectacular triumph in his first good part on Broadway, the part of a petty and despicable sponger in a very successful play of Harmon's that had run two years before. Harmon had picked him out of nowhere; and from that play Abbott had gone directly to a national reputation via Hollywood.

"What kind of fellow is he?" I asked.

Harmon looked out the window before answering. "I don't really know," he replied. "I don't honestly know."

"He certainly was good in the part of a heel," I said.

Harmon nodded. "He was perfect."

"And he owes you a lot," I added.

"No," said Harmon. "He doesn't owe me anything. He was so perfect in the part that without him I don't think we'd have had a play. Oh, that isn't false modesty. The play was there, but

I can't think of anyone else who could have played it; so he doesn't owe me anything, I don't owe him anything. It just worked out fine all around." Harmon raised his fork; but when it was halfway to his mouth, he lowered it. "Of course, I was a little sore when he walked out and went to Hollywood. If he'd stayed, we could have got a few more months out of it. However, I ought to know by this time what actors are like."

We dropped the subject of Abbott, and I asked Harmon what he himself was doing these days. He replied that he had been fooling around with an idea, and he told me a little something about it; but while he was talking, he seemed to have something else on his mind.

I couldn't help noticing, and I said, "Listen, Harmon, if you'd rather not talk about it—"

He smiled again. "No. I'm sorry. It isn't that I don't want to talk about the new play, but damn it all, that question of yours, what kind of guy is Norbert Abbott—I really ought to know more about him than I do. That's a serious oversight on a writer's part, to have worked with a fellow as closely as I did with him and still not know any more about him than I do." He didn't say any more, but through the rest of our lunch I could see he was bothered.

Harmon and I usually went to the library after these rare lunches of ours, but this time he suggested having our cigars at the table. Presently I saw why: Norbert Abbott finished his own lunch and was on his way out when he saw Harmon. He came to the table with a big smile and outstretched hand. "Why, hel-lo, Harmon," he said. Harmon introduced me, and Abbott accepted Harmon's invitation to sit down for a demitasse. They chatted comfortably for a few minutes. Not only was Harmon pleasant; he seemed to me actually respectful to the younger man. Then it came.

Harmon cleared his throat. "Norbert, I saw in the paper that you're going back to the Coast this afternoon."

"That's right. The Century."

"That's what I read. I was hoping I'd have a chance to talk to you before you left, but this is as good a time as any. Mr. Kerry here is an old friend, and he knows all my secrets. The truth is, Norbert, you know I haven't had a play since yours; and —well, bluntly, could you let me have a thousand till I finish the one I'm doing now? It'd be for only a short time, and I'm quite sure there's a picture sale in the new play, but right now—"

"A thousand," said Norbert Abbott.

"Less than half a week's pay, I happen to know," said Harmon.

"Yes, you're right about that, but you know it isn't all clear, Harmon. Taxes, expenses, and I have a lot of new cousins—you know how it is." He laughed feebly. "I'll tell you what I'll do, though. I'll talk to my manager the minute I get back to the Coast, and if he lets me have a thousand, it's yours. Of course, those managers are tough. He has me on an allowance, just as if I were a schoolboy, but I'll put it up to him as a special case. How's that?"

"Why, that'd be fine," said Harmon.

Norbert Abbott made his exit, and I looked at Harmon Gray. "I didn't know you were in a jam," I said.

"I'm not," he said, "but at least we got an answer to that question of yours."

"Well, that was pretty cruel of you," I laughed. "You had me convinced."

"Thanks. Incidentally I also proved something else to my own satisfaction, after two years."

"And what's that?" I asked.

"That I'm a good type-caster," said Harmon Gray.

PILGRIMAGE

Mr. Brennan pulled another sheet of yellow paper out of his typewriter, squeezed it into something like a ball, and shot it like a marble into the wastebasket. He put in a fresh sheet and typed out, "The Sports Whirl, by Tim Brennan. New York, November 8," and stopped. He reached into the basket and took out a couple of pieces of crumpled paper, read over what he had written, and tossed the papers back again. There was a tapping on the door of his hotel room and he opened it to admit a short young man who had "Valet" written on his uniform.

"Come in, son," said Mr. Brennan. "Got my suit all ready, eh?"

"Yes, sir." The young man hung the suit in the closet.

"What's the damage?" asked Mr. Brennan.

"Sir?"

"How much do I owe you?"

"You can put it on the bill or whichever you like. One twenty-five."

Mr. Brennan picked up the money from some stuff on the bureau. "One twenty-five, and fifty for you. O.K.?"

"Yes, sir. Thank you," said the young man. "Say, you're going to the game, huh?"

"Yes, covering the game."

"Oh, a newspaper reporter," said the young man. He examined the press ticket which was lying on the bureau. "What paper, may I ask?"

"The Centreport *Times,* Centreport, Indiana."

"Oh, yes. Indiana. That's where Notre Dame is. I had a friend in the Army worked in the Studebaker plant where they have Notre Dame College. The same town. I guess you get passes to all the fights and so forth? I never cared much about football, but baseball and fights . . . Of course, I follow all sports to some extent."

"Yes, so do I," said Mr. Brennan.

"I see. I guess they pay all your expenses on like these trips."

"Oh, yes."

"Uh-huh. That oughta be worthwhile, if a person cared about sports. I couldn't of done it, though. I was a very poor speller when it came to spelling words. I have my kid is seven years old and I wouldn't put it past him if he could spell better than me. Well, in a coupla years."

"Yes. I have a grandson about that age, and they're smart as a whip these days. Of course, they have different methods of teaching nowadays."

"Oh, yes. Yes, I guess so. Well, sir, anything else I can do for you?"

"No—uh. That's—uh—half a dollar is all right, I mean for a tip? I don't get East—"

"Oh, plenty, thanks. Yes, sir. Good night, sir," said the young man, closing the door.

Mr. Brennan would have liked to talk some more with the young man. Whether he was in Centreport, where he knew more people than any other man in town (the time he met Willkie, that was the way he had been introduced—Tim Brennan, knows more people than any other man in the *county,* not just the town), or on a trip like this or the other time he had come to New York, when Christian Keener Cagle was playing for the Army, Mr. Brennan liked to chat with people and get their opinions and different points of view and so forth. Great or small, it didn't matter to Mr. Brennan. Rockne, of course, he had known personally from going up to South Bend once or twice every year to get a slant on the new material. Zuppke, Stagg, Yost, Crisler— he had met all of them several times and had had long talks with them. He had corresponded with Eckersall. The big ones were just like anybody else once you got to know them, and it was the same in politics or business as it was in sports. On the other trip to New York, to see Cagle play, he had sat up till late talking to a citizen that only turned out to be a vice-president of the General Motors Corporation, that was all. One year, he got a smoked turkey at Christmas from Steve Hannagan, and whenever Mr. Brennan went to the five-hundred-miler at Indianapolis or the basketball tournament at Bloomington, they treated him like a king. You couldn't want better treatment. This trip—the boss, young Bert Leader, was the instigator of this trip, back in September. "Tim, this year you're going to the Notre Dame-Army game. How does that sound?" Well, how *would* it sound? He immediately contacted his friends at South Bend and they fixed him up with his press ticket and helped him with the hotel reservation. And tonight the Consolidated Press was sending one of its sports side to take him out to dinner and show him a little bit of the town, which just proved that the C.P. didn't forget that the Centreport *Times* was one of the oldest members of the C.P., from back in the days when the paper had a Morse wire.

Mr. Brennan's thoughts along this line led him to a startling awareness of duty; the fellow from the C.P. would be along any minute and he had not finished his piece. He sweated a little and then had his idea for his column. He wished he could have written more about tomorrow's game, with a little inside stuff from Blaik and Blanchard and so on, but the paper would be getting enough of that from the C.P. Instead, he wrote, in very fast time, a column on a favorite topic—recollections of Rockne from the angle of pleasant associations in the sports world generally. He finished the piece, folded it, and put it in his pocket. The young fellow from the C.P. would know which was the best Western Union place to take it to.

Mr. Brennan dressed with care. He had shaved—second time today—and bathed before starting to write his column. He removed his moiré silk dressing gown and gave his black shoes a rub with the inside of the dressing gown. He put on his white shirt and flower-patterned tie, and thought of his promise to his son's daughter, who had given him the tie for his birthday. His promise had been that he would save the tie for a special occasion, and if the night before the Notre Dame-Army game was not a special occasion, it would suffice until one came along. When it came time to spread his watch chain across his vest, Mr. Brennan had a decision to make—whether to wear the solid-gold basketball with the diamond on it that he had been given for coaching the Centreport High team to victory in its class at Bloomington, or the gold football that he had been awarded for coaching the only undefeated, untied team Centreport had ever produced in the Tri-County League. He decided in favor of the football and the Sigma Delta Chi honorary-journalistic-fraternity key. He had just got his coat on when the telephone rang. He walked over and lifted the instrument out of its cradle.

"Hello," he said.

"Hello, Brennan? This is Montgomery."

"Henry R. Montgomery of the C.P.?"

"Yes. I'm downstairs. Come on down and we'll have a drink at the bar."

"Wouldn't it be better if we had one up here? How're we going to recognize each other?"

"That's all right, they know me here," said Montgomery. "Tell them you're looking for me."

"You're the doctor," said Mr. Brennan. Mr. Montgomery had a youngish sound to him, but he could not be a very young man

to have been writing sports as long as Mr. Brennan knew he had
been. Another thing Mr. Brennan knew was that Mr. Montgomery was hardly one of the C.P.'s top men; Montgomery got
pretty good assignments, but not the best. The Centreport *Times*
sports department was not what you would call overstaffed, and
Mr. Brennan, many times, had written the headlines over Montgomery's stories, and as many times he had spiked Montgomery's
stories in favor of junior-high basketball-game stories of local
origin. These recollections did not add up to anything against
Montgomery, but they gave Mr. Brennan a little more self-
assurance than he might have felt if it had been Montgomery's
boss instead of Montgomery who was taking him to dinner. He
also thought that knowing more about Montgomery than Montgomery knew about him gave him an advantage, an advantage
that was slightly unfair, and he determined to put himself out
for Montgomery.

He was on his way to the door when the telephone rang
again. He was of two minds about answering it; it was most
likely to be Montgomery, impatient, but when he answered, it
was Mrs. Brennan, telephoning from Centreport.

"Why, hello. What is it, Nellie?" he said.

"Now, don't get upset, Tim. It isn't serious, but I knew you'd
want to know right away. Little Timmy broke his leg falling off
the garage roof."

"Broke his leg? How? Where?"

"I just said, falling off the garage roof at their place."

"No, I mean where's the leg broken? Is it a bad break?
How'd it happen?"

"Now, I wouldn't of called you if I'da known you'd let yourself get all upset. He's all right. It's a simple, clean break and
Dr. Hawthorne says it's nothing to worry about, the poor little
fellow. He and Miller's boy got a ladder and went up on the
roof, and little Timmy fell off."

"Where is he? Is he in the hospital?"

"He's at home. Dr. Hawthorne said it wasn't even serious enough to take him to the hospital."

"I don't care what Bob Hawthorne said, get the lad to the hospital! All Bob Hawthorne was thinking of was the hospital is overcrowded. Well, let somebody else move. A broken leg needs weights and casts and special equipment. You hang up and I'll call Bob Hawthorne."

"The leg's in a cast and Timmy'll get all the special attention he needs. Remember the child's mother was a registered nurse and she knows how to take care of him, and don't you dare call Dr. Hawthorne. He has enough to do without you—"

"Call Bert Leader. He's a member of the hospital board."

"I'll call no one, and neither will you. Jack is right here beside me and he says to tell you everything's all right. If it wasn't, I'd tell you to come home. I'd be the first—you know that. So stop worrying and go out and get your supper. It's an hour later there."

"I know that. I changed my watch on the train," said Mr. Brennan. They said goodbye and Mr. Brennan stood there for a little while before remembering that he was keeping Mr. Montgomery waiting. On the way down in the elevator, he thought of broken legs he had seen in his years in sport—ugly compound fractures on muddy football fields, for instance—and he knew of one case where the leg had had to be amputated, and at least two where the leg had had to be rebroken and reset.

"I'm looking for a fellow named Montgomery," said Mr. Brennan to the bartender.

"I'm Montgomery. I guess you're Brennan."

They shook hands. "I apologize for keeping you waiting, but I got a long-distance call." Mr. Brennan wanted to talk about his grandson, but he knew immediately that Montgomery was not the man he wanted to talk to. "Take a rye and a beer chaser."

"Get *him*," said Montgomery to the bartender. "Brennan,

you must be getting ready to knock one out of the ballpark. Well, that's for me. Give me another one of these, Fred. Where do you wanta eat, Brennan? We can go to the Colony if you want to. I've never been there, but I was told to give you the full treatment."

"That sounds too rich for my blood, and anyway, I don't want to take advantage, unless you'd like to go there."

"Well, frankly, any time I go to the Colony on the expense account—and believe me, that's the *only* time I'd go there—I'd rather take a broad with me. They say they have a nice fifteen-dollar blue plate there. Wait a minute! What am I doing? We could get a coupla broads. The office said the full treatment."

"No, thanks," said Mr. Brennan.

Montgomery looked at him and then said, "No, I guess not." He raised his drink and said, "Cheers."

"Happy days," said Mr. Brennan, on what should have been a happy day.

"You're in town for this Donnybrook at the Stadium, hey? What do you do, cover all Notre Dame games?"

"No, not all of them," said Mr. Brennan.

"Indiana? Purdue?"

"Occasionally. If I want to see Purdue play, I see them play. Indiana. Notre Dame. Northwestern. Whichever game I think'll make the best story." Mr. Brennan was not liking himself for putting it on for Montgomery, but several things had happened since he had decided to be nice to him, and one of the things was Montgomery himself. Montgomery's suit was a dark blue, the hat on the back of his head was an undistinguished gray, and his necktie was no fancier than Mr. Brennan's own, yet Mr. Brennan considered him a loud dresser. Montgomery's features were all right and neither his voice nor his accent was particularly offensive, yet Mr. Brennan did not like his looks or the sound of him.

"That's what I used to think I'd like to do when I first started out in this business," said Montgomery. "Stick around here awhile, then pull out for some small town, buy in on the local gazette, and more or less be my own boss. If I wanted to see Ohio State play, I'd go see them play. If I wanted to watch the high-school game, I'd do that. Or if I felt like playing golf and the hell with football, I'd damn well play golf. Brennan, you may have something, and I may yet do it myself."

"You better hurry," said Mr. Brennan to himself. "Why don't you?" he said aloud.

"Aw, Christ! I have a wife and two kids. We live out on Long Island and the wife likes the schools out there." He glanced at Mr. Brennan. "Forest Hills."

"Where they have the tennis matches. That sounds agreeable."

"I guess so. I'd probably blow my top in a small town. Let's have another strawberry jigger and go out and hunt up a steak."

Mr. Brennan and Montgomery finished their next drink during a quick discussion of a choice of restaurants, and went to the only place Montgomery recommended. "Every place in town'll have the rope up tonight," he said, "but I guess I can wink up a table, or sit with some of the mob."

It turned out that his second guess was good; Montgomery saw some people he knew, and he and Mr. Brennan joined them. Montgomery did not bother to identify Mr. Brennan, who stood alone while waiting for a chair. The chair was put between two of the men he had just met, and Montgomery, on the other side of the table, left Mr. Brennan to his own resources.

The men on his right and left did not stop eating even when their plates were moved slightly to make way for Mr. Brennan's silverware. Montgomery opened a conversation with a man at the next table, whose chair was back to back with his. Mr. Brennan could not hear a word they were saying, not even whatever it was Montgomery said that made the other man and Montgomery burst out laughing.

"Henny, what was the name of that project you were working on Wednesday or Tuesday night? The one used to be at the Copa?" This question came from the man on Mr. Brennan's left and was addressed to Montgomery.

"Why?" said Montgomery.

"I want to know her name, that's why," said the man.

Montgomery rubbed his chin and glanced around the room before speaking. "The one with the lungs?"

"Uh-huh."

Montgomery rubbed his chin again. "Gimme time to think up a phony name," he said. "Anyway, you can't score there, Charlie. I couldn't."

"I don't believe you, you son of a bitch, but even if you couldn't, I'd like to make a pitch," said Charlie.

"Her name is Dorothy De Vere and she's married to a very ill-tempered bastard, a detective, and she's five months pregnant and that isn't all that's the matter with her. Will that hold you?"

"You can have her," said Charlie.

"I have her," said Montgomery. "Will *that* hold you?"

"I'll find out someplace else," said Charlie, cutting his roast beef.

"All right," said Montgomery. "Now let *me* ask *you* a question."

"You're old, you ain't got any dough, you're one of these cheesy newspaper guys worse than musicians," Charlie said. "Why don't you give yourself up? Why don't you go home to Kew Gardens, you head-shrinker? I bet you a fifty-dollar bill I have a date with her by Sunday at the latest, and I don't even know her name. Now, what was the question you wanted to ask me?" While he was speaking, Charlie never raised his eyes from his plate.

"There's Grantland Rice," said Mr. Brennan.

"What was that, friend?" said Charlie, without turning.

"Grant Rice," said Mr. Brennan.

"Brennan's a newspaperman, too," said Montgomery.

"Yeah? What paper you on?" said Charlie. He leaned toward Mr. Brennan, ear first, momentarily suspending the knife-and-fork operation.

"Oh, you never heard of it," said Mr. Brennan.

"How do *you* know I never heard of it?" said Charlie. His smile was cold.

"I'll bet you never heard of it," said Mr. Brennan.

Charlie laid down his knife and fork and took out a bundle of money. He counted off ten hundred-dollar bills and laid them on the table in front of Mr. Brennan. "Any part of that, one to three."

"I don't want to bet you," said Mr. Brennan. He was trying to be affable, but not trying hard enough.

"Well, then, shut up, for Christ's sake." Charlie put the bills back in the bundle and the bundle back in his pocket, and while doing these things he inspected Mr. Brennan with an insolence that was a new experience for Mr. Brennan. It had been many years since Mr. Brennan had hit a man, but suddenly he felt the time had come. Then he knew that Charlie could see that.

"Well?" said Charlie. His hands lay flat on the table.

"Take it easy, Brennan, Charlie," said Montgomery. The others at the table were looking at Charlie and Mr. Brennan.

"Keep your nose out of it," said Charlie. The moment passed and Charlie formed a smile. "All right if I start eating, old-timer?" He picked up his knife and fork, and glanced quickly at Mr. Brennan's watch chain. "I never played no football." The others watched Charlie and Mr. Brennan, more Charlie than Mr. Brennan.

Mr. Brennan waited until he was sure his move would not be misinterpreted; then he rose. "I'll be leaving," he said.

"I guess I will, too," said Montgomery.

"No, you stay where you are," said Mr. Brennan.

"I'm blowing in a couple minutes, old-timer," said Charlie. "Stick around."

"No, thanks," said Mr. Brennan. He hurried out and got his hat and coat, followed by Montgomery.

"Where you going?" said Montgomery.

"Never mind," said Mr. Brennan. He heard Montgomery saying, "If that's the way you feel about it . . ."

ONE FOR THE ROAD

One for the road, kiddie. One for the road and I just happen to think of one happen to me only about a month ago. This might interest you. I doubt it, but it might. You've a rye, I'll have a rye. In my case, soda. In your case, whatever in the name of William Wadsworth Longfellow Shubert. You go right ahead and have whatever you prefer, and by the way, old chum, if I want to call you old chum or kiddie I shall continue to do so, because in my estimation I can always do and continue to do whatsoever I may please. You may be bigger than I, but I was telling you a story. Innaruptions not necessary. I stood here and listen to your dull goddam anecdote, so you will kindly remain here while I airy persiflage. Put in your own verb, son.

Mm. Hoom. Don't look at me if you don't want to, *mon vieux*. Also in any case don't patronize me. You're bigger, but by God I was always a better press agent than you are. I made more money and et settra.

Something you said a minute ago. I forget . . . Well, cheers, and here's how it was.

Wud I tell you? Happen a couple months ago? The hell it did. It happened quite a few years ago, but I thought I'd bring it up to date. No matter. Preten' it happened in the very recent past.

I had a couple shows then, doing a gray deal better than I am now, because in spite of the fact that I'm making more money

now, I didn't have to work hard *then* and *now* I don't have to work
at *all*. No week went by when I didn't extract a fast four or five
c's, even in July. Before that I ud been poor, 'tis true. I shall attempt to give you some background, *mon vieux*.

When I was a kid in this shoe town in Mass. where I come
from I was in love with a doll from the right side of the tracks. All
I can say about her was she was the loveliest thing I ever saw in
my whole life, which covers a great many years. Not beautiful. I
didn't say that, but what is worse than beautiful? I'll tell you. It's
lovely. This doll was sheer poetry, and I was a sheer nothing. My
background was I was poor, I din have any money, I was a mick.
My own grandfather couldn't read or write, my own grandmother
could read or write but just barely. And she was sheer poetry, this
doll. And to make the story worse, I was what you'd expect. A very
handsome young man from the wrong side of the tracks.

I met her, and it was whack! I can't snap my fingers, so you
snap your fingers. I'd a cousin worked for them in their garage and
I went up to see 'im one day and I met her. Whack! It use to be a
stable and they still had two horses, and a Mayo man by birth or by
ancestry, I knew a fetlock from a crupper, but if I didn't know a
fetlock from an I dono what—distributor—id still be the same.
We'd a moment's chat and then I said I'll see you tomorrow back
of the boat-club clubhouse, and by God she did.

Love, *mon vieux*, it stard then and it stard then and continued. I was a very bad little boy, acting up all the time, but vale-
dictorian of our class at St. Rose of Lima, the high school. I was the
unusual combination of bright boy and the girls' garters. I think
we had either fourteen or fifteen girls in my class. I don't know
what's the matter with you Pronnasuns. You certainly do miss a
hell of a lot.

They sent her to a school down in Connecticut, but she'd no
sooner be off the train than back of the boathouse or right on her
own front porch, so what could they do? I mean her family. They
finally said we could get married. They said, all right, marry Pat,

but first Pat has to earn five thousand dollars. Oh, sure. Go on, Pat, earn five thousand dollars. Not only earn it, but have it saved up. Sure. My old man was dead and my old lady was coughing blood, and I had a job clerking in the goddam shoe factory, and her family partly owned the shoe factory. Go right ahead, Pat. Embezzle yourself five g's. Wah-wah. I dono, you Pronnasuns have a wry sense of humor. They put it up to me. *I*, my old lady coughing blood and I pulling down the munificent sum of twenty-two a week, I'm suppose to amass the munificent sum of five thousand dollars. I couldn't amass fifty dollars, let alone any five thousand. On the two-two a week I was getting I could have made a showing, might have bought a car or go to Boston or New York, which I later did, but not while the old lady is alive. The doll and I figured it out one night and it was going to take me at the very least forty years, so the smart Yankees beat the smart mick.

The hell they did. Naturally she married some guy, not from our town, but he was helping his old man when they were putting in some new machinery in the shoe factory, and he was studying engineering, too. This doll's people, you know, they weren't any Governor Bradfords. Just Yankees. And no objection raised when this Ralph came along. A Canuck! Rafe, she called him.

I even sent them a wedding present, or her.

Then I ran for selectman, and I got it, and I thought aw the hell with this. I didn't think I'd get elected dogketcher, but I breezed in, so I went to the lousy Yankee that ran the paper and told him I'd prefer to be in the newspaper business. I got the lousy job, and if you can't learn the newspaper business in a year you might as well give up. This son of a bitch even offered me stock to stay, but no. Not me. I stashed a few bucks and came to New York and got to be a press agent.

Now we have two ryes to denote lapse of none of your goddam business how many years. I go around corrupting the press more and more, making myself more valuable by and large, to the

point where I can command a *pourboire* running around thirty
thousand dollars per annum. *That* was around the kind of money
her old man was extricating from his paltry shoe factory. She by
this time is in residence in the Province of Ontario. *I* have this
two-room suite, the same lousy two-room suite in the same lousy
hotel where I stayed the first night I got to New York. I got married one little time and it ran me around fifteen thousand dollars,
but we parted amicably when we decided—well, what we decided. The whole thing ran about five months, and we parted
amicably. It was all right with me, it was all right with her. I din
lose anything, barring the fifteen g's, and she didn't lose anything, unless you call losing me losing.

So, as they say, I played the field. More to my style anyway.
Then the night came I'm talking about.

I was around, talking to this one and that one. Stage door-
men, treasurers. Got a half promise from a kid in a show I had,
a musical, but I knew that wasn't going to amount to anything.
And I dono, aside from passing the time of day with a cop or
two, I didn't feel like talking much, or picking up tabs for the
newspaper crowd, and so what did I do? I went over on the East
Side. Spot where I knew the press corrupter and the barkeep. It
was too early to go home, and anyway I din have anything to
read at home. Barkeep and I exchange the time of day and I'm
about to end up reading the labels on the booze when this
worthy taps me on the shoulder. Calls me by name. Yeah, I said,
that's me. Clean-looking fellow, not looking for trouble. Standing
there and heard the barkeep call me by name.

"You know who I am?" he said.

"Your identity eludes me," I said.

"It won't," he said. "All I have to tell you is I married"—
mentioning the doll by name.

"You're Rafe," I said.

He laughed and he said yeah. He said he heard a lot about
me. So I tried to make polite conversation and bought the fellow

a drink. We had three or four mutually and in the course of the conversation I found out he was just in town on his way to another town. The other town is where his wife, my girl, or *old* girl, she was moving their things from Canada to—well, a little city not too far from right here. I asked him how she was, and the kid, and everything was fine. Then he got an earnest face on him and asked me, he said, "I understand you have something to do with such-and-such a show."

"That's right," I said. "Why?"

"Well, I saw the show last night," he said. "You know as one man to another," he said, "I'd settle for any one of those chorines."

"Oh," I said. I knew the show had about twenty minutes to run, and I guess he surmised that, too. "See what I can do about that," I said.

So I went to the phone, out in the booth. And if you think I called the theatre . . . I called the little city I was talking about, and I got his wife, my old girl. I gave her my addresses and phone numbers and told her for God's sake. "No, Pat," she said, "I could never do that."

I stard to tell her, I mean I was going to start to tell her what I was supposed to be doing in the phone booth, and then I thought—I don't know what the hell I thought. I went back and told Rafe it was no cigar. All the kids dated up.

Jerk probly thinks I'm a great friend of his. Mm. Hoom . . . Two ryes.

THE SKIPPER

Delaney, the middle-aged correspondent, was writing in his diary, which he called a journal because in the Navy diaries are forbidden. "I transferred yesterday by bosun's chair from the carrier to this ship, which I shall call the mighty fleet oiler *Mississinewa*, although that is not her name. Even in this short time I feel completely relaxed, or almost completely, probably because in a general way I am headed home, but there is more to it than that. I share a room with a j. g. and we have our own shower and all the water we want. We have three portholes for cross ventilation which in these latitudes is okay. In fact at this moment I can almost make myself believe that I am cruising in a private yacht. I paid my respects to the captain, a lieutenant commander named Clark, who seems like a nice enough guy. The exec also is a lt cmdr who made one crack yesterday after supper. He said: 'It aint a bad deal as long as you can forget you're riding around on a floating stick of dynamite.' When I said we seemed to be riding high out of the water and therefore were probably empty he told me something I'd never realized before: that an oiler is more dangerous empty than loaded, because of the vapor. He said he had seen an empty burning over a month one time in Florida."

At this moment Delaney heard a knock on the open door. It was a grinning Filipino. "Sir, Captain wish to see Mr. Delaney. You come follow me, sir?"

Clark was on the bridge. Delaney saluted because the day before the captain had seemed to expect it. Clark's face was again covered with some kind of white grease against the equatorial sun. "Thought you might like a cup of coffee. Go in and sit down, I'll be with you in a minute." Delaney followed the Filipino to the captain's quarters, a combination office, dining room, and sea cabin. The captain came in and tossed his khaki cap on the bunk. It was a weather-beaten cap; the sea air had long since got to the device so that it gave the appearance of being encrusted with salt.

"Did you get your baseball caps, Captain?" said Delaney.

"Oh, yes. Yes, thanks." He was washing his hands.

"Don't thank me, thank Captain Draper."

"No, you're wrong. Captain Draper asked me to be sure and take good care of you. He said you were a fine fellow and he practically told me the only reason I was getting the caps was because you were coming aboard my ship."

"Well, that was damn nice of him. He's a damn nice guy."

"*Who do you know,* Delaney?"

Delaney laughed. He named an admiral. "He's a cousin of my wife's. The word gets around, doesn't it?"

"The word always gets around, Delaney," said Clark. The Filipino served the coffee and cookies. "Maybe you'd rather have a Coke? The admiral's cousin."

"The admiral's cousin's husband."

"That's close enough. You all squared away? Anything we can do for you?"

"All squared away, thanks. I'm very comfortable."

Clark passed the cigars. They were not as good a brand as were available aboard the carrier. "Are you sure you can spare them, Captain? I'm not much of a cigar smoker, and as a matter of fact I have a few I'd like to give you."

"Give 'em to the exec, or pass 'em around among the chiefs if you have enough to spare. That's a better idea."

"I'll do that," said Delaney.

"They don't get many cigars, and I use mine up chewing on them." He lit the one in his mouth. In that brief moment, while he was lighting the cigar, Delaney had to rearrange his ideas of the captain's age. He obviously had been horribly sunburned, but until he raised the match to the cigar and looked down at the flame he had not appeared to be forty years old; now his eyes were tired and the relaxed face showed places where it never would relax again. He might have been fifty, he might have been more.

"One of them asked me if it'd be all right to invite you to their mess. The chiefs, I mean," said Clark. "Is it all right?"

"Of course it's all right. A pleasure."

Clark smiled. "That's what I told him. 'Why don't you just ask him?' I said. Well, it turns out he wasn't sure if it was the right thing. We never had a correspondent aboard before. He said he understood you rate two and a half stripes, so he didn't know whether to invite you or not. You know what I told him?"

"No."

"I told him if you didn't feel honored you didn't rate anything."

"And you were right. I feel honored, or will, when they ask me."

"They'll look you over for a day or so, but I guess they'll invite you." Clark smiled and watched to see how Delaney was taking it. Delaney smiled back.

"Now you have to excuse me. Paper work." Clark rose. "I guess you know what paper work is, but I'll bet you like yours better than I like mine."

The next day Delaney ate dinner with the chief petty officers' mess. They were Boston Irish almost to a man. They had not seen a white woman or touched any woman in thirty months. They apologized for the dehydrated potatoes and waited sensitively for Delaney to be surprised and appreciative of the steak. They passed the cigars. After dinner Delaney went back to his room and counted his cigars. There were not enough to go around. He wrote in his journal for an hour or so until he heard shots, rifle shots, they sounded like, and the Filipino came to the door again, grinning.

"Sir, Captain say if convenient you join him on flying bridge?"

Delaney followed the Filipino. Clark greeted him with a wave of his hand. "You like to shoot?" he said.

"Sure. What are you trying to hit?"

"Trying? Let's see you hit one. Those flying fish. Ever handle one of these?" He handed over a carbine.

"Yes. How'd you get hold of it?"

"I surveyed me a couple of them at Manos. The exec jettisoned his, so be careful of this one."

They fired about ten rounds apiece, hitting nothing but the sea. "I've had enough if you have. Let's have a Coke," said Clark.

They went to his quarters. They drank a couple of Cokes apiece and smoked cigarettes. Delaney kept feeling that he was being studied while they made talk about the carrier.

"Well, how'd you get along with the chiefs?" said the captain.

"Fine. They're a hell of a swell bunch of guys."

"They're every bit of that," said Clark. "I told you yesterday, the word always gets around. You didn't know I knew you had dinner with them."

Delaney laughed. "No, I didn't."

Clark got up and took an old magazine from his desk. "I just read an article of yours. How long were you in Hollywood?"

"I've been there a couple of times."

"What's it like out there? I never had any desire to go there. I'm a farmer. But if I ever did go there there's only two people I'd like to meet."

Yes, and I'll bet I know who they are, Delaney thought: one is Gary Cooper and the other is probably Irene Dunne. "Who are they?" he asked.

"Of the women, Irene Dunne."

"Uh-huh."

"The men, Spencer Tracy. You ever get to meet them?"

"Both of them, but the funny thing is I met both of them in New York when they were on the stage. I saw Tracy in Hollywood, but not Irene Dunne. Oh, I *saw* her. She used to go to the ball games once in a while."

"The ball games. Yes, I can imagine her going to a ball game. But you didn't know her very well. What about Tracy? Is he a nice fellow?"

"He used to be. It's a hell of a long time since I saw him."

"I don't think he'd change." Clark went to his desk again and brought back a pocket photograph case. "Here's a picture of my wife, taken last Christmas. This other one was taken just before I left home. Thirty-four months ago." He looked up at a calendar and Delaney followed his glance. The calendar was marked. "Do you think she looks anything like Irene Dunne?"

"Yes she does, quite a lot," said Delaney. "Are these your kids?"

"No, they're my wife's two nieces. We have no kids of our own. Are you married? Oh, sure, you told me. You ought to be home in about a week."

"Yes," said Delaney. "Where's your home, Captain?"

"My home's in a town in Indiana that you never heard of, on a farm. But my wife's staying with her folks while I—*aw aw!*" He stuffed the photograph case in his pocket and slammed on his cap and ran out of the cabin. From somewhere below came shouts of alarm. Delaney went out on the bridge and looked forward. A large valve was shooting forth a thick ugly stream that Delaney could not identify. Whatever it was was flooding the iron-plated deck, and two boys were screaming at each other but staying away from the valve. Clark jumped down the ladder and ran to the valve. In a few seconds he had closed it tight. He stood back and watched it a little while and then went to the other side of the deck and snatched a fire hose from one of the boys and began to pour water on the stuff that had come out of the valve, forcing the stuff to the scuppers. He motioned to one of the boys to take over, and then rejoined Delaney. His shirt and pants were soaked and so was his cap.

"What the hell was that, Captain?" said Delaney.

"If you want anything done around here, do it yourself," said Clark, examining his cap. "Well, now I can use one of those baseball caps . . . Why, I'll tell you. It's simple. The valve wasn't altogether dogged down and the ballast started overflowing, that's all. Be a different story if we had some of that hundred-octane in there." He winked at Delaney. "Somebody's gonna catch hell for this. I think you'd better not be here when I start eating their heart out. Come back later if you feel like it."

The next day Delaney was not summoned to the bridge and he was kept fairly busy taking addresses and messages from the officers for their wives stateside. He was all packed to leave the ship early in the morning on the day after that. The Filipino again made his appearance, but this time not smiling. "Sir, Captain say he wish to see Mr. Delaney." Delaney knew that the Filipino's reluctance to see him go was not on his own account. Delaney went to the bridge.

"Well, so you're leaving us, Mr. Delaney."

"That's right, Captain. I want to tell you how much I've enjoyed being aboard. You have a happy ship, sir."

"Thank you. Did the O.D. tell you? You go ashore in my gig."

"Yes, he told me. Thank you very much. I wanted to ask you if there was anything I could do for you when I get home."

"Anything you can do? I don't know," said Clark. "Why, yes. One thing."

"Fine," said Delaney.

Clark smiled. "Don't forget us," he said, and then the smile was gone. "That's all. Just don't forget us."

NOT ALWAYS

Dinner, the Langleys had been informed, was at seven, and the hotel manager's tone strongly implied promptly at seven. The Langleys' ship had been delayed in docking at Hamilton that day and they had got ashore quite late for lunch—so late, in fact, that while they were eating it in the hotel restaurant, Mr. Langleys' ship had been delayed in docking at Hamilton that They're *conferring* it upon us, like the O.B.E."

"What's the O.B.E.? I thought that was a Japanese kimono," said Mrs. Langley.

"It is," said Langley. In twenty-some years, he had not learned to refrain from little jokes, but he had learned not to try to explain them.

"It is not. It's probably something dirty. What does it mean? Is it something to do with fairies?"

"I'd rather not say," said Mr. Langley. They sat through the rest of their lunch in silence, most of which, Langley knew, was on his wife's part a thoughtful silence devoted to working up a naughty meaning for the initials of the Order of the British Empire. The Langleys were the only guests in the dining room, so there was nothing to do but eat and leave.

The hotel was not a licensed premises, but in the afternoon Mr. Langley had the foresight to buy gin and vermouth. He mixed a pint of martinis in a well-worn travelling cocktail shaker.

When the dinner bell rang, he was hungry and at peace with the world and with his wife. The food was not good, but it was edible and warm, and he listened to and agreed with his wife's comments on the way the dining room was done and how it could have been improved upon, and her comments on the other women in the room.

"Don't seem to be many people here," he said. "Quite a few empty tables."

"That's because a lot of people are going back on the boat we came on."

"I suppose so," he said. He felt good enough to refrain from pointing out that that ship was not sailing until the next afternoon.

"You can't see her, but there's a woman two tables behind you on your left. She looks exactly like that Mrs. — I-don't-think-you-know-her. I see her at the field trials."

"Mrs. Thursby."

"Yes! How did you guess?" she asked.

"Psychic," he said. "You ought to know that."

"You must have noticed her on the way in, except you don't know Mrs. Thursby. Only, it wasn't psychic, because it doesn't happen to *be* Mrs. Thursby. But I wonder what made you say that name. Tell me. I'm interested."

"Oh, I just happened to think that this was Monday, and the day after the day after tomorrow is Thursby."

"Oh, bushwah! Melvin, I'm interested."

"Well, if you must know, whenever I think of field trials, I somehow think of bitches, and that's what you think of Mrs. Thursby."

"I do not! I never said that," said Mrs. Langley. "I may have thought it, but I never said it."

"Precisely. I didn't say you said it. I said that's what you thought of her."

"How did you know that?" asked Mrs. Langley. "I don't

remember ever discussing her with you—or anybody else, for that matter."

"I told you I was psychic," he said.

"Psychic!" She jabbed her fork into piece after piece of the chicken à la king. "In a minute, I'll begin to believe you had an affair with her." She kept looking down at the food until she finished the sentence, then looked up quickly to try to catch him in a guilty facial expression. She always did that when she wasn't sure, and it never worked.

"You hit it," he said. "We're a big thing, Mrs. Thursby and I."

"Really? You must tell me all about it sometime. You always do."

"Oh, come on, Vic, let's cut this out," he said.

"You're a smug son of a bitch," she said. "*Aren't* you?"

"Yes. I always was," he said.

"No. Not always," she said, and her dim smile seemed faintly triumphant.

They had reached one more low point among thousands of low points of thousands of meals, but he did not dwell on it, because at that moment new life entered the room—a group of seven or eight young people, laughing and chattering from laughter and chatter that were continuing from a small cocktail party in somebody's room. They dispersed, two girls and a young man to a table for four, and two young married couples to two small tables like the Langleys'. The tables were not close together, but for a few moments the group chatter went on from one to the other, and there were no dark looks for their lateness or for the life they brought into the room. One of the couples sat quite near the Langleys, the young man facing Langley. The young wife's face was American-pretty, Middle Western-sorority-house-pretty. She was not the prettiest of the four girls, but she had distinction and dignity. She was a trifle taller than the run

of girls and she was proud—as she had reason to be—of her
bosom. In one respect, at least, she had been well brought up;
a wise mother, aunt, or grandmother had instructed her to take
advantage of her height, not to slouch it away. Langley had
noticed before she sat down that she was the same height as her
husband, which, of course, made her seem taller. Langley liked
her and more than liked her. He fell in love with her, and he
wished he could be sitting across the table from her. He thought
that he knew all the answers to any questions he might ask her:
how she stood politically (Stassen, very likely); on promiscuity
(a history of more or less conventional experimentation); on the
atomic bomb (hold on to the secrets until Russia became reason-
able, then share our information for the good of mankind); on
labor (coming around to her father's way of thinking lately); on
Sinatra versus Crosby (kid stuff). He also knew, in the very few
minutes since first he had seen her, that his knowledge of her
would remain pure guesswork, that in all likelihood he and she
would never exchange two words. But for a few minutes he
loved her.

He left off his consideration of her and gave study to what
manner of man she had married. Now, for the first time, he
looked at the young husband. As a chairborne commander in
BuPers in the recent war, Langley had met hundreds of naval
officers. Among them, it was easy enough to tell that a man was
a Navy flier, but a game Langley had played was to guess
whether a man was a fighter, dive-bomber, or torpecker pilot. He
had lost the game as many times as he had won, but his wins
were satisfying. He had no way now of knowing if the young
husband had even been in the Navy at all. His ruptured duck
told nothing. But if he had been anything, Langley decided, he
had been a night-fighter pilot. As a type, the night fighters had—
as he could see this young man had—extra intelligence and extra
courage, but besides that they had something else. They were
fatalistic, and they were loners. They had to be. So here was a

young man of intelligence, capable of "grace under pressure," who had been trained to kill and would have killed, and had the look of the loner. He was handsome in a mediocre way; that is, with no distinction. Langley wondered why the girl had married him. And then he understood.

They were sitting too far away from the Langleys for their conversation to be audible, but the girl said something, a long sentence, to the husband. While she was speaking to him, the boy's lips moved as though he were uttering the words with her, and in his eyes there was such love as to embarrass Langley. The courteous thing to do was to turn away, although the young man did not care, or did not even know that anyone else was in the room. But Langley did not turn away. He kept watching the young man, because what Langley saw was Langley.

The girl finished what she was saying and the young husband said, quite audibly, "No kid!," and puffed out his cheeks and laughed explosively. He bent down to his food again—his table manners had been neglected—and shook his head over and over, enjoying whatever his wife had told him. He kept on showing that he was enjoying it until she started in on something else. Again he stopped eating, again the lips moved, again the look of love, and now Langley began to understand something about the young wife. The boy had nothing to contribute. He probably never had had anything to contribute, and his wife was doing the talking to cover his shyness. All he had to offer was stupid love. "And that," said Langley to himself, "was the way I was." He sneaked a glance at Victoria; she was happy with her salad and her little—her enormous!—triumph; she had said neatly, beautifully timed, something she must have been waiting to say for twenty years.

All those years, all those women, all those lies. He had been as shy as the kid at the other table. She was the girl of distinction, and of beauty and money besides. He was the son of a New York Central conductor, and in 1918 he had worn a forestry-green uniform, with an ensign's boards, Navy wings, and gleaming leather puttees. And so they were married for just the reason that the kids at the other table were married, and Victoria had "brought him out," or "drawn him out," or both. She would tell a little story, and his lips would move with hers. She'd helped him to learn the kind of manners that he had not picked up in the Kappa Sig house. At the right times, she'd had his children, and again at the right time she had got him into a nice club. She had accepted the ferocity of his love, and had pardoned him the first couple of times he'd released the ferocity elsewhere; then came the phase during which there were scenes; then nothing and years of it. And all through the years, this humorless woman had had it in her to snub him with three words: "No. Not always." The Peal shoes, the Wetzel suit, the Racquet Club tie, the food before him, this trip to Bermuda, the people he called his friends—no, not always.

"I wish to hell we could get a drink in this place," he said.

"You mean now?"

"I don't mean Saint Patrick's Day," he said.

"Well, why don't I ask the manager? After all, Father used to—"

"Like hell you will," he said. "If I want a drink, I can get it myself."

"All right, all right, all *right*," she said. "*Get* it yourself."

NO JUSTICE

The old friends often had lunch at this place. One day, not long after Repeal, they had simultaneously rebelled at looking at the same old faces in that refectory known as the Yale Club grill, and they had wandered into Arturo's, a former speakeasy, which as luck would have it was that day having a fashion show. The place was crowded with debutantes, pretty and plain, but at least all female and all young, and so for ten years they had been coming to Arturo's, now and then hitting a fashion show, but always without fail seeing a fair share of attractive girls.

Merritt and Beckwith didn't have to talk. They knew all there was to know about each other. They had been born in the same town, gone to the same country day school, were together at New Haven for four years, been to Bermuda and Europe together, each had been best man at the other's wedding, and their wives saw each other just infrequently enough to allow the friendship between the men to go unmolested. The men never gave each other presents, but they exchanged something rather better: trust.

This day they were dawdling over their demitasses, interested in a party of five girls who were trying to figure out who owed what on the check. "The one that's collecting the money reminds me of Agnes Wentworth. Remember Agnes Wentworth?" said Merritt

"Yeah. Did you ever hear the wonderful story about Chief Justice Holmes?" said Beckwith.

"You mean, 'I wish I were seventy-five again'? What's that got to do with Agnes Wentworth?" said Merritt.

"It hasn't anything to do with Agnes because that isn't the story I was thinking of."

"Oh," said Merritt.

"It seems when he was in the Civil War there was a beautiful nurse, and all his life he'd been telling Mrs. Holmes about this nurse. Well, one day when he was on the Supreme Court he got a letter from the beautiful dame, asking if she could come and see him, and of course he said she could. He got all spruced up and of course told Mrs. Holmes about it. Oh, yes. He was going to somebody's house to have tea with this woman. That was it. After forty years he was going to see the woman he'd been talking about all those years. Well, he came home that evening and he was a depressed man. Didn't want any supper. Practically in tears, and then Mrs. Holmes said to him, 'I know. She's gotten fat.' 'That's right,' said Holmes. Isn't that a good story?"

"It's a swell story about Mrs. Holmes. But I don't see what it has to do with—"

"You will. The other night Pauline and I went to the theater and after the theater we went to 21 for a drink."

"That's a strange thing to go to 21 for," said Merritt.

"Do you want to hear this or don't you?" said Beckwith. "All right. Well, we sat down and as we were sitting down I thought I recognized the woman sitting next to Pauline. You know Pauline never knew Agnes Wentworth, but of course she's heard about her. Go ahead, say 'Yes, I imagine she has.'"

"I imagine she has," said Merritt.

"Thanks. Well, I wasn't going to say anything, but before I could stop myself I whispered to Pauline, 'I think that's Agnes Wentworth sitting next to you.' 'You mean right next to me, on my right?' said Pauline. 'Yes,' I said. So she tried to get a look at her and so did I. I wasn't sure I recognized her but it was a close enough resemblance, and also I had an idea the woman sort of recognized me. Well, we ordered our drinks and ordinarily Pauline won't take more than one highball when we're just on our way home from the theater, but this night she had three. We sat there without saying a word, trying to listen to this woman's conversation to determine if it was Agnes Wentworth. The only thing Pauline said was, 'I certainly hope it isn't, not with that laugh.' Well, if you remember, Agnes had a, uh, it was a loud laugh but I always thought it was rather charming, so I had to admit that maybe it was. Could be, I had to admit. Finally Pauline said, 'I'm not going to sit here getting tight without finding out if it is or it isn't Agnes Wentworth. Why don't you just say to her, "Aren't you Agnes Wentworth?"'

"'I can't do that,' I said. 'You can't say to a girl you were once engaged to, "Aren't you a girl I was once engaged to?"' If it was Agnes it would be insulting, and if it wasn't, well—"

"Uh-huh," agreed Merritt.

"So I got the check and we went home. All the way home in the taxi Pauline gave me hell. You're always reading and hearing about wives getting jealous because their husband and an old sweetheart met after many years and bango! the spark was rekindled."

"Bango! That sounds just like a spark," said Merritt.

"But not Pauline. She was giving me hell because I *didn't* recognize my old sweetheart."

"Oh! Then it *was* Agnes," said Merritt. "Say, I didn't know you had it in you. You mean you put on an act for Pauline and she fell for it. I honestly didn't know you had it in you."

"Had what in me? I wasn't putting on any act. I still don't know whether it was Agnes or not."

Merritt nodded slowly. "I see," he said. "Well, all I can say is I can't blame Pauline. By the way, what has all this to do with Mrs. Justice Holmes, or shouldn't I bring that up?"

"I don't know," said Beckwith, "but somehow I think she'd have understood."

"If I were you I wouldn't complain," said Merritt. "If you don't understand why your wife wanted to have a good look at her husband's old sweetheart, then, brother, you're no chief jus tice yourself."

"I still think—"

"Waiter, check, please," said Merritt.

THE LADY TAKES
AN INTEREST

[The following is a copy of an intra-office communication.
The original is presumed to be in the files and/or records, if
any, of Mrs. Robert Hooker, president of the Gibbsville (Pa.)
Standard and widow of the late "Fighting Bob" Hooker,
owner, editor, and publisher. The memorandum was written
by Doug Campbell, now managing editor, formerly city
editor, sports editor, etc., of the *Standard*.]

To: Mrs. Hooker
FROM: Doug Campbell
SUBJECT: Ray B. Hoffner Memorial

I hope you will forgive the delay in answering your memos re-
garding the Ray B. Hoffner Memorial, but I am sure you will
understand when I explain that due to our recent retrenchment
program and the difficulty your nephew Karl and I have been
having in getting newsprint, I have had to put off writing this
memo. Also I have been expecting to see you in the office and
left word downstairs that when you came in I was to be notified
immediately. I of course understand that aside from your duties
as president of the paper you have numerous other commitments
and, parenthetically, I trust that we have been handling the news
items to your satisfaction. We are all very grateful to you for
sending in these items, especially when you include lists of names

of the prominent women with whom you are associated in the charitable and other enterprises. Mary Dobbs, our new young society editor, has been doing a fine job and I know I speak for her as well as myself when I express my thanks for your sending the items instead of telephoning them. In addition to her job as society editor, Mary has been helping out "on the street," as we say, and it is almost impossible for her to take long lists of names over the phone after lunch. Our county edition goes to press at 2:50 in the afternoon, which means that Mary, for instance, is writing from about 11:30 A.M., when she comes in from her tour of news sources. Her deadline for society-page items is 12 noon, unless we have to hold for items of extreme importance. Another difficulty when some items are telephoned is that because of the nature of many of your charitable and civic enterprises it is desirable to have such news published not only in our paper but by our competition as well. I believe I explained to you that the *Leader* will not print an item which appeared first in our paper. But thanks to your new system of writing out the "stories" and lists of names we now are able to hand over the items to one of the stenographers downstairs, who makes a carbon which we shoot over to the *Leader* office. You thus get double, or complete, coverage for your charitable and civic interests. We all hope that you will drop in on us in the editorial room very soon, preferably after four o'clock, when we are under somewhat less pressure than at other times of the day, although I need not tell you we are always honored by your visits. Since we are a little short-handed at the moment I suggest that if you wish to bring friends who are interested in seeing how a newspaper is brought out, it probably would be pleasanter for them if you notify me a day or two in advance so that I can assign one of the staff to escort you and provide the necessary explanations. I also suggest that you wear old clothes if you wish to go through the whole plant.

And so to the matter of the Ray B. Hoffner Memorial. Unfortunately I have mislaid the originals of your memos to me, but

I have had several conversations with your nephew Karl and I
think I know substantially what you have in mind. Perhaps it
would be advisable to review the suggestions, before passing on
my comments, and, in so doing, check my perhaps faulty memory.

As I remember it, when Ray Hoffner died last January you
were in Phoenix, Arizona, and did not hear of his death until
your return to town. As I understand it, you were on your way
East by train when you read in one of the Denver papers that a
police officer had been killed in line of duty, and that the local
paper had created a fund for his family. This left so strong an
impression that you quite rightly decided it would be a good
thing if we were to do likewise, and when you learned, upon
returning to town, that Sergeant Hoffner had died, you decided
that this was an excellent opportunity to emulate our esteemed
Denver contemporary. You discussed the matter with Karl, who
of course agreed, and you thereupon wrote me the first memorandum, which I carelessly mislaid. I did, however, discuss the
matter briefly with Karl, who knew Ray Hoffner very slightly, if
at all, owing to his (Karl's) fairly recent residence in town and
also to the fact that as business manager his duties do not place
him in contact with police officers. In our first discussion I suggested to Karl that perhaps we would be wiser to postpone the
creation of a fund until another time. That is my belief now, and
I urge you to consider all the facts before issuing an actual order
in the Hoffner matter.

It is too soon after Hoffner's death to establish a fund for the
future without causing some comment. I suggest that privately
we decide upon certain conditions of an award, and then in the
regrettable event of a police officer's death, either in line of duty
or some such praiseworthy condition, we announce the award
simultaneously with the appearance of the story covering his
death. I respectfully suggest that to qualify for the award, which
should be given to the wife and/or family of the deceased police
officer, said officer shall have died as a result of injury or illness

sustained in police activity. We can work out details, but that, in my opinion, should be our guiding principle.

Sergeant Hoffner, unfortunately, would not qualify under those terms. I have known Ray Hoffner all my life and while what I am about to say is a confidential report, I have no doubt it would be corroborated by anyone who has had any connection with Police Headquarters or with Ray. The cause of death was correctly given as pneumonia. The preceding circumstances have, however, not been publicized. He had gone off duty shortly after two o'clock A.M., and paid his nightly visit to a house on Railway Avenue which since has been closed. The house is what we call in the paper a house of "ill repute." Shortly after four o'clock Patrolmen Wilkes and Velusky, on duty in the prowl car in the western end of town, received an order to go at once to the house on Railway Avenue to investigate the firing of shots. There they found Sergeant Hoffner, who had been drinking. He had emptied his revolver while taking target practice at a row of beer bottles. He was not in a belligerent mood and when the woman proprietor of the house assured the officers that he could pass the night there to "sleep it off," the officers relieved Hoffner of his revolver and departed. About an hour later, however, Wilkes and Velusky received a message to look for Hoffner, who had left the house in search of the prowl car in order to retrieve his revolver. He now was in a belligerent mood and before leaving had threatened and struck several of the inmates. In spite of the severely cold weather he left without his cap and overcoat. Wilkes and Velusky proceeded to search the neighborhood without success. They went off duty at eight A.M. and were relieved by Patrolmen Shea and Wintergarten, who continued the search. Hoffner was found asleep in the tool shed of the St. Stanislaus Polish Cemetery, more than a mile and one half from the house on Railway Avenue, when two part-time gravediggers appeared for work at ten A.M. Police were notified and Hoffner was taken to headquarters, although not booked, and then removed by ambulance to St. Mary's

Hospital, where he died three days later. Surviving were two sons by his first marriage, which ended in divorce. They are believed to be living in Allentown, Pa., with Hoffner's married sister. His second wife, from whom he was separated in 1935, operates a beauty parlor in Milwaukee, Wis. Hoffner was buried in the Odd Fellows Cemetery by the Police Benevolent Fund, after Milwaukee police reported to local headquarters that the second wife "wanted no part of him, alive or dead."

I would be glad to work out details either for some kind of coöperation with the Police Benevolent Fund or to establish a Fund of our own, but I think you will agree that to do so in memory of Ray Hoffner would not be to the best interests of the paper, and I am sure that if Mr. Hooker were alive he would agree. We are, of course, always delighted to receive your most welcome suggestions for the good of the paper, and perhaps as a small stockholder I may be permitted to offer one or two of my own at some future time. Your inspired wartime idea to run a cut of the American flag on the editorial page was typically patriotic and you no doubt recall how much I personally appreciated your suggestion several years ago that women's golf scores properly belong on the society page. Thus by tokens of your interest we are made aware that we are all pulling together—you in the mansion on the hill, and we here.

(Signed) DOUG CAMPBELL,
Managing Editor

INTERIOR WITH FIGURES

Ned parked his motorcycle in the garage, between the Buick and the Ford. The presence of the Buick indicated that his father was home early. He went to his room, took off his work clothes and laid them in a corner of the bathroom, took a bath, and dressed —that is, he put on his flannel slacks and a shirt and loafers, without socks.

In the living room, his father was listening to an old record, Fletcher Henderson's "Farewell Blues." When it was finished, Edwin Senior delicately replaced it in an album. "Good, huh?" he said.

"Swell," said Ned.

"How goes it at the airport?" said Edwin.

"Be finished up in another two weeks, they said today."

"Hey, then you'd better start looking for another job, hmm?"

"Oh, I've started already," said Ned.

His father went to the portable bar. "Do you want a cocktail?"

"Sure," said Ned.

"O.K. Go on up and get dressed, and I'll have one ready by the time you're back."

"I *am* dressed," said Ned.

"For what?"

"For dinner."

"Like hell you *are*," said Edwin. "Go on upstairs and put on a coat and tie, and what about socks?"

"Mom said I didn't have to wear a tie in this hot weather."

"She did? Well, *Pop* says you wear a coat. *I* wear a coat, so will you. When did she say you didn't have to wear a tie?"

"Last night. Why? Don't you believe me?"

"It's not a question of not believing you. I didn't hear her say it, that's all."

"You weren't home for dinner last night."

"I know that," said Edwin. He held the vermouth in his hand. "Well?"

"Well?" said Ned.

"Aren't you going to get a coat?"

"Look, Father, why don't you relax? You'd be more comfortable if you didn't wear a coat and tie. If I have permission, I guess you have, too."

"Well, I must say you have your crust. Permission! It isn't a question of permission. It's a question of respect. I wear a tie and a coat out of respect for your mother. And your sister. I'd be more comfortable in my undershirt—"

"No, you wouldn't. There's always a fly buzzing around in the dining room. It's more comfortable to wear a regular shirt like this. But not a tie or a coat. Why don't you try it?"

"Look, don't think I can't pick you up and *carry* you upstairs," said Edwin.

Ned waited a moment before speaking; then he got up and started to leave the room. "Maybe you can, but there'd be a hell of a racket."

Edwin also waited a moment. "Oh, all right. Sit down."

"Thanks," said Ned.

Edwin proceeded with the mixing of the cocktails. "But don't get any ideas about who's head man around here."

"You pay the bills, you're head man," said Ned.

"Here," said his father, handing him a cocktail. "Is that the only reason I'm head man? Because I pay the bills?"

"Well, it's reason enough, isn't it?"

Edwin considered a moment. "It's, I suppose, an adequate reason. Yes, that's exactly the right word. It's an adequate reason. A *fiscal* reason."

"Are you trying to get sentimental?"

"What if I am?" said Edwin. "It's a hell of a thing to be told that the only reason you get any respect is because you pay the bills."

"I didn't say it was the only reason," said Ned. He tossed off his cocktail. "Do you mind if I say something?"

"Go right ahead. The floor's yours."

"Well, it's pretty personal," said Ned. "Could I have another cocktail?"

"Help yourself," said Edwin. "Why don't you wait till you're good and stiff and then really let me have it."

"I don't get stiff during the week. That sun's too tough when you have a hangover."

"It's too bad you didn't think of that when you were at New Haven."

"That doesn't even make sense. I wasn't fired for drinking." He hesitated before refilling his glass, but went ahead with it.

"No, but it probably helped," said Edwin.

Ned sat down. "What I was going to say fits in with that last crack of yours." He held his glass before him, took a sip, and resumed. "You know, for a man with so many young ideas—no, that isn't the way I want to say it. You know, I go around to the houses of the fellows I know, and girls, too, and their fathers all seem a lot older than you. They don't seem to have any young ideas. By that I mean, take you, for instance, tonight. When I came in here, in this very room, you were playing a record—a jazz record—and enjoying yourself listening to it. Matter of fact, you get more pleasure out of that than I do, and yet you're my father and I'm the so-called younger generation. You know what I mean?"

"Yes."

"Well, what I mean is you have a lot of young ideas. You're about the only one of my friends' fathers that plays tennis. The others either play golf or don't play anything."

"Uh-huh."

"Well, you still like Victrola records and tennis, and another thing I noticed, you like an open car and all the other fathers have sedans. In fact, you even *look* younger."

"Well, thanks. This is all very complimentary," said Edwin.

"Yeah, but wait a minute. I haven't finished."

"Oh, I knew that all right," said Edwin.

"All that stuff I told you, that's why for a man with young ideas how can you suddenly change from black to white?" He took another sip of his cocktail. "Like wanting me to practically put on a tuck for dinner, and all that stuff about respect for Mother, and getting sentimental."

"You mean stuffy."

"Well—you're the one that said it. I didn't say it. Then you practically accuse me of getting fired out of Yale for drinking. I flunked out and you know it, but you twist it around as if I always went to class with a hangover. It's not only stuffy. It isn't logical. If you're gonna be young, be *young*. If you're gonna be old, be old. I don't mean you. I mean anybody."

"But, of course, it does happen to apply in my case," said Edwin.

"Well—I just hate to see you getting stuffy. And you're the one that said that word."

"I know. That is, I was the *first* to say it. It came in pretty handy for you just then."

"Respect?" Ned went on. "Respect is earned. My mother earned my respect by a lifetime of being a good wife and mother. Therefore I respect her. But I don't have to show my respect by wearing socks to the dinner table. I show it in other ways. By listening to her point of view when I know she's absolutely wrong. By—little things. By consulting her with minor problems that I know she'd like to be consulted on. By—well, little things here and there. That's what I mean by respect."

"And very good, too," said Edwin. "Well, since we're being frank, it all boils down to my being a stuffy, middle-aged character with some of the appearances of young ideas."

"No, but, for instance, the cracks you made when President Roosevelt died—"

"Oh, for Christ's sake, Ned. Two years *ago*."

"All right. I'm sorry," Ned said. "And I'm finished."

"Are you sure? I can take quite a lot more."

"No, that's all," said Ned. "But it's pretty important."

"Oh, I realize that. I'll think it over, and I might even make some changes, and thanks."

"Thank *you*. You took it the way I hoped you would," said Ned.

Edwin poured himself another cocktail. "Speaking of changes, this might be the appropriate moment to play the Whiteman record of the same name. Or would it?"

Ned laughed, and his father got out the record and put it on the phonograph.

"It's too bad you don't get as much out of these records as I do," said Edwin.

"Oh, well, *you* don't like *chess*," said his son.

Nellie, the maid, brought in the afternoon papers and handed them to Edwin. He did not immediately open them. While the music was playing, Ned's mother entered the room. "Hello, boys," she said.

"Ma," said Ned. Edwin bobbed his head.

She took the papers out of Edwin's hand and began to read. When the record was finished, she tossed one of the papers to Edwin. "I see where Mr. Donohue died."

"Yes," said Edwin, reading.

"Mr. Donohue?" said Ned.

"That Irish slob that lives out at the club," said Edwin. He looked up from his paper. "Well, won't *he* be missed! Walking up and down the club porch, trying to eavesdrop on everybody's conversation, and standing out there on the first tee, bothering the golfers, then down at the pool, watching the girls in their bathing suits, then to the bar, trying to horn in on more conversations. But at least that's where he belonged—in the bar. Behind it. He didn't even have the guts to be a bootlegger. He put up the money to start out other bootleggers in this town. Remind me to go to *his* funeral."

"What did you have against him, Father?" said Ned.

"He was just a horrible man," said his mother.

"Oh," said Ned.

"I never said two words to him," said Edwin. "It was what he represented. He wasn't fit to associate with decent people, and, believe me, if I'd been a little older, he never would have got in the club. It's funny you didn't know him. He was *always* around the pool and the bar, *always* trying to horn in."

"Oh, I knew him. He used to buy Cokes and drinks for us," said Ned.

"Now, I never knew *that*," said Edwin. "You took drinks from him?"

"Sure. Everybody did. I could tell you two of my friends that owe him money right this minute," said Ned.

"You can? Who?" said his mother.

"Well, that's confidential, Ma. All the guys knew, if they got in a jam, Mr. Donohue was good for a bite. He told one of the guys last Christmas, he said he didn't have any son of his own, and if any of the guys ever got in a jam where he didn't want to notify his family, why, just ask *him*. And one fellow did get into a certain kind of a jam and Mr. Donohue lent him three hundred dollars, and one other boy borrowed a hundred from him just to take his girl to a certain prom."

"Well, I'll be a son of a bitch," said Edwin. "Did *you* ever put the bite on him?"

"Not for money."

"What for, then, may I ask?"

"Well, he wired a friend of his in New York and got me hotel reservations. It was a big favor. We all liked him in our crowd."

"Well, by God," said Edwin. He addressed his wife. "You remember he was supposed to have bribed his way into the club. You remember what your father said at the time. But I didn't realize it extended to the kids. He really *was* all over the place, wasn't he?"

"Awful," she said.

"But he didn't do anything to you, either one of you, so I don't see what you have against him," said Ned.

"Then apparently you haven't been paying any attention to what I've been saying," said Edwin.

"Yes, I have, but apparently you didn't pay much attention to what *I* said. I mean before we started talking about Mr. Donohue."

Edwin looked at his son, then spoke to his wife. "Our son and heir thinks his father is a stuffed shirt."

"Oh, Edwin, he doesn't," she said.

"Oh, yes, he does. He explained in detail why he thinks so, just before you came down. Didn't you, Ned?"

"Ned, if you said anything like that to Father, I want you to apologize."

"Good God! Apologize? No, I won't apologize," Ned said. "I didn't say anything that wasn't true." He stood up. "I don't want any dinner."

"Ned! No dinner?" said his mother.

"Sit down, you fathead!" said Edwin.

"No, *thank* you. I'm not dressed right," said Ned. He went out of the room.

"What started all this?" his mother asked.

"Let's forget about it," said Edwin.

Frannie, the daughter, came into the living room. "Hi," she said, going straight to the phonograph and putting on a record. "Is it that I may have a slight libation?" she said.

"One," said her mother.

Frannie poured a cocktail, and they heard the spitting and barking of Ned's motorcycle. "Where, may I ask, is that one off to?" she said. She did not wait for an answer. She pointed to the phonograph. "Well, Father? Can't you guess?"

"I don't know," said Edwin.

"Not possibly!" she said. "It's Harry James."

"I was going to say Harry James," he said.

"Yes, but you didn't. You're slipping," said Frannie. She made a face at the cocktail. "Watery, and not even cold."

"Then put it right down and don't drink it," said her mother.

"I'll put it right down *and* drink it, in the same action," said Frannie.

"This family's getting awfully smart," said Edwin.

"Dinner is served, ma'am," said Nellie.

AT THE COTHURNOS CLUB

Although the Cothurnos Club was founded by actors a limited number of writers and painters are taken in from time to time, and that is how I chance to be a member. It is the pleasantest of places; in the reading- and writing-rooms pin-drop quiet prevails, while in the bar and billiard room and dining room there is very little likelihood of a man's feeling lonesome. Especially is this true of the dining room, where most of the members eat at a large round table. After I had been honored by admission to the club I took to lunching there nearly every day and that was how I happened to notice Mr. Childress. He always ate alone at a small table against the wall. He never seemed to speak to anyone, for surely the nod that he gave the men at the round table could not be taken as a greeting. A few days ago I asked Clem Kirby, who put me up for the club, to tell me about the reclusive Mr. Childress. "Has he been a member long?" I said.

"Oh, yes," said Kirby. "About thirty years, I should say."

"But was he always like that? I don't see why a man like that joins a club, he's so anti-social."

Kirby smiled. "Maybe it's hard to believe, but up till about ten or twelve years ago George Childress was just the opposite of what you see today. Full of beans. Witty. Here every day, down in the bar, drinking with the boys, and so on."

"What does he do?" I asked.

"He paints, or did. He was what's commonly called a fashionable portrait painter, and he made a lot of money, and while I don't think anyone could call George stingy, he took care of his money. He hasn't done anything in recent years. That's probably why you've never heard of him."

"Vaguely I have," I said.

"He married Hope Westmore," said Kirby.

"Oh, of course," I said. "That's where I've heard of him. Hope Westmore's husband. She was one of my all-time favorite actresses. So that's George Childress. Are they still married?"

"Married, yes," said Kirby. "But of course—" Clem did not finish his sentence. His eyes turned sad. "I'll tell you about George.

"He wasn't exactly a practical joker, but he was something of the sort, especially with, well, someone like you, a new member. He'd find out all he could about you, and then before being introduced to you he'd discuss your work, whatever it was, in your hearing, and I may say the opinions he'd come out with would be devastating. He did it, of course, to get a rise out of new members. A cruel trick. What you younger fellows nowadays call a rib. He had several little tricks like that. He also invented another one, with a new twist.

"He would join a group of fellows in the bar, all old members except one. Everybody was on to the trick but the new member. George would be introduced and he'd be his most charming, affable self. Then slowly he would get the conversation around to the theater and he would say, 'What was the name of that actress a few years back. Terribly good actress. Beautiful. But drank herself out of every job she had?' And he'd pretend to rack his brains, trying to recall the name. The fellows who were in on the trick would also pretend to search their memories, and of course what would happen would be that the new member, trying to be helpful, would volunteer a name. Now George's point was that he never got the same answer twice, or did very seldom.

"Well, I see you know what happened. You're right. One day

we were down in the bar and there was a new member, a young fellow, and when George couldn't remember the actress's name the young fellow popped up with a name, and of course the name was Hope Westmore."

"Good Lord," I said. "What happened?"

"Well," said Clem Kirby, "there was a stillness that I thought would never end. You've seen for yourself, George is a powerfully built man and I've never seen anyone exercise such self-control. But he took a deep breath and said, 'You see, gentlemen, I never get the same answer twice,' and then he excused himself. As far as I know that's the last time George has been in the bar."

"What about Hope Westmore. Was it true?" I said.

Kirby looked at me long and steadily. "I don't see that that makes the slightest difference," he said.

THE LAST OF HALEY

Haley's boat, the *Yelah,* was the last one in. He throttled down to idling speed at the yacht-club landing, tossed his fifteen-year-old cousin a line, and stepped up to the landing. The kid had been earning spending money, working at the club during the summer, just as Haley had done twenty and more years ago.

"O.K., Cousin, put 'er away," said Haley.

"O.K., Cousin," said the kid. "All right if I use up what's left of the gas?"

"There isn't an awful lot left."

"Yes, I see. Just up to the Point and back?"

"I hope you *get* back. The gauge says empty," said Haley.

"I know this gauge. Boy, you were out all afternoon."

"No, only since half past three," said Haley.

"Well, you know me. Prone to exaggerate," said the kid. "But you were really pouring on the coal."

"Well, it's almost the last chance I'll get this summer. Take it easy."

"Oh, sure," said the kid. "See you at the dance."

"That's right. I owe you some money, don't I? I haven't any on me at the moment."

"That's all right. I'll catch you there—if you get there before eleven o'clock. You know. They make us kids go *home* at eleven, just about the time *you get* there."

"I get it. You'd like to have the dough before you go to the dance. O.K. I'll phone your Ma and tell her I owe you two bucks and she's to pay you for me."

"I'd appreciate it very much," said the kid.

"Permission to go home and take a bath, sir?" Haley saluted.

"Permission granted," said the kid, returning the salute.

Haley went home and took off his khaki shirt and pants, souvenirs of the submarine base at Pearl, and rolled them into a ball with his skivvies and tossed the ball into the laundry hamper. He was lying in the tub when Willa came in, wearing a dressing gown he had brought back from Gump's.

"What ever happened to that rule we used to have? *You* know."

"*I* know," she said. "Don't come in the bathroom without knocking. I thought you'd probably fallen asleep."

"A poor excuse is better than none. Or is it?"

"Do you want to lie there while I do my legs?"

"No." He got out of the tub and dried himself in their bedroom, and put on his old tuxedo. He was unable to close the top button of the pants, but he covered that with the cummerbund, which also was pretty snug. He was inspecting himself in the full-length mirror of the bathroom door when Willa opened it. She was naked, carrying the dressing gown, and the contrast between the lingering beauty of her body and what was happening to his own brought him a sense of defeat that he did not need. It was piling it on. He was still strong enough, but he was beginning to look like an old-time brewery-wagon driver, and she continued to look like a girdle ad. She walked past him, slightly amused at catching him in front of the mirror.

"Don't you think it'd be a good idea to go downstairs and greet your friends?" she said.

"They aren't here yet, and why call them *my* friends? They're just as much yours."

"They're always very prompt. Punctual. Especially since

Katie found out you're in love with her. Just remember, they'd never be coming here if you hadn't made me ask them."

"I certainly twisted your wrist this summer. Tonight'll make the second time since June they've been in this house."

"That does me," said Willa.

"What do you want to drink?"

"Scotch on rocks. That'll make it easy for you. It's what they drink. 'Scotch on rocks'! Oh, brother! How quaint can you get?"

He hesitated before closing the bedroom door. "I've heard you order a Bloody Mary. How disgusting can you get?"

The Muldoons were punctual, and Willa was still upstairs. Haley greeted them and asked them what they'd have, and they said Scotch on rocks. "I think that's what Willa wants, too," said Haley.

"Can I help you, Bob?" said Muldoon. He was very tall, very thin, and he had not yet sat down. He was nearly six feet four, and Haley wished he would fold up in a chair.

"No, thanks, Gerry. Easiest drink this side of a glass of water." Haley made four and served them, leaving Willa's drink on the coffee table in front of the davenport where Muldoon was sitting. Haley sat on the other davenport beside Katie.

"We're sitting next door to the Vandersmiths," said Haley.

"Who?" said Muldoon.

"Who? Who? Who?" said Willa, making her entrance. "Gerry, you sound like an owl. Hello, Katie."

"Hello, Willa," said Katie. "My, you look nice."

"Thank you. Hello, Gerry. Don't possibly get up." There was an unmistakable sharpness in Willa's voice and manner. "What have you two been doing lately?" She made it sound as though they had been smuggling, without implying the charm of smugglers.

"Oh, I don't know," said Katie.

"Nothing to speak of," said Muldoon.

"We haven't been doing much either—at least, I haven't," said Willa. "Course Robert's been all over the place with that boat."

"You want this drink or shall I—?" said Haley.

"If you'd hand it to me where I could see it, I'd drink it," said Willa. She sat down in a chair across the room from the three others. "Well, I saw the seating plan and we four're sitting next to the Vandersmiths' table. They have twenty-four and they'll all be drunk by the time they get to the club. Let's us get drunk, too, and shout—"

"Oh, no. Let's not," said Haley.

"I say let's," said Willa.

"I'm willing," said Muldoon.

"If you want to see a man get drunk," said Haley, "if that's all you want to see—"

"I didn't exactly say you," said Willa. "I mean all of us. Those Protestant snobs, every week they come storming in—"

"I'm a Protestant," said Katie.

"Well, I know, but your name is Muldoon," said Willa.

"Well, then, don't say things like that," said Haley.

"Katie knows what I mean. It's the end of the summer, and we weren't asked to the Vans' party," said Willa.

"Isn't that too goddam bad?" said Haley.

"Well, except we *were* asked, Willa," said Katie. "But you asked us first."

"Time out for an awkward pause," said Haley.

"Oh, come on," said Muldoon. "Grown people—"

"I apologize," said Willa. "I'm a louse." She rose and left the room. Haley acted as though nothing had happened, as did Muldoon. Katie got up and followed Willa out. In a couple of minutes, the two girls returned.

"It's agreed that we're all going to have three more drinks," said Katie.

"Except me. Six," said Willa.

"Yes," said Katie. They had had their arms around each other's waist when they came in, and now they laughed and sat again where they had been sitting. "You two dullards ought to start mixing drinks," Katie added.

"I'll do it," said Muldoon. "Easiest thing this side of a drink of water."

"Go right ahead," said Haley.

They all had several drinks apiece and drove to the club, to go to their table for four, near the empty table for twenty-four. "Cleared the air, anyway," said Haley, parking his car.

"Sure," said Muldoon.

A Paul Jones was in progress. Little boys were running away from little girls they were stuck with, and little girls were looking around for partners and then running off the floor, suffering the final, unendurable pain of not being wanted. Two young fathers with murder in their hearts got up to dance with their rejected daughters, and were rebuffed. Revenge was in the air, and a great group of adults came in and took their places at the table of the Vandersmiths. Behinds bumped chairs, pardons were begged, dresses were ruined by clear soup and red wine.

"That's a great little group you've got there," said Haley.

"Not my group," said Muldoon. He was cutting his filet mignon, but he knew what group Haley meant.

"Oh, they're nothing," said Katie.

"I say they're absolutely nothing at all," said Willa. "We're more exclusive."

"Than what?" said Haley.

"Than they are," said Katie. She did not look up. She was one of those well-trained persons who eat everything that is put on their plates. She concentrated on her food; her white dress was cut so low as to give a recurring reminder of her breasts. Haley looked at the four-hundred-dollar dress, at the husband who had paid for it. They were both eating away. He looked at

Willa, crushing peas with her fork, and at his own plate, empty of meat.

"Did anybody see what I just saw?" said Haley.

"No, what was that?" said Willa.

"A hobo in a grocery staw," said Haley. "No, if you didn't see it, it'd take too long to explain."

Katie went on sawing and chewing. Muldoon likewise. "Ask Fred if we can have some Scotch," said Willa.

"Say, Fred," said Haley to the waiter, "whenever you get through with those Protestants, put a bottle of Scotch on this table, please."

"Oh, stop that Protestant talk," said Muldoon.

"Listen, kid, I'll stop all talk," said Haley.

"Well, that wouldn't be a bad idea," said Muldoon.

"Listen, Gawkie," said Haley.

"Bob! Please!" said Katie.

"Let's have that Scotch," said Haley.

"Right, Mr. Haley," said Fred. He departed.

"Katie, we dance," said Haley.

"Let's wait till we get some coffee," said Willa.

"How about waiting till we mind our own business," said Haley.

"Yeah, how about that, Bob?" said Muldoon.

Katie put down her knife and fork. "All right. How about it? If you think you want to, I'll dance with you, Robert."

"Please do," said Haley. "I do." They got up and he held her and they moved to music. For once around, he said nothing; then he looked far away and said, "I'm sorry, Katie."

"Oh, well," she said.

"More than you think, though," he said.

"Maybe. I don't know."

"I love you. You love Gerry."

"Yes," she said.

"He doesn't do anything. I keep on loving you."

"I don't know what to say to that," she said.

"But you know I love you?"

"I think so. I guess so," she said.

"All right, then let's go back to the table."

"All right, Robert," she said. "I love you, too. Once around?"

"You mean for goodbye. But you said it. Say it."

"I love you, and let's go back," she said.

"Yes. Are you going to be here next summer?"

"Not if I can help it. I don't want to ever see you again," she said.

"I think I can fix that," he said.

"That was a short one," said Willa.

"I ran out of conversation," said Haley.

"Oh, I'll bet," said Muldoon.

"Now, if you'll excuse me if I leave while I'm still up?" said Haley.

"Loud protests," said Muldoon.

"I didn't ask you," said Haley. "You know, Gerry, you haven't got very much."

"Oh, no? You think that?"

"Excuse me, one and all," said Haley.

On his way to the bar, Haley tripped a couple of times. After a couple of drinks, he found his kid cousin. "How'd it go, Commander?" said Haley.

"Fine. I'll remember you in my will, Cousin," said the kid.

"Oh, you got the two bucks? I didn't mean that. How's the Big E?"

"The Big E? Oh, you mean the *Yelah*. Well, that gauge said empty, and it's empty now, I can tell you," said the kid.

"Now, think of that," said Haley. "If five bucks would be worth anything to you, I know where you could get five bucks. It's too late to get gas on the dock."

"You mean siphon out some gas? Whose car?"

"Anybody's."

The kid made considering faces. "Five, huh?"

"Five bucks," said Haley.

A little girl came and stood beside the kid cousin. "Uh, Barbara, this is, uh, my cousin, uh. Mr. Haley, this is Barbara Wilderming. Well, I guess not, Cousin."

"Yes, I see what you mean," said Haley. "Nice to've seen you."

He left the club and walked until he took a spill. He laughed and got up and continued walking until he took another spill. There seemed to be no necessity for rising in a hurry, so this time he waited till he was good and ready. He resumed walking and now sang about McNamara's band, which made the distance seem shorter. Sometimes he called out that his name was McNamara and that he was the leader of the band. He was humming that much of the song, of which he did not know the lyric, when he stepped off the yacht-club landing. The cold water revived him so that he was able to swim out almost all the way to the can buoy, where his boat would be tied up. Some feet short of that, it didn't seem worth the effort.

MEMORIAL FUND

Miss Ames came in and stood silently in front of the desk in an annoying way she had, waiting for him to speak.

"Yes, Miss Ames?" said Russell.

"There's a Mr. Jarwin outside to see you," she said.

"What about?" said Russell. "Who is he, and what does he want? You know how busy I am, Miss Ames."

"I do know how busy you are, Mr. Russell, but this man said he was a classmate of yours and wanted to see you about the Duke Brady Fund."

"Jarwin? . . . Oh, Lord, Jarwin," said Russell. "All right, I'll see him in five minutes."

Miss Ames went out, and Russell got up and took down his college yearbook from one of the crowded shelves. "J. Jarwin. Economics Club. Candidate for track in sophomore year. Played in band in junior and senior years." That was all, that was the recorded collegiate history of J. Jarwin. It was the opposite extreme from Russell's own and Duke Brady's lists of campus achievement, with their fashionable clubs, prom committees, athletic endeavors. Russell studied the picture of Jarwin, who had a thick pompadour and thick glasses and a high stiff collar, and he remembered the one time he had seen Jarwin away from college. That had been the summer vacation between junior and senior years. Russell had gone to visit some friends in the White

Mountains, and in the intermission at the hotel dance Jarwin had come over to him: "Hello, Russell, do you remember me? I'm Jarwin. In your class."

"Oh, yes. How are you?"

"Fine. This is my band playing here. We're here all summer. How's Duke Brady?"

"Duke's fine. He's working as a lumberjack, keeping in shape for football." In September, back at college, Russell had kidded Duke Brady about running into his friend Jarwin, and the Duke hadn't had the faintest idea who Jarwin was. But there was one thing about Brady that Russell never quite liked: the Duke was by way of being a campus politician, and for the remainder of his days in college Brady had made a point of speaking to Jarwin. That was from September to April. Brady had quit college in April 1917, joined the Army, and matched his football and hockey reputation with a D.S.C. and a Croix de Guerre with a couple of palms. And now, in another war, the Duke was dead, killed in the crash of an Army transport plane.

Russell signalled to Miss Ames, and presently Jarwin bustled in. Russell rose and the two men shook hands. Jarwin's unfortunate pompadour was gone, and the glasses were perhaps a trifle thicker, but it was recognizably Jarwin, a curiously pushy little man whose pushiness had not got him anywhere in college. It was going to be just like that time in the White Mountains and the so-familiar mention of Duke Brady.

"You've got a nice office here," said Jarwin. "It's more like the kind of offices you see in England. I mean, the books all over the place and so on."

"Well, we're in the book business," said Russell.

"Yes, but not only the books. I mean the old furniture, the pictures. I almost expect you to serve tea."

"We do serve tea," said Russell. "We're not terribly high-powered, I suppose."

"Oh, don't get me wrong. I like it," said Jarwin.

Russell refrained from commenting that that was nice of

him. "What are you doing these days?" he asked.

"I have my own business now. Jarwin Manufacturing. We make certain parts for guns, and that brings me around to the Fund, the Duke's Memorial Fund. I got your letter, the committee's letter, and I was wondering if you had the right idea, establishing a scholarship in his memory."

"Why, yes. I think it's a very good idea. We all thrashed it out pretty thoroughly and a scholarship seemed like the best idea."

"I don't," said Jarwin.

"No? That's interesting. Why not?"

"I'll tell you why not," said Jarwin. "First of all, from a purely business point of view, if you start a fund now you aren't going to know how to invest it to yield a uniform sum every year, therefore you don't know how much the scholarship will be worth from one year to another, and that isn't even taking into consideration inflation."

"How about war bonds?"

"Oh, don't think you have me there, Russell. I buy plenty of them for myself, but in this case I don't think it's a good idea. You certainly don't want to cash your war bonds, you want to hold on to them, so that means you wouldn't have what you might call a 'live' fund for some years to come, and in my opinion the memorial to the Duke ought to start right away. Have you thought of a marble shaft?"

"Naturally that came up."

"That's what I'm in favor of. Something permanent and something we can see in a few months' time. That's the kind of memorial the Duke ought to have. An inspiration, just as he was an inspiration to me."

"I see. Well, I think the committee have already made up their minds, Jarwin."

"Yes, probably have. That's why I came to see you, to see if I could get you to change their minds."

"I'm afraid not," said Russell.

"I didn't think you'd agree with me, but I have a counter-proposition. How much did you plan to put in the scholarship fund?"

"Three thousand dollars."

"Uh-huh. You call that enough for the memory of Duke Brady, with all the money there is in our class?"

"You sound as if you had some pretty big ideas," said Russell.

Jarwin smiled. "Not too big. You see, Russell, I was very fond of the Duke."

"He was my best friend," said Russell. "I, uh—"

"Go ahead, say it. You didn't know he knew me. Well, he didn't. He merely spoke to me, but he was an inspiration to me. I wanted to be like him, and if I couldn't be like him in college at least I could keep punching when I got out of college. I consider him to a great extent responsible for whatever success I've had in business."

"Is that so?"

"Yes, that's so, Russell, and that's why I want to make this proposition: you fellows on the committee can have your scholarship, but will you let me match the three thousand with another three thousand of my own so that you can build something permanent as a memorial to the Duke?"

Russell hesitated before answering, and then he spoke deliberately: "Jarwin, I think you ought to be reminded that I am only a member of the committee and not the whole committee, but I'll tell you now, quite frankly, that I'll take your proposition to the committee, but with the recommendation that they turn it down. You see, my dear fellow, I don't think you ought to be allowed to overwhelm us with your money. And I'll tell you something else, if there were to be any really large gifts to the fund, I think they ought to come from people who were close friends of the Duke's, not from someone that he didn't even know existed for three years. If it hadn't been for me, Duke Brady never would have known you existed."

"Do you think I don't know that?"

"Oh? How did you know it?"

"In senior year he started speaking to me and one day I asked him why, and he said you told him I considered him a friend of mine."

"He did?" said Russell.

"Oh, I guessed how it happened, Russell. That time in the White Mountains when I asked about him, you probably went back to college and you probably laughed about it and said you didn't know he was such a great friend of Jarwin's. That's true, isn't it? Isn't that about the size of it? It's all right, Russell, it was so long ago you wouldn't be hurting my feelings."

"To tell you the truth, it was," said Russell, ashamed.

"Yes, I was a sort of joke in college, but Duke Brady was nice to me, so here's a cheque, and you can do as you please with it." He took out a chequebook and wrote quickly while the two of them sat in silence. Jarwin tossed the cheque to Russell, and rose.

"And you know, Russell," said Jarwin. "If it had been you instead of Duke Brady, I think I'd have done the same thing. In a funny way you were good for me too. So long, Classmate."

THE HEART OF
LEE W. LEE

I laint a little more about Lee W. Lee a while ago. You remember me telling you maybe a year ago, maybe two years ago I told you. This group come into the Copa and Joe Lopez like he knew them, he gave them a table, desirable table one back of ringside, but not ringside, and the faist thing I got fascinated was by his size, this one guy. Enormous in size. He could of easly tipped the scales at three-ten if not more and his heightth was in proportionate. You know what I mean on him it looked good? Take off like a ceytain amount of the weight and you easly could end up with one of them Southwest Kentucky State Teacher College centers. On the other hand, take off a ceytain amount of the heightth and you have on the order of Tony Galento. Well, that night I faist saw the party in question I took particular interest in studding how he ate from the standpoint of quantity. It was all right. To scale. All he did, he sat down at that table and put away more food than any white man—white or colored, I don't care which—that I ever saw, and you know doorn my brief but long enough sojourn with the Army I saw some great eaters. Just now reminds me of a cute little yarn I heard a while ago about this guy is a songwriter out on the Coast. Hollywood songwriter. I don't remember what his name was but call him Harry Jones. Harry was a big man, too, but fat, because all he lived for was to eat. Eat, eat, eat, eat, eat. Diamonds Brady, whatever they called him, the old-timer back for

God's sake at the tain of the century? Diamonds wasn't in it with
this guy. This Harry. Harry? Harry? I know the name because
it's a common name like Jones, but not Jones. No, not Jones. But
call him Harry. In any case Harry took the greatest *pride*, you
know, in how much he could *eat*. You know what I mean? He
was *proud* of it. The *amount*. How some people take pride in
accomplishing one thing? And some another? *That's* the way it
was with Harry and what he took pride in was how much he
could eat.

Well, Al Hitchcock, the great English director boasting like
with Madelon Carroll that picture. "The Steps." A number of
steps. Thaity-nine! That's right. Al boasted that one and countless other psychological and thrillers. You haid of Al Hitchcock.
But he had another propensity similar to Harry the songwriter's.
He loved to eat, too. So when Al signed for Hollywood somebody
mention to Harry. "Harry," they said. "You know this Al Hitchcock that they recently signed. They tell me he's quite an eater.
Quite a knife-and-fork man." "Yeah?" says Harry. "I tell you what
I'll do. I'll eat everything Hitchcock eats, and *then*," Harry says,
"and then I'll eat Hitchcock!" Cute story don't you think, if you
never haid it before? Nothing to do with Lee W. Lee but it just
happened to occur to me, and we're not doing anything more
important.

I'd still like to tell you about Lee W. Lee, though. After the
faist night I watched him eat he must of come to the city to stay,
becuss I bunked into him numerous places here and there at the
various spots. I didn't get to meet him at faist but I inquired who
he was. Lee W. Lee, they said. That meant little or nothing to
me. To tell the truth I never haid the name before. A while I
figured him for one of the black markets or other, but then they
went passé so I figured him for a fix man in like football, basketball, and them. But the trouble was, one night he'd be around
stashing away a few steaks with the sports mob and the next
night he'd be chumming with Garsong, you know the tubercular
Frenchman making the deals for sending cars to his native

France. Then the next night he'd be buying the wine for little Mildrene Shalimar, the little song stylist on the radio. Then the next night after that he'd be sitting there alone at a small table for two and the other chair he'd have tilted against the table, vaitually the equivalent of putting a sign "No Visitors" up. Always a bundle, mind you! Oho! Brother! You know what he was? You haid of Bill Gorman the sport writer being a fast man with the lettuce. Well, I never happened to witness Lee W. Lee reaching for a check for the simple reason there *was* no check. Not that he was cuffing anything. He paid. Always paid. I inquired from the various waiters in this spot and that spot and I was assured he wasn't running up any tabs. But when he came in the place, any place, it was the understood thing, wherever he sat down the bill at that particular location was for Lee W. Lee and nobody else. Not even if like a party of four or five'd be going for the full treatment, meats and wines—if Lee W. Lee happened to sit down for a momentary double brandy or two and then powdered out, the bill was his. And the people would never find it out till finally they asked for the check, and always the same story. The waiter: "Sorry, sir, taken care of by Mr. Lee. No, thank you, sir. Tip, too, Mr. Lee's pleasure." Always paid on the way out, you know what I mean? Never at the table. Later he told me why this was. He said he couldn't entertain in his modest quarters these lovely people but he didn't like to flash a bundle out in a public restaurant, so he made it a habit of remunerating without any ostentation, you know what I mean. Of course as a side remark I might hazard the thought that if I was carrying around a stack of bills this here thick laid out flat I wouldn't remunerate with any ostentation eyether myself, and physically I'm a much smaller man than Lee W. Lee.

In that connection was how I happened to meet him finally. I was standing chatting with Ben the doorman at Eywin's Chop House and Lee W. Lee came out. One of his nights alone. He had his usual heater in his kisser and Ben went over and asked him if he wanted a taxi, Mr. Lee. Mr. Lee: "I think not, Ben, thank you. A nice night for a stroll." Then all of a sudden what did he do but he pointid over at me and says, "Little man, I'd like to stroll with *you*." "Me?" I said. I never met the guy in my life before. Saw him countless *times*, you know what I mean, but never had two waids with him. *One* waid! But he was so god-dam enormous, even ten feet away like he was standing, I had the feeling he could reach over and pick me up if he so desired. So I—I went over and I said to him, I asked him what was it, Mr. Lee. He didn't say anything only handed Ben a piece of money, folded up, wished Ben good night, and said, "Let's stroll." We strolled till we got to Sixth Avenue and then tained down Sixth and suddenly he stopped at some bar-and-grill gin mill. Paddy's or John J. McGillahooley's or I don't know. They're all alike to me. I never frequented them in my whole lifetime. On Sixth Avenue they can't do me any good. "Let's drop in here and chat," he said. Well, at least that proved the cat didn't get his tongue, which I thought but didn't say. It was the faist time he spoke since we left Ben.

We went to a table in the back and he ordered something and I ordered something, I don't know what. I didn't know *then* is how I felt, waiting for him to broach whatever he wanted to broach.

Mr. Lee W. Lee: "Now, then, what's your name and what do you do for a living?" he said.

Me: "My name? My name is Milton Black and what do I do for a living? I imagine you'd call me an account executive," I said.

Him: "No, I wouldn't," he said, "becuss I don't know what the hell that is, an account executive."

So I explained to him I was account executive with an independent advertising agency where I handle the advertising for some various night spots and restaurants.

"Oh," he said, and then he thought a minute. Then he asked me a question, how much did that pay me.

Me: "Now, wait a minute, Mr. Lee," I starred to say.

Him: *"How much?"*

So I named him a figure, upped it a little in case I didn't know maybe he might be going to make me an offer, but not too much in case I didn't know maybe he was a tax man.

Him: "Married?" he asked me.

Me: "Divorced," I said.

"You pay alimony?" he said.

"I do," I said, and he asked me how much and seemed very sympathetic to the situation, till suddenly.

Him: "I want to tell you something, you—" He called me some very profane and obscene things that I liked to take the ketchup bottle off the table and give it to him right then and there, but of course he would of known that in advance and anyway I doubt if a bottle of ketchup would break on him. He ripped me up and down, but never raising his vaice, till finally what he tains out he was sore about, he didn't like the way I kept looking at him in all the spots. What develops is he had a Kodak memory for faces, and especially if they exposed any curiosity about him. Displayed. "You've been displaying a lot of curiosity about me and everywhere I go I see your—your face. I want to know why. You don't worry me. You just bother me," he said.

Well, it took me the best part of an hour and a half to tell him my life history, my likes and dislikes, who I went around with, and one thing or another. Finally I was telling him about when I was a little boy in school and people used to take advantage of my size and pick on me, and all of a sudden he made like spitting, only no saliva came out. "Finish your drink and never mind finishing your story. I feel like taking in a club."

He meant I was to go with him so we got into a hack and went over to the Copa to catch the twelve-thaity show. There was a large group of young couples outside waiting to get inside and it wasn't the regular bobby-sockers. Couples, they were. Dressed up. Then I remembered it was high-school graduation time. These young fellows and gals, they were like you make a date six months ahead of time for Commencement and you're always reminding the mouse it's you and nobody else or no Copa at Commencement, and that keeps her in line, the mouse. With me it wasn't any Copa, becuss one thing when I was in high school it was Rudy Vallee's place, not the Copa, and secondly and fifthly and tenthly, we didn't have big ideas about coming downtown to a night club when I was at Evander.

Lee W. Lee: "Look! They giving away milk or something?" he said. I explained to him and he laughed. All of a sudden he went over to the crowd and picked out two kids and said, "Come on, you're going in and be my guests."

Well, two more surprised kids you never saw. A big groan went up from the ones ahead of them that happened to be standing in line longer, but one look from Lee W. Lee and silence reigned supremely. He took the kids in and as if Joe Lopez wasn't surprised enough seeing me with Lee W. Lee, what about these two kids? But Lopez played it straight, and gave the kids a ringside table. Not for four, just for two. The kids. I and Lee W. Lee sat at another table.

Well, the kids ordered Cokes and got up and danced and had steak sandwiches and watched the show and had the time of their life, and Lee W. and I just sat there watching them. Two kids really stuck on one another, you could tell that. We didn't talk much, becuss I didn't feel like intruding my thoughts, and Lee was studding them. Then he said, "She has a nice pair of jugs, that kid." Aw-haw, I thought to myself. Here it comes. He'll put away ten or a dozen more highballs and start moving in. But I was wrong. He kept looking at her, but he didn't go over to the table, at least right away. Once in a while he'd say, "A beautiful pair of jugs. Do you think he's getting any of that?"

"I don't know," I said. "Kids nowadays."

"*I* don't think he *is*," said Lee, very sad. Then he watched them a few minutes more and said. "He isn't, and it's a goddam shame." Then a few minutes later he called our waiter and ordered a bottle of champagne. "Don't bring any bucket. Cool it off outside and bring me the bottle." So when the waiter came with the wine Lee took it and went over to the kids' table. I stayed at our table but I could hear the whole conversation. He pulled up a chair and sat down and held the bottle in his hand and said, "Are you having a good time?" And they went into rhapsodies and he said for them to drink up their Cokes and have some of this, meaning the wine. The young fellow didn't want to take any, but the gail did. I mean she pretended like she didn't, but she wasn't drinking wine, she was drinking a waid called champagne. Lee poured their glasses full of bubbly and left it there and then came back to our table. He didn't say anything till they got up and danced again. Lee said, "I think he's in."

Me: "He is if he wants to be."

He tained on me. "That's a hell of a thing to say!" he said.

"Don't get me wrong, Mr. Lee," I said. "Maybe he's in love with her and they don't want to do anything till they get married or engaged."

He didn't say anything only snarl at me and then a little while later the kids came over and thanked him, and one thing I could see, the young fellow was in all right, if he wanted to be, becuss Lee could of been, or I could of, or Joe Schmo from Kokomo. Anybody. I guess that's a lot of champagne if you're not used to it, what she drank. I noticed there was only like a fingerful left in the bottle. They knocked that over fast.

They went home, or wherever they were going, and I said I guessed I would likewise take a powder about fifteen or twenty minutes later. All that time he sat there thinking. "All right, go ahead," he said. "But answer me this question."

"Glad to accommodate," I said.

"I think maybe you're right," he said.

"About those kids?" I asked him.

"Yes," he agreed.

In other waids, he was considering the possibility such as I pointed out, where we have the situation of a young couple not wishing to do anything till they get married, very likely. It just shows you one thing: I happen to've come across a lot of mysterious talk about Lee W. Lee and the whereabouts of his source of income, but you must say for the man, he's got a heart. That's what I laint about Lee W. Lee, my friends.

THE BROTHERS

Smith stood at the window, looking down at the late-afternoon thousands in Times Square. Among them he recognized, without any particular friendliness, about a dozen men and women that he saw pretty nearly every day: two detectives, two cops, a dancer with whom he had had an affair, three horse-players, an advertising solicitor for a theatrical paper—people he would have spoken to if he had been down there, but people he was just as glad not to be chinning with just this minute. Seeing the horse-players reminded him that he had a bet down at Fair Grounds. He looked at his watch, a narrow gold number curved to fit his wrist; it was too early for the results of that race. He put his hands back in his hip pockets and continued to look down at the people.

He looked where the dancer ought to be by this time if she had made normal progress in the crowd, but she wasn't there. Then he took another look and saw that she had been stopped by a man and was chinning with him. Probably a musician. Somehow or other Smith resented her presence on the scene, and in all honesty he knew why. She was a good kid, but there she was as a reminder that he was no rose himself and on this day, this afternoon, he did not want to be reminded that he was no rose. He wanted to have an absolutely clear conscience today. Just for now he half wished he was a priest, had never been married, never been divorced, never had known the dancer or anyone like her. Then he called himself a hypocrite and aloud he wished her luck.

He got a shoebrush out of the bathroom and went back to the window. He brushed his shoes, which did not need it, and went back to the bathroom and washed his hands, without rolling up his shirtsleeves. He took a whiskbroom to his coat, which was on a wooden hanger. He was going back to the window when the phone rang.

"Yah," he said.

"Joe, this is Pat. Pat Walsh."

"Yah, Pat," said Smith.

"He's here. He just come in the place," said Walsh.

"Who's he with? Is he with anybody?" said Smith.

"No, he's by himself, but he's sittin' in a booth, so I guess he's probly meetin' somebody."

"Is he sober?" said Smith.

"He looks all right to me."

"Is he wearing his uniform?"

"Oh, sure," said Walsh. "Yeah, in his uniform."

"He didn't ask for me or anything, did he? Did he mention me?"

"No," said Walsh. "All he did was he just come in, said hyuh to me and went over and sat down in one of the booths. Andy the waiter took his order. He ordered a bourbon and soda. That was less than five minutes ago. I called you right away the minute I was free."

"Okay, Patty, thanks very much. I'll be over," said Smith. "Oh, listen, when I come in—"

"I ain't been in touch with you. I understand, Joe."

"But don't make it look like I'm a stranger. You know, be casual. I come in every day. Like that."

"Sure, sure. Like it was nothing out of the ordinary, you just dropped in."

"Right, Patty. Thanks very much."

"Right, Joe."

Smith looked at himself in the chiffonier mirror. He put on his coat and hat and overcoat and went downstairs. He made himself walk slowly to Patty Walsh's, so that when he got there he was convincingly casual, unhurried.

He was glad that there were so few people in Walsh's. It made it look more natural when he looked around, after ordering his drink, and spotted his brother in the booth. He pretended to do a take. He set down his drink on the bar, looked at Patty Walsh and grinned and then looked at his brother. He went back to the booth, his hand outstretched.

"What *is* this? When did *you* hit town?" said Smith.

"Hyuh, Joe. Wuddia know?" The younger man shook hands.

"Just got back from the vawdaville show. What is it, Jerry. When'd you get in?"

"I got in yesterday," said the younger man.

"You didn't see Mom," said Joe.

"No, I didn't."

"You didn't go over the hill, did you?"

"Do you wanta see my pass?"

"No. No. Well, how about if I buy a drink?"

"Sure," said Jerry. "Sit down. I'll buy *you* one."

"Why'd you wanta come here? Why didn't you go to my joint and save yourself some dough?"

"Well—I guess you know the answer to that."

"You mean you didn't want me to know you were in town?"

"That's right," said Jerry. "What'll you have?"

"I just ordered one," said Joe. "Maybe I'm not welcome."

"Well, it didn't exactly fit into my plans, but you're here, so what the hell."

"What's the matter with me? You in some kind of a jam?"

"No, I wouldn't say that," said Jerry.

"Kind of embarrassing in front of Patty and Andy, them

seeing me run into you here. Christ, if you didn't want Mom to know you were in town I wouldn't of told her. But you shoulda figured, you come to N'York and you come here or Malone's or any one of a half a dozen places and I'd have heard about it. I'm in here four, five afternoons a week."

"You are?"

"Sure."

"Since when?"

"Since I don't know how long. Half the time I don't ever take a drink in my own place. If I did that I'd be loaded every night before the dinner crowd was gone."

"How's it going?"

"It's going all right. Scotch and gin, hard to get, but they all know about that now and anyway I don't get as much of a call for Scotch and gin as some of the other joints. Butter is murder. Steak—well."

"What about the black market?"

"What do you think? I couldn't stay in business if I didn't do business with them. But the hell with that. What about you? You're *lookin'* all right. You put on a little weight."

"Uh-huh. How's Mom?"

"You oughta go see her and find out."

"Uh-huh. When did you see her the last time?"

"I don't know. Four, five weeks ago. I talk to her on the telephone."

"You're *here. You* don't go to see her, so don't complain if *I* don't."

"It's different with you. You're closer to her than I am. Have something?"

"I'll have a bourbon and soda," said Jerry.

"That's for me, Andy," said Joe.

The two men looked at each other. There was no doubt about it; he was a handsome kid. Joe was sure he could still take him in spite of the good shape the kid seemed to be in and in spite of any trick stuff they taught him in the Army. And now he knew that Jerry was reading his thoughts and grinning.

"Do you wanta go outside?" said Jerry, still grinning.

"Listen, kid, it's too cold outside. If we wanted to tangle I guess Patty'd let us push back a couple tables and chairs. What put that in your mind?"

"It's what you were thinking, wasn't it?" said Jerry.

"Yeah, I guess so. It's only natural. The day I can't handle you that day I'll admit my age."

"Well, that day is here. It was here a long time ago, Joe. How old are you?"

"The hell with that kind of talk," said Joe.

"I bet you're close to forty-five."

"Not quite, not quite. You're what? Twenty-nine. I guess I can still spot you say fourteen, fifteen years if it came to that, but wuddiasay we hope it doesn't come to that, Jerry. What I'm inttarested in is why the hush over your trip to N'York."

"How'd you know I was in town?" said Jerry. "That's what I'm inttarested in."

Joe decided to be frank. "I heard it from three or four different sources. Are you in trouble? Did you go over the hill?"

"You know so much, you figure it out."

"I don't have to figure it out. I know. You had your load on last night, all over town. I could name a half a dozen different spots where you were shooting off your mouth how you felt about the Army. What do you wanta do? Go to Leavenworth? You wanta kill Mom?"

"Listen, fella, *you* didn't kill her."

"I was different. I was never home much anyway. Also don't overlook the fact that she's a lot older than she used to be. As far as I'm concerned, listen, you can go up and spit in MacArthur's eye, that is if you ever get close enough to him. Which I doubt."

"I remember those pictures of you in that little sailor suit.

Where was it you were? Pelham Bay. You were a big hero. Yeah, you fought a hell of a war . . . Why—don't—you—stop."

Joe took out a pack of cigarettes, lit one, put the pack back in his pocket, and for a long time he smoked and slowly sipped his drink. He said nothing, but every once in a while he would look at his brother and then look away. Finally Jerry spoke. "I got a date," he said.

"Goo-ood," said Joe. Then: "With a *girl?*"

"Don't be funny."

"I'll just stick around and see what she looks like."

"Stick, and see if I care," said Jerry. He picked up his drink and went to the bar. Joe watched him finishing his drink; by the time Patty served him another the girl came in. She was about twenty and one of the current crop of very pretty dancers. Joe could not hear what they said to each other, but the girl looked over at him coldly and with hate. She turned away again, then Jerry came over and took his coat and cap off the hook. He dropped two dollars on the bar and Jerry and the girl went out together, walking close together arm in arm. Joe watched them out of sight and then joined Patty at the bar.

"Well, I guess I certainly fixed that," said Joe.

Patty rubbed his chin and looked out toward the street. "Yap. Well, that's the way it goes," he said.

"What the hell can I do? Does he have a pass, do you know?"

"Yeah. Three days. There was two M.P.'s in here last night checking up. I guess he's in the clear so far."

"Maybe I ought to turn him in," said Joe.

"Oh, you wouldn't wanta do a thing like that, Joe. Not turn him in. Hope for the best, Joe. Hope for the best."

"I get it. You don't think I handled it right."

"Well, I don't know, Joe. I don't know. That ain't for me to say."

"Who was the dame? Do you know her?"

"Nope. Never seen her before. Some chorus girl she looked like."

"If I could get to her—"

"Well, I don't know, Joe. If I was you, if you want my advice I'd just leave things the way they are. You just gotta wait and see and hope for the best."

"Yeah. Wait and see. You're a hell of a lot of help."

"Oh, now don't start taking out your abuse on me, Joe. I did you the favor of calling you up if he happened to come in the place, but I don't have to stand here and take your abuse, no more than he did. No sir." Walsh was all dignity. "Andy, take over a minute, while I go down the cellar, will you?" Walsh left and Andy stood behind the bar, but at the far end of the bar away from Smith, and Andy concentrated on his paper to show that he didn't want to talk.

Joe put a couple of bills on the bar. "This is a hell of a place," he said, and left.

HE THINKS HE OWNS ME

About once every hour I make it a habit to make a sort of a tour of my club, or saloon. That way I get to say hello to the ones that think I ought to say hello to them, and I get a general picture of how things are going, like is the orchestra playing too loud and are the waiters standing around not paying any attention to the live ones that have a thirst. But when I finish my tour I make it a habit to go back and sit at the same table near the entrance and near the bar. I have good reasons for that, too. One thing, I can see everybody that is coming in and when there is somebody that Theodore, my headwaiter, may have his doubts about, he can look over at me for a signal whether to leave the parties in or tell them we're all filled up. Another thing that may sound corny because it has been in the movies and stories but is true, I been in this business a long time. A very long time. And when I started out in it it wasn't legal and I always have to keep it in mind that some guy from twelve–fifteen years ago might take it in his head to pay an unfriendly visit, so I always like to not only know who is in my club but to see them coming in. When I am taking my tours naturally I have to leave it up to Theodore, but when he is in doubt he makes them wait till I get back to my table near the bar.

This one night recently I came back to my table and there was a few people standing outside of the rope waiting for

Theodore to leave them in. Five people. Two couples and a guy around my age alone. Why Theodore was holding them up I could see right away because I know how Theodore's mind works. He was stalling the young couples because they didn't look as if they would have enough money to pay the bill and also they wouldn't of decorated the place. I leave plenty young people in that have very little moola but at least they decorate the place and also ones that maybe have not got much money now but will have when they get a little older. But then I noticed these two young couples were sober and quiet and so I gave Theodore the nod and he left them in. That gave me a chance to look at the older guy, the guy my age.

I knew I saw him some place before. He looked sober and as if he had money in his pocket and the kind of guy generally that Theodore would of left in to have a couple drinks at the bar. But it made me smile, because I knew what was going on in Theodore's mind. The same thing that was going on in mine. What I said before: we have the same kind of mind. Meaning I didn't want him in and Theodore wasn't leaving him in because the both of us knew we saw him before but couldn't place him. If we didn't think we saw him before he would of got in right away.

I sent for Theodore. "Who is that fellow?"

"Boss, I been trying ever since he got here, but I can't place him."

"Did he ask for me?"

"No, all he asked for was a table in the big room and I told him we were all filled up and anyway he couldn't sit in there if he didn't have a lady with him. He offered me five bucks and then ten, and when I turned him down he asked me if it was all right if he stood there and waited, maybe he'd see somebody coming in that he knew. So I said if he wanted to wait, okay."

"You're not supposed to do that."

"I know, Boss, but he seemed all right. If he was a total

stranger I'd of let him in to the bar, but I wanted you to get a look at him."

I thought a minute. "Give him a table and keep an eye on him. I want to find out who he is." Theodore let him in, but we didn't find out who he was, not that night or the next or the next, and so on till of course we finally did or I wouldn't be telling this story.

He would come in every night and stay till we closed. He was a good customer, although I don't like to see a middle-aged guy alone at a table, but he aroused my curiosity. He would spend about the same every night. His checks would come to around fifteen bucks and he gave the waiter five bucks and five bucks to Theodore. He drank enough Scotch so that he wouldn't leave as sober as he came in, but the only difference was when he left he always looked pleased with himself, sort of smiling. We tried several ways to find out who he was. His hat, for instance, it came from a New York store but no initials in it. He had three suits. Conservative, but not any particular kind of conservative the way some of my Yale and Harvard customers' are. His hair was just about all gray and he was a man that had put on weight. That much I figured out for myself: when I knew him before he was thinner. I went through all the kinds of business I could think of to try to place him. Actor, athlete, aviator, banker, broker, doctor, et cetera. The funny thing was that he fitted every one of them. I'd say to myself he was an all-American football player, and I could easily see him in a football suit. Or I'd say to myself he was a lawyer and I could easily figure him for that. I had him down for a reporter, and I was sure he was that, but a lot of newspaper guys come in my place and as a matter of fact I asked two of them to take a look at him and they both said the same thing, namely, that they saw him before but couldn't place him. A lot of help that was.

Of course there were two things I could of done. In my business if you're any good at it you get the knack of making yourself agreeable to a customer like this guy, stopping by his table a few times and getting him into conversation. Most people will ask you to sit down and start telling you their life history, but this fellow gave me no encouragement. I asked him a couple times if everything was satisfactory and he said thanks it was but that was all the encouragement I got. Also I didn't want to crowd him because by this time I was sort of playing a game. The second thing I could of done was have him tailed and one night I did through one of the hack drivers outside my place, but the stranger only went some place for something to eat and the hackie didn't wait. I was sort of ashamed of that because I was only cheating myself. I got so I wanted to remember him without any help and I stopped asking people who he was. Theodore had the same feeling. He took it as sort of a game too. We even made a bet which one would place the fellow first. Fifty bucks.

Well, Mister Mystery kept coming in, getting a little plastered, but not giving anybody no trouble till one night Sue Sutton, the singer with the band, said to me: "Mister Mac, who is that character comes in alone every night?"

"Why do you ask?" I said.

"I don't know."

"Does he bother you? He send you notes?"

"No, he just looks at me."

"Well, you know, Sue, a lot of guys look at you. I look at you myself. It isn't all that torchy voice." That was true. Sue had had a couple of shots at Hollywood but no cigar. She never got anywhere there, but she was a good little band singer and what looked like fat in her screen tests looked just right in front of a band. If the Mystery Man had to look at anybody he could do a lot worse than Sue, and that includes a majority of the customers. But then Theodore told me that Sue had asked Frank, one of the waiter captains, to give the Mystery Man a table where she wouldn't see him, which Frank did. She said the man would sit there grinning at her, making her feel creepy. This was very unusual for Sue, who never let anything like a man grinning at her bother her. Finally she came to me again and said she wanted the fellow barred.

"What for?" I said. "I can't just suddenly bar a guy without telling him why."

"I won't go on while he's in the club. If you want to fire me, okay, but that's how I feel."

"Take a couple nights off. You're getting stale."

"I'll take the nights off, but if this character's here when I come back— It isn't as if he did anything or said anything. I just have the feeling he thinks he owns me or something."

Sue took the next two nights off. The second night the Mystery Man asked Frank if the girl singer was sick or had quit and Frank told him no, she was only taking a couple nights off. That made up my mind. Curiosity or no curiosity, this guy had what they call a fixation about Sue and I had a hunch it would lead to some kind of trouble and Sue was too good a kid for that, so the third night, when she was coming back, I left word with Theodore that the Mystery Man was barred. Theodore took it hard and asked me if the bet was off and I said yes. The Man turned up as usual and Theodore wouldn't let him in. The fellow took it all right the first time but when it happened a second and a third time he said to Theodore, "Am I barred? Is that it?"

Theodore stalled. He said: "The management doesn't like to serve gentlemen without ladies, sir."

"That isn't it," the fellow said, and left the club.

Then two nights later he turned up again, but this time drunker than I ever saw him, and nasty. Theodore and the doorman had to throw him out and the cop on post helped them. The second night after that I was reading the morning papers and I found out all I wanted to know.

Here's what the paper said: "Ellwood Dale, 47, hero of many silent pictures, committed suicide early yesterday by leaping from his room in the Hotel Blanque . . . Dale, whose career

as a screen lover was matched by his marital adventures, retired from the screen with the advent of talking pictures. In
recent years he had been living on a small ranch near Hollywood.
He was first married to Marie Latour. This marriage was followed in rapid succession by brief unions with Hazel Harkness,
Charlene Munsey, and Renee Case . . ."

I was studying the old photograph of the Mystery Man
when Theodore came to my table. "I see you got the papers,
Boss."

"Yeah, tough. But one angle I don't get. Sue."

"Sure you do, Boss. Charlene Munsey is Sue's mother."

"I didn't know that," I said. "In a way I guess I owe you
fifty bucks." However, we still haven't settled that.

THE DRY MURDERS

When Kirschner went into the dining room for his breakfast, Julie and the cook were in conversation. Julie was dressed up. She turned, and so did the cook, but neither spoke to him; they concluded their conversation and the cook left. Then Julie spoke: "Do you want anything in Beverly Hills? I'm taking the children in to see Dr. Mull."

"No, unless you can get me a new pair of these," he said.

"Huaraches? Why don't you get them yourself? Nobody can buy shoes for somebody else," she said.

"They don't have to fit perfectly, you know. And I could draw an outline of my foot."

"Not this morning, you couldn't. This morning you couldn't draw flies."

"Ha ha ha," he said.

"Ha ha ha yourself," she said. "You don't think I'd waste a good gag on you, do you?"

"Not unless you were sticking it in my mouth, ha ha ha ha ha," he said. "Tell her I just want coffee." He nodded toward the kitchen door.

"You can do that yourself," she said.

"Be a kind, considerate helpmeet, gentle Julia. Take pity on your errant husband. Do this one last thing, make this final gesture . . ." She heard only half of what he said; she was in the kitchen.

She came back.

"You know damn well she hates me," he said. "She's only deaf when I ask her to do something."

"We're lucky to have her at all. I'm surprised she stays. You stiff every night since we've been down here, walking around the way you are now. Look at yourself."

He walked to a pier glass, and suddenly put up his hands in exaggerated horror that was not meant to be funny. "No, no! Don't force me to look at that—that—*thing!* That which was once a man."

"What are your plans?"

He sat at the table. "A cup of coffee, and then I have no plans."

"Well, just remember Fay and Allan are coming for lunch."

"I've just made some plans," he said. "I'm going for a swim."

"All right. I'll be back before lunch," she said. "Wait a minute. When are you going for your swim?"

"The minute I see Fay and Allan stepping off their porch."

"I *thought* so. You can't do that. You know they don't like to sit on the beach."

"That's one thing I know, all right," he said. "That's one thing I'm counting on."

"Oh, well, there's no use arguing with you. Your disgusting bad manners. Alienate those two and see who speaks to us." One of the children—they were hers by another marriage—called to her. "Go for your swim," she said to Kirschner. "I hope you drown."

"And so—do I," he said. "You know who writes dialogue like that? Do you know how much writers get? That write dialogue like that? I think I'll be a writer. The two of us team up, Julie. Both be writers." She hurried out, but he went on talking as though he were addressing a panel of prominent cameramen. "Take it away, Ruttenberg. Take it away, Daniels. Take it away, Shammy. No more a cameraman I. Take it away, Cronjager." The cook, carrying the coffee things, halted with the swinging door half open.

"Don't you want the coffee?" she said.

"Oh, sure. I was just trying to use extrasensory perception on my great friend Professor Leon Shamroy. He's miles away."

"I don't believe in that stuff. Telepathy."

"Oh, you mustn't say that, Mrs. Quinn. Professor Cronjager, Dr. Ruttenberg—"

"Mr. Kirschner, if it's all the same to you, my own husband, Mr. Quinn, he didn't used to sit around with his bathrobe open in front of me and I don't think you have any right to either."

"But I'm wearing bathing trunks, too, Mrs. Quinn. I really am." She saw, obviously to her surprise, that he was telling the truth and stalked back to the kitchen.

Kirschner smoked while drinking two cups of black coffee, and left the house, taking with him cigarettes and sunglasses.

He dropped his bathrobe and huaraches on the beach in front of the house and began to walk away from his place and Allan's. In ten minutes he reached a promontory at which the beach narrowed, and beyond which he could not be seen from his house. Ahead of him there were shacks and cottages less elegant than the one in which he lived. He sat on the beach, his back against a rock, and remembered when there were no houses, elegant or otherwise, along this entire stretch. "This may well be the suburbs of Santa Barbara, or the Peninsula, or something," he said. He lit a cigarette and stretched his legs, and rested the back of his head against his clasped hands. "This is a rather unusual way to go about planning a murder," he said. "That's what you want to be by yourself for, isn't it? To plan a murder?" One murder, he was convinced, would be enough. If he were to murder Julie he would be rid of her, and automatically free of her cold, superior children. Their father could have them all the time then, if that's what he wanted—and it seemed to be, since he was always fighting to get them.

If he were to murder Fay, she would not be around to be wanted, to enjoy being wanted, to get excited with the knowledge of how very much she was wanted. "I was told," she once had said to Julie in his presence, "that I was the only actress Kirsch ever photographed that he didn't have an affair with. Star, of course, I mean. Or leading lady. I don't think it was a compliment, either. He never even made a pass at me, did you, Kirsch?"

"I *looked* quite a few, I remember," he had said.

"I guess I was too frightened of your reputation," Fay had said.

"As a cameraman or as a bum?" he had said.

"Both, I guess. I don't mean bum. Wolf."

It must have been a tiresome conversation for Julie, although she never had referred to it. Her friendship with Fay was of such a nature that it suited her, at various times, to believe and not care that he had had an affair with Fay, or to believe that he had not, which was the truth. It was also true that on their only picture together Fay was sleeping with the director. She then married Allan, who was not in pictures, and Kirschner likewise married out of the profession.

"If I murdered Allan she'd fall right in my lap," he told himself. (He had not worked out any murder plans beyond planning to make it, in any case, look like an accident.) As the bereaved she would not want to do anything so gauche as to return to pictures, and she never had made much of a hit with Allan's friends, so she would be right in his lap.

Of his three possible victims the only one he wanted to murder with any violence was Allan, and that was Allan's own fault. Once in an embarrassing moment of frankness Allan had discussed the friendship that gave him such happiness: "One thing I do know, you Kirschners, and that is this—we're not friends just because I happened to marry a famous movie star. You especially, Kirsch, because you've had that almost all your life. I honestly, sincerely believe you like Fay for herself and me for myself. Julie and I, we're just a couple of Pasadena people, to begin with, but the funny part is, the four of us, we're all like

just ordinary people together. You see what I mean, Kirsch?"
Kirsch saw what he meant, all right, and he also saw Fay taking
a sun bath almost every day.

There would be no murder, he well knew, and there would
be nothing else. His wife and his un-had woman would hold
towels in front of them when he appeared on the roof of his sun
porch. The woman's husband would take him to football games
and keep the conversation clean and faithful, if not exactly trust-
ing. In two more weeks, Kirschner would start work on a new
picture, and if there was anything there it would be all right, if
it wasn't too much trouble. As for now, if he started back immediately, he probably would get to the house in time to shake
up a nice Dubonnet cocktail for Fay and a nice Dubonnet frappé
for Allan. Now one deep, health-giving breath of sea air before
getting to his feet.

"Hullo."

Kirschner, abruptly aware that he had been half asleep,
turned and saw a boy, perhaps three years old, standing to his
right. "Hello, there," said Kirschner.

"What's in that package?"

"Cigarettes."

"Do you smoke them?"

"Oh, yes. Quite a good deal."

"I'm going to smoke, too," said the boy.

"Well, I think you ought to wait awhile."

"Is that a lighter that you turn and it lights up and you hold
it near your cigarette?" said the boy.

"Zippo. Do you want to try it? I'll show you how. See? Now
you try it."

The boy operated the gold lighter and held it to Kirschner's
cigarette. "Thank you," said Kirschner.

"What's your name?"

"Paul," said Kirschner.

"My name is Billy. Do you want to see the famous splash in the water?"

"I do indeed," said Kirschner.

"Now watch." The boy ran to the water, spread out his arms, and flopped down. He came back.

"That was some splash, all right," said Kirschner.

"Oh, look, you have *white* hairs, too." The boy pointed to Kirschner's chest.

"That's right."

"Where do you live?"

"Way down the beach," said Kirschner.

"We don't. We live *that* way."

"I see. One of those white houses."

"No, no. That's the way we *came*. We came in our *car*."

"Oh, I get it," said Kirschner. "Is that your mother coming this way?"

"Yes. I have to go with her."

He went a little way in the direction of the young woman who was calling him, but then he turned around and came back to Kirschner. "I want to kiss you," the boy said.

"Please do," said Kirschner. The child kissed him on the cheek.

"Goodbye," said Kirschner.

"Goodbye, Paul."

"I have to go, too," said Kirschner. He stood up and waved a little while before going his own way. For the last time that day he spoke to himself aloud. "Nobody in Christ's world would believe it," he said.

EILEEN

All morning the flowers had been arriving, and the telegrams, and some of them had been there when Joe Stone appeared at his office, at twenty past nine. The messages all made little jokes on his completing his first year as a producer, the jokes not always in direct ratio of intimacy to the cordiality of his relationship with the senders. Some of the agents, for example, seemed to think that if they called Joe their pal, that meant he was their pal. Some of those people knew better, and still others would never, never know better, and for them he felt a little pity. They were the ones who could not really afford to send anything—not even telegrams—and sent large baskets of flowers. His fellow-producers on the lot likewise sent baskets of flowers, but their cards said things like "Nice going," or made gags of a complimentary nature based on the titles of Joe's two enormously successful pictures or the one that was at the moment in work.

He did not wonder long how so many people had hit the anniversary right on the nose. Joe was not yet in *Who's Who,* and hardly anyone had remembered his birthday a month ago, but his first anniversary as a producer was a date that got remembered; and of course there was Elsie, his secretary, who knew her way around the studio. Elsie would expect other secretaries to remind her of their producers' anniversaries (unless their producers happened to be on the way out), and so she had reminded them of this big milestone in Joe's career.

Elsie had put the flowers in his private office, and she followed him in. He turned around to her and smiled. "How do you think it looks? You know all that stuff. Am I on the way out, or is it just the right number? Not too many, or not too few?"

"Just exactly the right number. Pile of telegrams on the desk," said Elsie. "I've started a list of telegrams and another list for flowers."

"Good girl. Thank you."

"That's part of my job. I didn't send you anything."

"If you had, we couldn't have kept a straight face."

"That's more or less what I figured," said Elsie.

"How about a kiss to celebrate?"

"Stop. If you ever wanted a kiss from me, you wouldn't have to ask for it."

"Well, in that case . . ." he said.

"No, now. Don't put on an act. It's an insult when we both know it's an act. The square basket's from Mrs. Stone. I'd better not tell you what the flowers are, because she'd know I told you."

Joe took off his lapel-less jacket and hung it in his bathroom closet. He replaced his sunglasses with his reading glasses and went through the telegrams rapidly. "You say you have a list of who sent flowers?"

"The name you'd be looking for isn't on the list, so far," said Elsie.

"You could be wrong, you know."

"I don't think so. The big boss's name heads the list. The other name isn't on it. Am I wrong?"

"Never," said Joe.

"The young lady'll be here in person at three-thirty, you know—or how dull can I get?"

"Where do you think I ought to send these things—Cedars of Lebanon?"

"Send some to Los Angeles General. I'll take care of it. I'll call Transportation just before I go home, and get a studio truck."

"Why not before that? This'll be like trying to work in Forest Lawn."

"Look, Mr. Stone, I can't help it if the young lady's going to be embarrassed because she didn't send you flowers. There'll be people that did send flowers coming in and out of here all day and they'll expect you—"

"All right, all right."

"And you *have* to be here at six, because they're planning a little surprise for you in the executives' dining room. The big boss'll be there."

"How to start the day wrong," said Stone.

"How to end it wrong, if you're not in the execs' dining room at six."

"When *have* I been off the lot at six? I'll be on hand."

"Well, it's a living," said Elsie. She flipped open her notebook. "Forrest Bedford wants thirty-five hundred and a ten weeks' guarantee or he won't leave the Cape. He says he's working on his play, and he also wants the studio to get him a house at Malibu. No? . . . The table at Romanoff's is O.K. for eight-thirty. . . . Research says you were right and they didn't wear spiral puttees at the Mexican border in 1916. . . . Washington says it's no use trying to talk to General Pershing. . . . General Funston died in 1917. . . . I'll get it." She answered the telephone. Joe Stone was in his second year.

At three-twenty, Elsie spoke to Joe over the intercom. "Miss Eileen Clancy is here."

"Ask her to come in, please," said Joe.

He stood up when she came in, and held out his hand. "Nice to see you, and always punctual."

She shook hands. "That's the way I was brought up, and I want to get ahead."

"You will," he said.

"What's the big occasion? Is it your birthday?"

"The one that counts around here. One year ago, I became a producer."

"Well, if what everybody says is right, you'll be spending a lot more of them around here. Congratulations. At least I could have sent you a telegram. I will when I go home."

He knew, because he often had waited for other people's decisions governing his own career, what she must be going through, and yet she seemed to be enduring no anxiety. She seated herself at the left side of his desk, in a large, comfortable chair—large enough to rate its own little table, cigarette box, lighter, and ashtray. The afternoon sun came in on her, but she had nothing to fear from it, even though nobody's hair could be genuinely that color. It was almost the color of her skin. But, at least for a while, no one would want her to change it. Her features were of such regularity as to be next to uninteresting, and they were interesting because they were perfect. Her mother and father had been in show business and they had taught her makeup; they knew, and she knew, that she could use that much lip paint, which on anyone else would have been too much. She was wearing a good, plain white dress, left unbuttoned in a frank display of her breasts. The only jewelry she wore was a tiny wristwatch with a heavy gold snake band.

"Well, I wanted to tell you myself, Eileen. I have good news for you." Joe could not resist making her wait a few seconds. The corners of her mouth showed the beginnings of a childish smile, but her eyes showed something far from childish, which had shown up in her last picture, a bit that had been cut out and that he had seen before the picture was cut. "In fact, a lot of it," he said.

"Tell it to me slowly," she said.

He picked up a paper knife, held it by the forefinger of his right hand and the forefinger of his left hand. He spoke slowly. "You are getting a new contract," he said.

She lit a cigarette and inhaled faster than a worried horse-player. "Uh-huh." She nodded twice.

"You're being tested for Sara Duval," he said.

"Yes," she said. She could tell from his inflection that there was more.

"And a very good break. I persuaded Franklin Ames to make the test with you. He never makes tests with anybody—not since he's been a star."

She looked at him in a way that at first was difficult to understand. He had no feeling that she was seeing him—and then he recognized the expression. He had seen it before, on a few women with whom passion took the form of sadness. There are those who cry. He was witness to the end of the life she had led until now and watching the beginning of the new life, as a star, that she had always wanted. It was probably more intense than any passion she ever had experienced, and she was helpless. And he was closer to her now than he ever had been before. All he had to do was touch her, yet if ever there was a time not to touch her, this was the time. Now, this minute, it wouldn't have made any difference who touched her, but it would be better to have her remember later that he had not.

The moment passed and her expression changed. "I think you cut your finger," she said. She stood up.

"Why, God damn it, I did," he said. "I'm bleeding to death."

She put her handkerchief over the two tiny drops of blood where the paper knife had pricked him. "May I keep the handkerchief?" he said.

She nodded. "Do you always have that much self-control?"

He looked up and saw that he could hide nothing from her. "I've never had to before."

"Then the more thanks for having it now." She sat down. "I didn't have any of my own, but I have now. Joe, I'm in love with somebody, or I think I am. He isn't anybody you know. He isn't even in pictures. I guess I'd better get off this lot. I wouldn't be any good to you, and you've been good to me."

"I wouldn't bother you."

"No. I could count on that, but I know I bother you. If they want me that much here, I can get work someplace else. You can get me my release."

"I could, but I couldn't stand it with you not here. Let's try it and see how it works out," he said.

"You know what's sensible? It's for me to shake hands and say thanks and goodbye."

"That wouldn't have been the case if you hadn't read my mind. Try it, Eileen. See how it works out."

"I have my car. I think I'll go for a long ride." She stood up.

"I'm sorry if I spoiled your big day."

"I'm sorry if I spoiled yours, Joe."

"You didn't."

"Shall I come in Monday?"

He smiled. "Same time, same station."

She went out.

There was someone else waiting to see him, and someone after that. It was a little past five-thirty and he was alone when Elsie came in and laid a telegram on his desk. It was from West Los Angeles and it said: "I have thought it over and have decided it will work out all right." It was signed "E.C."

"Any answer?" said Elsie.

"No," he said. The answer was not up to him, but he could not tell that to Elsie—any more than he could tell her that the future looked bright·

THE WAR

The electric refrigerator, in its own room off the kitchen, was of a size that could be suitably recommended for a small hotel. The young man held a quart bottle of homogenized milk in one hand, the while he inspected other contents of the refrigerator.

"Now who the hell are you?" said a deep voice.

"Sir?" said the young man.

"I just asked you who the hell you were," said the man, who was overweight and past his youth.

"Me? Why? Who are you, for that matter?"

"Somebody owns this establishment, and I could be the one."

"Nuts. You could, maybe, but you're not," said the young man.

"Listen, kid. Identify yourself. I don't like to see my friends' iceboxes being raided by some unidentified squirt."

"Go away, mister, whoever you are. I was invited here. And don't try any funny stuff or I'll crack you with this bottle."

"I see you would, too," said the man. "What's your name?"

"Oh, shut up and go away. My name is Frank Ankle. Does that suit you?"

The middle-aged man looked at the young fellow and then burst out laughing. "Frank Ankle?"

"That's good enough for you, mister."

The man put his hand over his entire face, over and over

again, bending his nose, roughing up the grain of his eyebrows. "Is your name—now tell me the truth—is your name Something Wheelwright?"

The boy frowned. "Why'd you pick that name?"

"Are you a nephew of Bob Wheelwright's?"

"Yes," said the boy.

The man shook his head. "All the characteristics. All the characteristics. You are—Ed Montgomery's kid. Your mother was Ellen Wheelwright."

"Yes sir." The boy nodded.

"Frank Ankle. I haven't heard of Frank Ankle for twenty years at least. Put down the milk bottle, son. I could have taken it away from you any time. Like this." The man put his left arm in front of the boy's right arm and grabbed hold of the back of the boy's coat at the same time he gently but quickly put the heel of his right hand under the boy's chin, and gently kicked the boy's left foot, throwing him off balance. "A little respect for your elders, son. If you hadn't said Frank Ankle I was about to put you back in the icebox, you and the bottle of milk." He tapped the boy's chin a few times.

"I'm convinced," said the boy.

"One of these little taps would break your neck."

"I'm convinced," said the boy. The man released him.

"One thing," said the man. "Never *threaten* to hit a man with a milk bottle. Hit him. Now tell me about Bob Wheelwright. What's happened to him? I haven't heard anything from him for four-five years."

"Uncle Bob's dead," said the boy.

"Dead? When'd he die? I mean, Bob Wheelwright died?"

"Yes sir. He died last spring. May the twelfth, I think it was. By the way, my name is Ted Montgomery."

"My name is Joe Rutledge." He took a cigarette from an old-fashioned curved case. "Have one. Look at what it says in that case." He handed over the case and rested on a kitchen chair.

The boy read: " 'To perhaps the best man. June the twenty-second, Nineteen-twenty-three.' I see."

"You know, you lose track of those things," said Rutledge. "I mean, Bob did, and I did. But I wonder where the hell I was last May? Where have I been since, that I didn't know about Robbie?"

"Uncle Bob died in a sanitarium."

"Well, I knew that. At least I knew he was off his rocker, but at least somebody should have told me and not just find it out from somebody out of the blue. That's a hell of a note. Did your Aunt Angie go to the funeral?"

"No sir. Mother and Father went, but not my grandmother. It was very private."

"Didn't they send it to the alumni paper?"

"I think they did. I'm not sure," said the boy. "I don't know. Maybe they didn't. I thought maybe Father did, but I don't know for sure. You know—Uncle Bob was given up."

"I know, but how didn't I happen to hear he was even dead? Where was he?"

"Near Poughkeepsie. But nobody could ever see him," said the boy.

"I suppose you know why, don't you? That little cigarette case, I was best man. Grosse Pointe, Michigan. That girl was not very good. She was not. No. Not a very good girl. But old Robbie was stuck on her. All those kind of people used to take advantage of your uncle, and he'd let them get away with it . . . Save the goddam world! Help every son of a bitch that breathes the breath of life, but when it comes to where you can help somebody you love, you can't tell him anything, you can't advise him, you can't do anything for him. You just sit on your prat and keep your yap shut! You can't even go to his funeral."

The boy crushed the cigarette butt in a saucer. "Mr. Rutledge, sir, I was in the Navy. I got security-conscious."

"Are you trying to tell me to keep my trap shut?"

"Yes sir."

Rutledge lighted another cigarette. "What is going on in your mind is what I said about saving the world. Right?"

"Yes sir, but that's not all."

"Oh, and the fact that last May I didn't know your uncle was dead?"

"Yes sir," said the boy.

"Well, you have a point there," said the man. "You mean I must have been in some part of the world where I wouldn't hear he was dead?"

"Yes sir," said the boy.

"What else?"

The boy stared at him accusingly. "About how you could break my neck."

"Oh, is that so? That impressed you?"

"Yes sir," said the boy. "That isn't the way we were taught."

The man nodded. "Suppose I told you I haven't been out of this country since 1940? That would deflate the hell out of you, wouldn't it?"

"Yes sir," the boy said.

"I mean and convinced you that I haven't been out of the country since 1940."

"Yes sir," said the boy.

"Oh, stop. Now you think you're talking to rank, don't you?"

"Yes sir," said the boy.

The man stood up, and walked to the icebox. "Did you happen to notice who made this?"

"No sir. These kind of iceboxes—I don't know."

"What about your girl?" said the man.

The boy grinned. "Sir, I told you I was in the Navy."

"Never mind about the Navy. I asked you a question."

"Oh. You mean seriously. I thought you were trying to trap me again. My girl's here and she's hungry. That's what I was doing when you came in. Trying to get her a sandwich. If you see any roast beef . . ."

The man sat down. He looked unhappy and as though he were trying to hear distant sounds, of music, from God, of nothing falling on nothing. Then he stood up again, and his voice was musical. "All right, Ted. You'll come and work for us, won't you?"

"Yes sir," said the boy.

"That's good," said the man.

NIL NISI

All morning and all afternoon a Coast Guard plane, sometimes
two, had been flying low over the sea, circling, making eights
around imaginary pylons. Half a dozen powerboats, some official
and some private, stood by or cruised in a small area. A com-
mercial diver sat in the stern of one boat, wearing his suit, but
puffing on a pipe while his helmet lay on the deck and he awaited
the order to descend. In the morning, people stayed out of the
ocean, partly through fear, but mostly out of decent respect for
the woman whose body had not been found. They stood around
awkwardly, looking toward the focal point, a Coast Guard cutter,
and conversed in subdued tones, even, or perhaps especially, the
few small children. A couple of times when pieces of driftwood
the size of a railroad tie were washed up on the sand, it was an
adult and not a child who cried out. At lunchtime nearly all the
people on the beach went to their houses or to the Club. It was
not a very good day for the beach, but the sun did appear,
weakly, at about one-thirty. By three o'clock there was a larger
crowd on the beach than there had been in the morning, word
of the drowning having reached everyone on the island by that
time, and only a few persons were not in bathing dress. Someone
said, "If they haven't found her by now I don't think they ever
will, not around here." This thought was acceptable to most of

the people in swim suits and a large number of them went in the water.

George Whittier's house was less than a hundred yards up the beach from the point off which the cutter was standing by, and since nine-o'clock breakfast he had been watching the goings on from the roof. There were chairs and pillows and a *hikiee* on the roof so that he and his wife and their guests could take sun baths. It was no day for sun-bathing, and in any case Whittier's right arm was partly enclosed in a cast. He had broken a small bone in his wrist while trying to crank McCandless's Bugatti. Whittier had got the news of the drowning from Edgar, the colored houseman, who had to help him with breakfast. Edgar spread the marmalade on the toast and opened the eggs. "They was a lady drown last evening," said Edgar.

"Where? Here?"

"Yes, sir, somewheres right off the Hobson property. Your Mrs. Chaplin or Chapman, whatever the name is. Took place somewheres around eight o'clock last evening, near as I can find out."

"Mrs. Chapman? Good Lord! How'd it happen, Edgar? Did you hear? There's nobody in the Hobsons' house now."

"No, sir. They arrive Friday," said Edgar. "According to all the information I received, this lady and gentleman decided to go for a swim around eight o'clock last evening and it was mighty rough all day yesterday, and I guess eight o'clock, it may be she ate an early dinner and went in with a full stomach. Very likely got awful cramps and the gentleman couldn't save her. People rented the house next door to the Hobsons', they was seated having their dinner and heard the gentleman calling for help. They got a son, strong young fellow about twenty years of age, and he *dashed* right out and just thrun his coat on the sand there and removed his trousers and I imagine took off his shoes and dove right in that ocean and swam out there lookin' for who was looking for help. Just about pitch dark then, you know."

"Uh huh."

"He located the gentleman and brought *him* back, half drowned, but no sign of the lady. They never did hear the lady calling for help. According to my way of thinking, maybe she had one of these heart attacks and, glub, down she goes. They got the sheriff and the Coast Guard, but she was gone. Yes, sir, *she* was *gone*. They was up all night, though. They stayed right on the job. They're out there now. You and Mrs. Whittier and Mr. and Mrs. McCandless, you was in Palm Beach, and I guess that's how you didn't hear nothing about it. I didn't hear nothing myself till I went up the Club to fetch the mail."

"I saw lights on the beach, but I thought it was a picnic."

"Some picnic," said Edgar. He held a light for Whittier's cigarette. "They got must be a dozen or more boats out there lookin', and an areoplane flying around since early morning."

"I was wondering what the plane was doing."

"I never been up in one of those, but that ain't gonna do much good, that areoplane. Not the way that ocean is acting up. Too dirty to see anything no matter how high up or how low. Poor Mrs. Chapman, she'll probably get washed up at Daytona, or Stuart. Better be Stuart. I don't see them fish leaving her alone till she get to Daytona."

"Who?" said Ann Whittier, appearing at the door in her dressing gown.

"Sit down and eat your breakfast and I'll tell you later."

She slumped into a chair. "All I want is some tea and lemon. Those planters' punches! Just some tea, please, Edgar." Edgar went to the kitchen. "Did you hear me upchucking? About three or four o'clock. Some people were having a beach picnic at that hour. I wonder who."

"Some picnic," said Whittier.

"Hmm? You sound grim. What is it?"

"Millicent Chapman was drowned last night. The lights on the beach were people looking for her body. Apparently they haven't found her yet." He told her what Edgar had told him. She drank her tea slowly.

"I wonder who the man was," she said.

"Probably Ed. Ed Willard. Or Charlie Fox. We'll find out in a few minutes."

"Whoever it was, it was a dirty, nasty thing to do to him. And typical: Characteristic."

"You mean you think she committed suicide?" said Whittier.

"Of course she did, and just like those people that jump out of buildings and kill people walking on the street. If people are going to commit suicide, all *right*, that's their privilege, but why involve other people? Like that what's-his-name friend of yours that shot himself with his wife in the next room. Messing up other people's lives. Selfish, inconsiderate, just because they can't take it themselves."

Whittier studied his wife for a moment. "I'll find out who was with her. Will you dial the Club for me?" They left the dining room and she dialed the number.

"This is Mr. Whittier, Frank. Do you happen to know who was with Mrs. Chapman when she drowned? . . . I see. Thank you." He hung up. "It was Ed Willard." He studied her again. "I should have found out where he is. Do you want me to?"

"Not particularly. There's nothing we can do, and if he was as badly off as Edgar thinks, the doctor probably gave him something to put him to sleep."

"I suppose so," said Whittier.

"I guess we'll have to tell Mac and Betty. They're planning to play golf with me. Still, I don't know why they shouldn't play. They didn't know her. Just met her to say how-do-you-do to."

"We didn't know her so well either, but I don't think *you* ought to play golf."

"Why not?"

"Well—she's been here. We've entertained her. We've seen a lot of her every time we come down here."

"Yes, for two or three years, but in a small place like this you can't be very selective. The hell with her. I'm going to play if Mac and Betty feel like it."

"No, I don't want you to. You'll be the only people on the golf course, and I think Mac and Betty'll understand if you don't. They've some sense of the fitness of things."

"Even if I haven't. All right. What are we supposed to do? All put on bathing suits and go out and dive for her? Or wear black or something? You could be a little more considerate of your guests, if you ask me. You with your hand, you can't do anything anyway, so everybody else has to be marooned in this house while you go into deep mourning." She sang the words of the hymn: " 'For those in per-rill on the sea.' "

"God damn it, this isn't the only golf course in Florida. Take Mac and Betty to Palm Beach and we won't tell them anything about Millicent."

"All right, I *will*. What about you?"

"I'll stay here. Naturally, with my hand and so forth."

"You want to be alone," she said.

"Yes, as a matter of fact, that'd suit me fine," he said. They glared at each other and then he went to the roof. About an hour later, leaning against the parapet and watching the search, he heard the departure of his car.

He stayed on the roof all day and most of the time he looked out at the little fleet. He had Edgar bring up binoculars along with the sandwich and coffee he ordered for lunch, and every now and then, when the boats seemed to be gathering together, he would look through the glasses to see what he could see, but there was nothing new—only more of the same. Still, he stayed on the roof, because he had things to think about.

Until Ann had mentioned her suicide theory, he had not given suicide a thought, but after the word had been spoken (and he had been the first to speak it), he believed nothing else.

"I like you," Millicent Chapman had said. "I never thought I would." That had been on the train going North almost a year before, when his winter vacation was at an end.

"What's different about me now?"

"Your mind's on your work," she had said. "Instead of being on a train, you're practically in your office. Florida's nothing to you."

"Florida's a hell of a lot to me," he had said. "So is Maine."

"I don't believe it. Your work's the most important thing in the world to you."

"No. If I could make as much money playing golf as I do practicing law, there's no doubt in my mind which I'd choose."

"Naturally," she had said. "But you can't. Hogan and Snead and those people, the top ones, can't make as much money as you do, and don't tell me you'd like to be one of them and scale your living accordingly. You'd rather be what you are, a successful lawyer. Let me like that about you, will you, please?"

"Why, sure. Only you're wrong. From now on, I'll be thinking of Maine. After Maine, I'll start thinking about Florida."

She had shaken her head. "My life is what you think you like. No work. All play. Dull girl."

"No, not a dull girl. Will I be seeing you in New York?"

"You know you will, as much as you like. I was going to Arizona next week, but now I won't."

He had seen her in New York, but after a week she had called him at his office to talk of love, and that night he had told her, angrily, never to do that again. "All right," she had said. "You can go home now, and I can go to Arizona tomorrow. Go on, go home."

"Don't be unreasonable."

"Go home!"

In the hall that night, waiting for the elevator, he had been glad to be out of it with so little damage done, but months later, in Maine, he often thought of the coming autumn in New York and the inevitability of seeing her again, even though he had heard nothing from her or about her. In the fall, he had looked for her at parties, restaurants, and the theatre, but did not see her again until Florida, in his own house, the first afternoon of his winter vacation. "Ed Willard and Charlie Fox are coming for dinner," Ann had said. "And Millicent Chapman and a new couple from Chicago, very nice, named Valentine."

"That'll be nice," he had said, and it was. It gave him a chance to talk to Millicent. She rode with him after dinner when they all went to a party up the beach.

"I'm awfully glad you're here, Millicent."

"I'm here because I knew you'd be here. Otherwise I hate the place. The phony simple life. I'm going to Palm Beach tomorrow afternoon and I'll be there tomorrow and the next day and the next, too, for that matter, if you like. It's somebody I know named Sylvia Crown and she won't be there. Are you interested?"

"Yes."

"At least one day come, whenever you can make it. Please? I love you. I won't leave the house."

But he had not gone. Two or three times he could have gone. Once, in fact, Ann had asked him to go to West Palm Beach to the hardware store and he had told her to send Edgar. On the fourth day, Millicent had appeared on the beach, and she had been there every day thereafter, and he had never been alone with her again. She had seen to that.

It was getting dark when he heard his car, and in a few minutes Ann and the McCandlesses trooped up to the roof.

"Have you been up here all day?" said Ann. She glanced at the binoculars, which were hanging around his neck.

"Yes. They still haven't found her," said Whittier.

"That's a morbid occupation," said Ann. "I told Betty and Mac that a swim'd be out of the question, so we're having drinks up here. Unless that's out of the question, too?"

He ignored her. "What would you like, Betty? How about you, Mac?" They told him what they wanted and he called down to Edgar for the ingredients. He again addressed the McCandlesses, inquiring about their golf, and they were voluble about that. Edgar brought the Martini things and placed them on the table. "Understand they recovered Mrs. Chapman," he said.

"Oh? Where?" said Ann. They all looked out to the boats.

He laughed. "Oh, them boats. You don't see no Coast Guard boat out there. Cutter, he went down the island about four-five mile. He got the instructions by the radio when they found her. Them boats don't know about her yet, but I do. Up at the Club, they know, but them boats don't know. They got her about an hour ago. Frank at the Club told me she was—" He hesitated and looked at Whittier.

"What?" said Ann.

"Like I was afraid of, Mr. Whittier. You recollect my fears if she had to go all the way to Daytona?"

"Oh, God," said Whittier.

"Mutilated?" said Ann.

"Yes, ma'am. Some. Not altogether. I didn't see her personally, but according to Frank. He didn't see her either, but according to the way he heard it . . ." He left.

Ann sat down and lit a cigarette. She gazed at it reflectively. "I suppose that more or less disproves my suicide theory," she said.

"How so?" said Whittier.

"A woman as vain as she was, about her looks, she'd take into consideration that—well, just what happened. The fishes'd chew her up."

"Would somebody going to commit suicide take that into consideration, Ann?" said Betty.

"You can be sure Millicent would," said Ann.

"You won't give her a break either way, will you?" said Whittier. "She committed suicide and made it nasty for the fellow that was with her, or she didn't commit suicide, because she was too goddam vain."

Ann looked at him. "Can you think of any reason why I ought to give her a break? Think hard."

He looked back at her. "Thinking hard, no," he said.

THE TIME ELEMENT

At about five minutes to three the man appeared on the little balcony beneath the annunciator, and as if he had all the time in the world, seated himself in the high-backed old chair. In a minute or two he rose and stood with his eye on the clock until fifteen seconds before three, when he set off the bell that rang until precisely three. Then it stopped, and trading on the Stock Exchange was closed for another day.

Wilson had watched the ritual from a jump seat at one of the posts in the center of the floor. He could have left the floor earlier; from experience he knew at two-thirty that business for the remaining half hour was not likely to keep him occupied. At a quarter to three he began to want a cigarette, but he did not leave the floor. For years he had been saying—without full justice to himself—that maybe he wasn't the smartest member of the Stock Exchange, but at least he was always there. It was an unfair assertion, because he was not the stupidest member either; and it was only partially accurate, because there had been days when he had been physically present on the floor, when he might more conscientiously have been elsewhere. Sometimes it had been a hangover that resisted all known remedies; other times, more recently, it had been the simple mysterious thing that was going on inside him. The thing, whatever it was, was simple because it seemed to be nothing more, in its manifestations, than that he was tired, beat. It was mysterious, though, because neither medical check-ups nor introspection had disclosed any reason for the way he so often felt.

As the clanging ended Wilson looked up at the balcony and said, "And that, said John, is that." No one heard him. He said so-long to the men in his immediate vicinity and walked toward the checkroom, automatically unfastening his badge as he went. He turned in the badge, got his hat, and stepped out into Broad Street and proceeded to Wall and his firm's office. He avoided encounters with friends by assuming an interest in the vehicular traffic. In the tiny room which he shared with Ned Dell, one of his partners, he hung up his hat and seated himself at his desk.

"Pretty quiet, wasn't it?" said Ned. He stopped work, putting down his fountain pen and lighting a cigarette.

"Uh-huh," said Wilson. "Now and then you could hear a commodity drop."

"You got a new suit," said Ned.

"Every time I wear this suit you say that," said Wilson. He opened the coat and put his hand down in the inside pocket and turned out the label that gave the date the suit had been delivered. "I happen to know it's April, 1946, without reading it."

"Well, every time I say that you show me the label, so maybe we're both in a rut."

"That—is for certain," said Wilson. "Or maybe you're hinting that I *need* a new suit. Think I ought to dress up more, like Wakely or one of those guys?"

"Yeah. Wakely's just the guy. Or Fenimore. Maybe you ought to dress more like Fenimore. What this office needs is more double-breasted vests."

"All right, if we can get Fenimore's mother-in-law's business I'll wear double-breasted vests. I'll wear an uplift bra if that'll get her business." He glanced at the mail that had accumulated since his early-morning call at the office. Dell picked up his pen and bent over his desk, but did not resume working. "Say, Marge called and she wanted to make sure about Saturday. Are you coming?"

"As far as I know," said Wilson. "Phyllis made the date, and as far as I know it's all set."

"Marge wanted to be sure. She called Phyllis this morning but I think she said Phyllis was in town. But as far as you're concerned it's okay?"

"Absolutely," said Wilson.

"Because—now not like the last time, Rob."

"Oh, what are you beefing about? I apologized to Marge, and she understood," said Wilson. "I told you at the time, hell, you were better off without me that weekend. I was stewed by four o'clock in the afternoon."

"I know, but this time don't have one of those late lunches. You asked me what I'm beefing about? I'll tell you. Beef is one thing. Marge bought a twelve-pound roast just because the last time you came out to our place you said you'd like to eat nothing but roast beef for a whole weekend. Then you didn't show. You know how much Marge likes you. She wasn't sore, but you know she loves to be the hostess and so on. Why don't you come out Friday night with me?"

"I know we can't Friday," said Wilson. "I'll be there, Ned. Don't worry. Don't worry, boy. Take it easy, boy. I'll be there. I'll be there." He stood up. "I think I'll knock off. This mail can wait till morning. Does anybody want to see me about anything? If not, I think I'll shoot uptown."

"No. Unless you want to stop in Fred's office, he might have something, but not that I know of."

"He had somebody in there when I came in, so I think I'll pass him up. Goodnight, Doctor."

"Goodnight, Robert," said Ned.

The letters he was leaving behind were—some of them— just important enough to give Wilson a briefly satisfying feeling of truancy. The letters could be taken care of in the morning, but properly they should have been attended to before he left the office, and in the subway on the way uptown he enjoyed the sensation of running away. But when the train was slowing down for Grand Central that rather juvenile pleasure ceased to be. When he left the office he had intended only to go home early, but by the time the train had stopped he had decided not to take the four-ten. All he knew was that he was not going to take the four-ten, and he was not going to the Commodore Bar, the Biltmore Bar, or the Yale Club, the three places in the vicinity where he usually dropped in for a drink. He came out onto Forty-second Street and while he was making up his mind which direction to take he noticed an airline bus discharging passengers. It was not an event that he ordinarily noticed, but his attention was attracted by four men who were getting out of the "limousine." They may or may not have been traveling together, but they all were wearing those rainproof transparent covers on their hats. It was not raining on Forty-second Street, although it could have been out at the airport. Wilson had a non-violent but firm aversion to the hat covers, and he never had happened to see four of them together. The four men walked around to the back of the bus to repossess their luggage, and Wilson was about to move on, actually had taken a step, when he saw the last passenger, a woman, getting out of the bus. He knew immediately who it was, and he hurried away until he got to Lexington Avenue. He turned south on Lexington and entered the first clean-looking saloon.

He sat at a table, took off his hat and laid it on a chair.

"Yes, sir?" said the waiter, a man in his late fifties.

"I'm alone. All right if I sit at a table?"

"Sure. Suit yourself," said the waiter.

"I'm tired, but I'll be out of here before your dinner customers start coming."

"Yeah, it's a kind of a muggy day." The waiter held his napkin with both hands.

"Have you got a telephone here?"

"Yeah. There's somebody in there now, but I guess they'll be out."

"I hope so, eventually," said Wilson.

"If you're in a hurry I guess you could use the house phone," said the waiter.

"No, I was joking. Hoping whoever's in there wouldn't be there permanently."

"Oh, uh-huh?" The waiter did not like jokes. "You, uh, wanta order now?"

Wilson ordered a Scotch and soda and the waiter withdrew. He brought the full shot-glass, the highball glass, and the club soda. "Will I mix it for you?"

"Not this one," said Wilson. He drank the whiskey straight. "Another of the same, please."

"Uh-huh," said the waiter. He brought the second whiskey and said: "How do you want this one? Straight or mixed?"

"This one straight too," said Wilson.

"Okay." The waiter watched him down the second drink and held out his hand for the empty glass. "Same?"

"Same thing," said Wilson.

This time the waiter held out the replenished glass, expecting Wilson to take it and down it.

"No, I crossed you. I want to mix this one."

"Okay," said the waiter. He went back to the end of the bar, leaning against it and talking sideways to the bartender. Wilson knew they were talking about him, but what they thought or said was of so little consequence in his present frame of mind that they could have put on Hallowe'en masks and he would have ignored them. He was only waiting for time to pass.

He looked at his watch again and again, and then he went to the telephone booth and dialed the number of the Barclay. "I'd like to speak to Mrs. Dunbar."

"Mrs. Richard Dunbar?" said the operator.

He waited, and then the voice of the woman from the airline bus: "Hello?" It was a questioning, faintly surprised voice.

"Kit?" said Wilson.

"Who's that?"

"It's Rob."

"What?"

"It's Rob," he repeated.

"Who *is* that? Is this Norman?"

"No, it isn't Norman. It's Rob."

"If this is somebody trying to be funny I wish you'd stop. Who is it?"

"Rob Wilson."

She did not speak for two seconds. "Say that again," she said.

"Rob Wilson."

"So it is," she said. "What do you want?"

"I don't know."

"Why did you call me?" she said.

"I don't know that, either."

"How did you know I was in this hotel? Were you in the lobby or something?"

"No, I saw you getting off the bus," he said. "At Forty-second Street."

"And then followed me?"

"No. And this is the first hotel I called."

"Well, that's natural. What do you want?"

"Well, I'd like to see you."

"Well, of course *that's* impossible."

"Why?"

"*Why?*" she said.

"I'm not very far away. I could—"

"Oh, but you *are*. You don't *know* how far. Oh, one of those planes could go for *days* and not be as far."

"Will you come downstairs and have a drink with me?"

"No, of course not. Are you downstairs now? If you saw me at the bus you know I wasn't with my husband, but how do you know he wasn't here ahead of me?"

"I never thought of that, but now I know he isn't. Please see me for ten minutes. Downstairs."

"Ten minutes? For nine years my life's been wonderful because I didn't see you for *one* minute. Why did you call me? Why didn't you pretend to yourself it wasn't me?"

"I couldn't *do* that, Kit. And I did run away."

"You what?"

"I was quite close to you when you got out of the bus, with those four guys with the hat covers. But I beat it. I got out of that neighborhood, but here I am telephoning you. Nine years, Kit. You've been lucky if you didn't want to see me."

"*If* I didn't want to see you? You say *if?*"

"Kit! You've *got* to see me for ten *minutes.*" There was more desperation in his tone than he would have permitted if he had been able to control it, but the trouble was he had not known in advance that the desperation was there to control. She was silent again, and he could almost see her at her old habit, chewing her lower lip while confronted with a problem. Then:

"All right, ten minutes. I'll be downstairs in fifteen minutes. But someone's coming to take me out to dinner, so don't think I'll be with you any longer than ten minutes."

"Yes, I know. Norman," he said.

He paid his waiter at the bar, gave him a good tip, and had luck getting a taxi. It was not far to walk, but he did not want to look tired or hurried when she saw him.

She was punctual. She was wearing her traveling suit but no hat. She was thinner than before, but that was the way he had said she would be: thinner, when she was thirty-five, and achieving her true beauty. He had been right about the beauty, too; people in the lobby made a pleasurable point of looking twice at her.

They met and she said "Hello," with no mention of his name and no handshake. "Let's sit in here, not in the bar. I don't want a drink and I'd rather you didn't too."

"All right," he said. They found two vacant chairs.

"I've given up smoking," she said.

"I suppose I ought to," he said. He smiled. "We haven't much time, so—who's Norman?"

"We won't have any time at all if you're going to ask that kind of question. I gather you're still married to Phyllis."

"Isn't that the same kind of question?" he said.

"Perhaps it is, but I can ask them, and you can't. I didn't ask to see you, you know."

"That's true. I wonder why you did?"

"Because of an overwhelming curiosity to see what you looked like," she said. "What are you now? Forty-three?"

"Yes."

"What did you do in the war?"

"I was in Washington, in the Navy."

"You didn't get overseas?"

"No."

"How many children have you?"

"Three. The same three. Two boys at South Kent and my daughter's at Westover."

"I knew where she was. I saw her name. I went there myself, you know."

"I know."

"Are you living in the city?"

"No. Stamford."

"Are you making a lot of money?"

"Not much. All right."

"Well, I guess that's all I wanted to ask you," she said. "Ask me questions if you want to, but the right kind."

"Well, I know about you."

"Do you? What? How do you know about me?"

"I have a partner in Chicago, and my wife gets the Junior League magazine. You have two kids, and your husband's a doctor."

"Yes, he's also the finest man I ever knew. And rather than

have you go on with your nasty little suspicions about Norman, he's my husband's brother."

"I see."

"My husband would like to meet you sometime."

"Oh, he would?"

"Yes. To beat the hell out of you."

"Why?" he asked. "He didn't know you when I did."

"Just on principle. He thinks a married man that pretended he was single and—well, just what you did. Almost made me commit suicide. I hope you never meet him, because it wouldn't be a fair fight, now that I've seen you again. Well, our ten minutes aren't up, but I guess you're as anxious to end this as I am."

"I guess so," he said. They both got up. "Well, I guess this makes us even."

"Does it?"

"Doesn't it?" he said. "You came back in my life at just the right time. This little interview makes me want to commit suicide."

"But you won't."

"No, I don't suppose I will. But you didn't either, remember. Now you're absolutely free, and I'm stuck. You know all about me that you want to know. You've seen me—and you *used* to think I was a pretty good-looking guy. And you've certainly brought home to me that I'm not any more. And one more thing, which makes us *not* even."

"Tell me."

"I love you, and I will as long as I live. So it isn't even, is it?"

"No," she said.

"You did one good thing for me, though. Now I know what's been the matter with me."

"Really?" she said. "Well, now why don't you just go and get drunk?"

"All right. Well, goodbye, Kit."

"Goodbye," she said.

He took a taxi and returned to the saloon with the sour waiter, who, however, had liked the big tip. "Back again the same day?" said the waiter.

"Oh, sure. I couldn't desert this place, my home away from home."

The waiter laughed. "Yes, *sir*. Same thing?"

"The very same," said Wilson. But when the drink came he drank it, looked at his watch, and paid for the drink.

"Not going away mad?" said the waiter.

"Oh, nothing like that," said Wilson. He would be late for dinner, but not very late.

FAMILY EVENING

"Mother," said Rosie, "who's the fourth for dinner tonight? Are you planning some neat surprise for me, like Gregory Peck? Fat chance, end parentheses."

"It just so happens that Gregory Peck backed out at the last minute," said Mrs. James. "No, we're having Bob Martin, a friend of ours from home."

" 'From home,' " said Rosie. "Mother, isn't this home? This is where we live, isn't it? I was born in New York City. What about Mr. Martin?"

"He's what you used to call one of the B. D.'s."

"*I* used to call the B. D.'s? I never even heard the expression. It rings no bell here."

"Well, I remember it, and so does your father," said Mrs. James.

"Then lift me out of this suspense. What does it mean?"

"Oh, a few years ago when we were all spending the week-end at Aunt Ada's we overheard you and Kenny and the rest of you talking about B. D.'s." Mrs. James waited. "You were referring to me, and your father, and Aunt Ada, and Uncle Archie, and people of our age."

"Oh, yes! The *Better Deads*. I must have been at the Brearley then," said Rosie.

"Yes, and it made me cry," said Mrs. James. "I was only

thirty-five or thirty-six then. Only. I don't suppose thirty-five seems like the prime of life to you even now."

"A girl in my class quit college to marry a man thirty-*four*. That brings thirty-five much closer to me. I'm capable of marrying a man thirty-five. What's to stop me? You, of course, but I mean theoretically. What about Mr. Martin? Is he attractive?"

"He used to be. I haven't seen him for years."

"Well, I like that. Every Christmas vacation you make me spend one evening at home with you and Father, then you go and invite some total stranger. I call *that* consistent."

"We don't *make* you spend an evening at home. We ask you to because we want to see something of you, and Bob Martin is not a total stranger. He was an usher at our wedding and he's somebody we've known all our lives. He called up this afternoon and it's the only time we could see him. He wanted to take us to 21."

"Three good parties I passed up to be with the bosom of my family. If he's remotely presentable can't we all go to Larry's later?"

"Larry Who?"

"Larue's," said Rosie.

"Let's see how it works out," said Mrs. James.

"Maybe you're right," said Rosie. "A little caution now."

Martin turned up in evening clothes and when Libby James chided him he made the old joke about dressing for dinner in the tropics. It was neither old nor a joke to Rosie, but she noticed he wore pumps, of which she definitely approved. He was heavy but not yet fat, so that his regular features were not altogether lost in cheek and chin.

"Martinis okay for you, Robert?" said Rosie's father.

"They better be. It's what I've had a string of," said Martin. "Why don't you pour Rosie's in the cup I gave her and she can catch up with me?"

"Oh, a tragedy, Bob," said Libby James. "Your cup was lost

in the fire. We had a fire when we were living on Fifty-first
Street. Luckily most of our things were in storage, but the cup
Bob gave you when you were born, Rosie, that was one of the
things we lost. I was convinced the firemen stole it, but Norman
said I was crazy. I still think I was right. Firemen are honest,
they look honest, but with the thousands of them in New York
City there must be one or two."

"Well, I'll give Rosie another one when she has her first
baby," said Martin. "Or will you settle for a cocktail shaker now,
Rosie?"

"I'll settle for a cocktail shaker," said Rosie.

"Why, Rosie!" said her mother.

"Well, Mr. Martin suggested it, and I haven't got a cocktail
shaker."

"You'll have one tomorrow afternoon," said Martin.

"No such thing, Bob Martin," said Mrs. James.

"There'll be no more discussion. This young lady needs a
cocktail shaker, and it's Christmastime, and that's what middle-
aged friends are for. E. R. J. I *know* somebody, so I can have it
engraved right away."

"I don't use the 'E,'" said Rosie. "Too much confusion."

"Okay. R. J.," said Martin.

"Let's have dinner," said Libby. "We're letting the servants
off early."

"I'll take mine in with me," said Martin.

"We all will," said Norman James.

Throughout dinner Rosie could see that Martin thoroughly
approved of her and of her mother. She was less sure that she
approved of him. He told the story of the time he broke his leg
while skiing at the country club, and of the time Libby's father
forbade her going out with him because he kept her up so late,
and of the time they drove seventy miles to a dance that was not
to take place until the following evening. Libby James remembered almost all of it in the same detail as Martin's. Norman

James smoked a good deal and kept his champagne glass empty and full, supplying a name or a date when he was called upon, or admitting total ignorance of an entire episode. Once or twice Mr. Martin began stories with the statement that Rosie would like this item, if she wanted to know what kind of person her mother was at *her* age. The martinis and the wine, in addition to the string of martinis he had had before his arrival, had no apparent effect on Mr. Martin. This was not quite the case with Rosie's mother and father. Rosie herself did not like to drink much.

"Wanta come in here, Robert?" said Norman James.

"Why sure, if you do," said Martin.

"I do. I do indeed," said Norman James. Rosie and her mother went to Rosie's room.

"Well," said Rosie, "I'm getting a bird's-eye view of an old romance."

"How do you mean, dear?" said her mother. "Bob Martin? And I?" She laughed.

"Stop giggling. You've been giggling all through dinner. I'll bet it wasn't Father that asked him here."

"As a *matter* of *fact*, it *was*," said Libby James.

"Well then, he was just being polite."

"Oh, stop. I was thinking I might put on my new evening dress and you could put on yours, and we could step out. Not if you're going to be disagreeable, though."

"Well, if you think I'd wear my new evening dress for this occasion, pardon me. I'm in favor of lights and music, especially if Mr. Martin wants to pay for it, but I'll wear the pink I got last summer."

"Wear what you please, my dear. Could you do something about my hair? Does it look all right?"

"Mother, Mr. Martin hasn't said anything about going out. Besides, he probably has a late date."

"You're such a child. I know he hasn't said anything, but

what if he hasn't? I'll merely suggest it to your father, and if Bob Martin has a late date I'll take great pleasure in watching him wriggle out of it." She studied herself in the mirror, at first arrogantly, chin up; but then that disappeared. She looked at the mirror's reflection of Rosie's face. "How do I really look?" she said.

"You look fine," said Rosie.

"No, I don't," said her mother. She turned away from the mirror. "Do me a favor, Rosie. *You* suggest it."

"Me! . . . All right, if you stop feeling sorry for yourself all of a sudden. You and the rest of the B. D.'s."

Her mother smiled. "*Dear* Rosie. It hurt, but it worked." She got up and followed Rosie down the hall, humming "Do It Again," a danceable number of 1922.

REQUIESCAT

It was about nine-thirty in the morning when the first car passed the big white house slowly, but not too slowly, went up the street a hundred yards or more, and turned around and came back and parked under the chestnut trees, but still a respectful distance from the big white house. For a little while it was the only car. It was an old LaSalle sedan, from which the rear half of the body had been cut away and a drop-delivery-truck body substituted. On the sides was painted "Brainard's Garage, Claude Brainard Prop., Tel. 391." It had a hoist, and old headlights had been added that could be used as searchlights. The fat man behind the wheel was Claude Brainard. He stayed in the car until a Chevrolet coach passed him, went up the street, turned around, and came back and parked close behind him. Claude got out and walked back to the Chevy. As he walked, he unbuttoned his overcoat and took a pack of cigarettes out of his suit-coat pocket, and out of the pack he took one cigarette. He made a big thing of getting one cigarette to jump up from the others; by shaking the pack and squeezing it in a certain way one cigarette, and one only, was made available. He put the cigarette in the very left corner of his mouth. Lighting the cigarette was like anyone else's lighting a cigarette, except that his hands were so fat and big that the cigarette disappeared inside the globe his hands made.

The man in the Chevy got out. He was small and thin, and the leather jacket he wore had been worn by someone taller before he ever got hold of it, someone in the Army Air Forces, someone younger than he. "It don't look to me like they was anybody here before us," he said. The car doors had removable leather signs that read, "Heber Smallwood, Plumbing & Heating, Tel. 305."

"Not so far," said Claude. He put his right foot on the running board of the Chevy and fondled the door handle with his right hand. The two men looked up at the big white house. No car stood in the driveway; the shades were lowered in all the windows. The fat man took a deep, sighing breath, and the little man did likewise.

"Smoke coming out of that chimley," said Heber Smallwood.

"Uh-huh," said Claude. "This looks like Frank Duviller's truck. . . . Yes. It's Frank." Claude and Heber waved to the man in the Model A station wagon, with the lettering, "Frank Duviller, Florist, Landscaping, Tel. 333." The station wagon made the same turn that Claude and Heber had made, and parked behind the Chevy. Frank joined the others, who were somewhat younger than he. He wore a mackinaw and felt-and-rubber boots.

"Claude, Heber," he said. "Confirm anything, boys?"

"Just got here ourselves, Frank," said Heber.

Now the three of them looked up at the house, each busy with his own thoughts. Then Claude, in some ways the shrewdest of the three, looked at the others. He scraped some snow off the roof of the Chevy and made a ball, but instead of throwing it at anything he let it drop and break. "Here's the three of us," he said. "First, I come and went up about Willoughby's and turned around, then Heber come and done the same thing."

"Yeah, that's right," said Heber.

"Then along come you, Frank," said Claude

"Correct, Claude," said Frank.

"Yeah. I got here right after you, Claude. Then Frank come," said Heber.

"Well?" said Claude, looking questioningly at one, then the other.

"Well what?" said Heber.

"I didn't ask you what you was doing here, Heber. You didn't ask me what I was doing. And nobody asked Frank what he was doing, and Frank didn't ask nobody," said Claude.

Frank nodded and smiled understandingly. He studied Heber. "Catch on to Claude's meaning, Heber?"

"I do not. If I was to say I always caught on to Claude's meaning, I'd be the biggest liar in this part the state," said Heber.

"What Claude is getting at is, here's the three of us, nobody asking any questions, nobody volunteering any information, but here we are all right, and all seem to—I don't know—take for granted why we're here," said Frank.

"Say, that's right," said Heber.

"What did you hear, Frank?" said Claude.

"Well, I guess I heard about the same thing you fellows heard," said Frank.

"What was that, Frank?" said Heber.

"Well, now you ask me a point-blank question like that, I hate to put it into words," said Frank.

The others nodded. "If you're worried because you got an idea it'd be bad luck to put it into words," said Claude, "you don't have to worry about that. I'll relieve your mind on that, Frank. What you heard's true."

Frank looked at the ground.

"I know it's true, too, Frank," said Heber. He tried to sound comforting. "What do you know about it, Claude?"

"Ada told me. My sister Ada. That has to be a Lodge secret, or Ada'd get fired for telling me. She didn't tell anybody only me, and if it ever got out she told anybody, she could never get another job with the phone company," said Claude.

"Lodge secret," said Frank.

"Lodge secret," said Heber.

"Ada handled the call to the doc and the Governor and all them, and what she heard she had to tell somebody, so she figured it was safe to tell her own brother," said Claude.

"You don't have to worry about it getting traced back to Ada, Claude," said Frank. "What I heard I probly heard before they put in any call to the Governor. I was sitting in Police Headquarters talking to Ed, on my way home from the post office. About half past eight this morning. Just passing the time of day with Ed and the phone rang. Ed answered and right away started in acting like I don't know what. Put his hand over the mouthpiece. 'Frank,' he said, 'you gotta beat it. This is a private call.' Or maybe he said official. Or secret. Anyway, he shooed me out before he'd do any more talking. Well, hell, you know that kind of thing never happened to me before. I was a deputy sheriff in the county when Ed was in short pants. On the school board a good many years. Founding member of the Village Improvement and Protective. Holy smokes, I know more official secrets and unofficial secrets about this community than Ed'll ever know, so I stood outside debating with myself what I was going to tell Ed Wheelwright to take the starch out of him. Then Ed come out himself. 'Frank,' he said, 'I'm alone here and I have to go out on an emergency call. Will you take over till I come back and keep your mouth shut about anything you hear? If anybody calls, you're a police officer. I hereby swear you in.' Well, he swore me in like that, without telling me anything more, and I said, 'Listen here, Ed, it's all right for me to be dumb like a police officer, but I don't have to be stupid like one, too.' So Ed, he asked me to be dumb and stupid till I heard from him or till he got back, and then he got into his car. Not the police car, you understand. His own car. That I considered meaningful, but I asked no questions. Went back in his office and sat down.

"I'll be honest with you. I looked at his scratch pad on his desk, thinking he'd of left some scribbling, but all was there was the name. Joe Hubbard." He tossed his head to indicate the big white house, and Claude and Heber nodded, glanced up at the house, and nodded again.

"Perhaps five minutes went by before the phone rang. 'Police Headquarters,' I said. Woman's voice. 'Mr. Wheelwright,' she started to say, and I started to tell her I wasn't Ed, but she didn't pay any attention. 'Thank goodness you're still there,' she said. 'I want to ask you a favor. Would you mind please don't wear your uniform?' It was her, up the house there."

"How'd you know that, Frank?" said Heber.

"How'd I know that? Well, I've known her since she was born. Couldn't mistake her voice. Know every tree on the place. Put in that back hedge last summer. Helped her start her first flower garden when she went there a bride twenty-some years ago. She and I worked many's the time eight, ten hours a day together. And when I heard her voice, I naturally connected up the name on the pad. I said to her this wasn't Ed Wheelwright, it was me, and she hung up. Not another word out of her, but there didn't have to be. I sat there worrying about her about a half an hour, till Ed called up and said Bob Hoffman was coming in to take over Headquarters."

"What did Ed say otherwise, Frank?" said Claude.

"Thanked me," said Frank.

"Didn't volunteer any more information?" said Heber.

"Yes, he did," said Frank. "He said there was an accident and I'd hear all about it, but for the time being that was all he could say. Well, if there was an accident, I knew it had to be Joe, what with his name on the pad and all, and I guess deep down I even knew what kind of an accident it was. When a man takes on the worries of the world . . ."

The others nodded. "He stopped for some gas at my place yesterday, late afternoon," said Claude. " 'Well, Claude,' he said. I waited for him to say something, usually some joke or other. I waited a couple minutes, but like he forgot I was there. Off he drove. I said to myself, 'Joe really got something on his mind.' "

"No doubt about that," said Heber.

"What about you, Heber? What'd you hear, and how, and when?" said Frank.

"What'd I hear? I heard what you two heard. I heard Joe took and put a bullet through his head about eight o'clock this morning. When'd I hear it? How'd I hear it? Well, this don't have to be no Lodge secret. Either you two happen to have anybody working in that house?"

"Forgot about that," said Frank. "Rhoda."

"I happen to have a sister cooking in that house over fifteen years," said Heber.

"I didn't think to ask you about Rhoda," said Claude.

"The natural thing when you hear a shot go off and a couple minutes later one lady of the house lets out a scream, you do what Rhoda done. You go upstairs and see what's wrong. Call Doc Tanner. Then the natural thing, you call your closest relative, your brother. That's what Rhoda done."

"Sure," said Claude. "That's what Ada done."

"Rhoda was all upset and crying," Heber went on. "Said Joe'd shot himself. She had a look at him and he was too far gone for any Doc Tanner. But I said now was the time when Mrs. needed her the most, so get off the phone and go back to *her*. In a situation like that, you have to talk sharp to a woman or otherwise they go to pieces, so I said to Rhoda, 'You go back there where you're most needed.' "

Frank took out a pipe and tobacco, and Claude and Heber watched him as though filling a pipe were an unfamiliar operation. When the tobacco had been properly tamped down and the oilskin pouch put back in his mackinaw pocket, Frank slapped the loose grains off his hands, and Claude had a book of matches waiting for him. Frank lit the pipe, and as he was handing the matches back to Claude, a black, enclosed-drive limousine drove down the street and made the turn into the driveway. There was a liveried chauffeur on the box, and in back were a man and a woman.

"Governor's car," said Heber.

"That's him in it," said Claude. "I guess that's his wife."

"He made it quick," said Heber.

"He oughta make it quick," said Frank. "I don't give him anything for making it quick."

"You gotta give him something for making it quick," said Heber. "Joe made speeches against him, remember."

"And Joe was right. When Joe was governor, he was a better governor than this fellow," said Frank. "Hell and damnation, Joe was better than anybody."

"Granted," said Heber, "but it shows this fellow's decent to get here in this short a time. He wasn't the kind of man Joe was, but he knew a good man when he saw one."

Claude cleared his throat. "I don't give the Governor anything or I don't take anything away from him. I voted *for* this fellow, and you two know it. I don't give him anything more for coming here than I give myself. But I don't take anything away from him, either."

"Well, that's a pretty good point, Claude," said Frank.

"I never voted for Joe in my life, but that don't take away from the fact that Joe himself was the best man we ever had in this goddam state in *my* lifetime. And maybe the whole goddam *United* States." Claude was a little out of breath when he finished.

"Some more cars," said Heber. They watched two small sedans coming up the street. The group of three nodded to the drivers of the sedans. "Harry Parker," said Heber. "Representing the Legion, I guess."

"Will Gallo, representing Gallo's Pool Room," said Frank.

"That's no kind of a remark to make," said Claude. "Will Gallo, representing *me*, as far as that goes. I don't represent anything."

"Yes, you do," said Heber. "You represent the Lodge."

"The Lodge?" said Claude. "i didn't come here representing the Lodge any more than you did, or you, either, Frank. No more than Harry's representing the Legion or Will Gallo's representing the Ladies Aid Society, for Christ's sake. Why don't you bastards face a fact when you see it? We all come here because we wanted to see if there was anything we can do, and there goddam ain't. What was I doing when I decided to come? I was putting a new set of plugs in Clarence Bond's Pontiac. 'The hell with Clarence Bond's Pontiac,' I said to myself. 'Joe Hubbard's dead.' I locked up and come out here. Did I think there was anything I could do? No. I didn't even think anything, but you couldn't of stopped me from coming, and the same with you and you and Harry and Will Gallo. Well, there's one thing I can do, I can get the hell outa here. There's gettin' too many of us, cars lining up, standing around." He turned to the newcomers. "Hello, Harry. Hello, Will. So long." He got in his car and drove away.

"Hello, Harry. Will," said Frank.

"Frank," said Harry. "Terrible thing about Joe."

"Yes," said Frank.

"Jesus," said Gallo, "it tells you what a terrible shape the world is in, a man like him knocks himself off."

"It sure does," said Harry.

"And he *knows* more than we do—I mean he knew," said Gallo. "He got to hear things we didn't get to hear, a man in his position. Think of *that*." He offered cigarettes; nobody took one, and he decided not to take one himself. "I don't think I'll stay here. I don't know why I come in the first place. So long, fellows." He left.

"What undertaker do they have, Frank?" said Harry.

"Search me. Dawson Brothers, I presume. They're the biggest in the county, although Prescott buried Joe's father and brother."

"I'll get in touch with Prescott," said Harry. "If he isn't handling it, he'll know who is. You know, the Legion'll have to provide a firing squad. Is the Lodge having a service, Frank?"

Frank and Heber looked at each other.

"Harry, you don't have to make no excuses," said Heber. "You didn't come here for the Legion."

"Yes, I did. Who else *did* I come here for if I didn't come for the Legion?"

"Claude was right—just about everything he said," said Frank, to no one.

"You heard Joe was dead and you didn't want to believe it," Heber said, "and then when you had to believe it, you *still* wouldn't believe it. So, just like me and Frank, here, Claude, Gallo, you got in your car and come out here to fight it, only there don't happen to be anything to fight."

"I guess so," said Harry.

"Here comes Prescott in the dead-wagon," said Frank. They watched the undertaker's car turning in the driveway. "There's getting too many of us," Frank said. "See you later." He went back to the station wagon and drove away.

"More cars," said Heber.

"Yes. Beginning to come on foot, too," said Harry.

"Mm-hmm."

"I guess there'll be a steady stream back and forth all day," said Harry.

"Well, there oughta be. Joe's entitled to it," said Heber.

"Poor Joe."

"Poor Joe?" Heber hesitated before getting in his car. "I don't know's I see it that way. He's out of it."

"The world, you mean?"

"Honest to God, Harry, I don't know what I mean."

THE FROZEN FACE

The father and son followed the captain to a window table for two. They were at one of the daytime clubs in the financial district. Pad and pencil were placed in front of the father, menus laid on their service plates. The father wrote the figure "1" beside the word "Members" and another figure "1" beside the word "Guests" and held the pencil poised while the younger man read the menu.

"You can have a cocktail if you want one," said the father.

"I couldn't remember. I was looking around on the way in and I didn't see anybody drinking."

"Well, they don't much, but have one if you like."

"You're not trying to talk me into it, are you?"

"I don't give a damn. I don't take one because it doesn't look well. That's the theory. If you're handling other people's money —that idea. And some big shot's liable to drop in and see you with a double martini in your hand, and he won't make you president of United States Steel. That's the theory."

"Do you *want* a cocktail? If you want one, why don't you have one? Are you afraid?"

"I'm scared to death," said the father. "But you go ahead. Nobody's going to offer you the presidency of Steel. Do you need those patches on your elbow? That coat's only a year old, isn't it?"

"If you make cracks about my clothes, I'll make them about

yours. If you're going to wear a stiff collar, why don't you get the right size? That one's choking you. Your neck squeezes out, like a fat woman with a girdle."

"What do you know about a fat woman's girdle? Are you going to have a cocktail or not?"

"No, thanks," said the boy. "I'll have the liver and bacon."

"What do you want to start with?"

"Asparagus soup."

The father wrote down the order for himself and his son. The soup was served, and the father said, "God! You eat fast."

The boy ignored the comment and went on eating through their silence.

"Are you going to have some dessert?" said the father finally.

"The chocolate layer cake," said the boy.

"You could use a little less chocolate layer cake, it seems to me."

"The decoration? That's from my beard. It's an ingrown hair. I get them."

"You've got one now, all right. All right, chocolate layer cake. Coffee?"

"Sure. Please," said the boy. He looked at his father and forbore to comment on the scratches of middle age around his eyes, and the deep hollow above his Adam's apple, and the gray-and-yellow hair that now barely reached down to the forehead.

The dessert dishes were cleared away, and the father and son poured coffee and lit cigarettes. "Well," said the father, "what's the big problem?"

"I didn't *say* I had a *problem*," said the son.

"That's what I understood you to say."

"No, I said I had something important I wanted to talk to you about. It isn't a problem. It's no problem at all. Not even a decision."

"Well, apparently you can go on all afternoon telling me what it *isn't*. Why don't you tell me what it *is*?"

"I will if you give me a chance," said the son.

"O.K., I'll shut up. Now's your chance."

"Well, Emmy and I are going to get married."

"Emmy Channing?"

"That's right," said the son.

"Well, congratulations. If you're not going back to New Haven tonight, I'll break out the champagne."

"Thanks, but I'd rather you broke into a smile or something now. Jesus! My little announcement laid a big egg."

"Well, I'm sorry I didn't display the right enthusiasm, but I assume this is an announcement of something far in the future."

"Well, the hell it is. We're planning on getting married in June."

"June? This June?"

"Right after graduation. The week after."

"Have you said anything to your mother about this?"

"No—but I wish I had. I thought I'd tell you first."

"I see," said the father. "Thanks."

"If I'd known you were going to give it the frozen face, I'd have told Mother and let you find out from her. What the hell!" He waited for his father to say something, but when nothing was said, he went on, "You'd have been God-damn good and sore if Mother and her husband knew it before you did. Well, thanks for the lunch anyway." He pushed his chair back.

"Sit down. I'm sorry. I honestly am. I apologize, if I can apologize. Congratulations. I think you're getting a swell girl and I think Emmy's getting a good man. I mean every word of that, and I hope you forgive me for the frozen face. I don't want *you* to get sore at me. I don't give a damn about anybody else. Don't you know that?"

"I *thought* I knew it. That's why I told you first."

"Well, it was nice of you, and I appreciate it," said the father. "Emmy's a nice girl. I've known Joe Channing for thirty years. Over thirty. I knew him when he was younger than you are, before he ever met Edith. When I first knew Joe Channing, he couldn't draw a straight line. Maybe he still can't, judging from some of his pictures. But I like Joe. He has his own ideas, but I'm not saying he's wrong."

"Practically," said the son.

"No, I'm not," said the father. "I'm *not*. I believe in following your own ideas, and I could no more follow Joe's than he could mine, but that's not saying he's wrong or I think he's wrong. Far from it. I'm practically saying Joe'd have been wrong if he didn't follow his own ideas, and disappear and live in Vermont. I think you're a little too sensitive. You think a criticism of Joe—if I'd made one—you'd think it was an implied criticism of Emmy."

"It would be, too, because she thinks her old gent is wonderful."

"A very comforting thing for a father to know," said the father. He looked at his son, welcoming, and then demanding, some such comfort, but it was not offered. "Well, I don't suppose the job situation's improved over the last time I saw you."

"No."

"I still can't offer you anything in my office. I'd like to have you, but your mother would raise hell. I know she would. If you came down here, she'd say I was trying to take over. I can hear her. Twenty-one or not, she'd say I was violating the spirit of the custody agreement."

"Well, nobody has to worry about that. I'm in Emmy's custody."

"Yes? Just don't use those words when you break the news to Mother. That'd be Strike Two on Emmy," said the father. "But what *are* your plans?"

"Well, we're going to have a kind of an elopement," said the son. "We decided that after going to a couple of big weddings this year. No families, no tribal customs or any of that stuff. A legal ceremony, and a fellow I know and his wife for witnesses."

"I can see where it'd be embarrassing, having two sets of parents at the nuptials."

"No. That's the way I grew up, isn't it?"

"That's true."

"I guess *you'd* be embarrassed, but *I* wouldn't," said the son. "Listen, do you have to go back to the office this afternoon?"

"Of course I do. Why?"

"Why couldn't you say you broke your leg and knock off for the afternoon? I'm loaded with dough. We could go someplace uptown and maybe tie one on, in a mild way."

"No, you come for dinner and we'll tie one on in a big way."

"No, thanks. It wouldn't be the same. It wouldn't be what I meant."

"Not this afternoon. I can't," said the father.

"O.K.," said the son.

"I'm glad to hear you're loaded with dough. Did you have a winning horse or something?"

"I have money, you know that," said the son. "I cashed a check."

"What do you call 'loaded'?"

"Ninety-some dollars."

"Are you spending that money from your grandmother?" said the father.

"Uh-huh."

"I thought I told you to hold on to that."

"I'm holding on to it, but today was a special occasion, and I thought I'd give you a surprise, a treat. I could have invited you to lunch uptown, but I'd have had to tell you what the occasion was over the phone. Come on, wuddya say?"

"I couldn't possibly, not till after work," said the father. "But listen, have you been dipping into that legacy?"

"I bought Emmy a ring."

"How much of it have you spent?"

"I don't know exactly. About thirteen or fourteen hundred dollars."

"That leaves about seventeen thousand."

"Around that," said the son. "Why not? It's mine. It's been mine for nearly a year. What do you think Emmy and I are going to live on the first year?"

"That's exactly what *I* was going to ask *you*," said the father. "You're so vague about a job, and I know Emmy hasn't got much, if anything. Joe's lucky if he has as much as you have."

"He hasn't. Not in cash. He owns his house and a car, and he's having a show next year, but he told me he had to borrow money from an art dealer to keep Emmy in college this year."

"Let me get this straight. Aren't you even going to try to get a job?"

"Not for a year," said the son.

"What are you going to do for a year?"

"Nothing," said the son.

"Nothing? How do you do nothing? What's your idea of doing nothing?"

"Well, I'm going to read *War and Peace*—"

"Oh, Christ!" said the father.

"Did you ever finish it?"

"Listen, I never even started it," said the father.

"I'm going to finish it. I'm going to read Clausewitz, Mahan, Freeman, *Mein Kampf*, Seversky—"

"I could have got you into West Point and saved myself a lot of money," said the father. "What's this preoccupation with war?"

"It isn't a preoccupation with war. I'm going to read Huneker, Craven, Shaw, and a lot of guys that are just names to me. I have a bookstore working on getting me the whole Modern Library."

"And where are you going to live?" said the father.

"On a farm near the Channings' place."

"In Vermont? Are you going to do any farming?"

"I'm not going to do anything, I told you," said the son.

"I suppose if Joe Channing needs a thousand or two, you'll be glad to help out?"

"Naturally," said the son.

"Nice for Joe," said the father.

"You didn't have to say that."

"No, but I couldn't resist it. It's *damn* nice for Joe."

"Wait a minute, Father," said the son. "Mr. Channing hasn't asked me for any money and I don't expect he will. You asked me if I'd help him out *if* he needed money, and I said I would. The other side of the picture is I'd be a jerk if I *didn't* help him out, if I was able to."

"It's very nice that you're able to."

"Listen, take it easy. Remember what we said about implied criticism of Emmy. I don't want to have a quarrel with you, but we've been picking at each other all through lunch."

"Are you above criticism? Am I supposed to keep my mouth shut while you announce that instead of going to work you're going to sit on your prat in Vermont for a reading period of one year? Maybe two? Depending on how long it takes you to get rid of that money your grandmother left you. Joe Channing did this."

"Oh, nuts!"

"That's what I'd expect you to say to me. Oh, nuts!"

"Listen to me, will you please. *Listen to me!* Mr. Channing doesn't even know Emmy and I are getting married. I didn't want to be disrespectful, but you started it. I was so *damn* respectful that I came down here and told you first, before Emmy told her own family."

"Channing and his ideas! I can see the two of you, hitting the old hard cider and cursing Wall Street. Well, don't look now, but your grandmother's money was made in Wall Street. Who supports the art dealers that support Joe Channing?"

"All you seem to worry about is a mythical loan from me to Mr. Channing."

"That's about as deeply as you can think, too. I don't give a damn what you do with your money, but I sure do hate to see a son of mine going for that simple-life stuff of Joe Channing's."

"Well, this isn't getting anybody anywhere. I'm shoving."

"I'll write you," said the father.

"Don't do me any favors," said the son, departing.

The father lit a cigarette, and the elderly waiter came to the table. "That was your son, wasn't it?"

"Was. Is. Was."

"I could tell that after I got a good look at him. Nice-looking young fellow."

"Thank you, Henry."

"A fine specimen. You can be proud. Some fresh coffee? A pot of fresh coffee?"

"All right," said the father.

LAST RESPECTS

Someone in Fairview Falls had once remarked that it took a big funeral to bring Harry Longden back to town. It was a remark that became a local truth, and after three or four of Harry's visits the comment was reworded to make room for an additional observation: Harry Longden, they said, only came back to town for funerals of people that in the old days wouldn't have Harry in their houses. Both remarks had been passed on to Harry by his older brother Charlie, the dentist, who was moderately proud of Harry's success, principally because Charlie had made it possible for Harry to go to law school and get out of Fairview Falls. Between the two brothers there existed a rough-and-tumble mutual respect, and a kind of formal, conventional affection that owed its continuing existence to the fact that neither was ever likely to make any demands on the other. If the two men had not been brothers they might have been good friends.

Harry, of course, could not have gone so high in his world without the equipment to be a smart apple, and he was a smart enough apple to concede the accuracy of what the Falls people said about his homecomings. But Harry alone in the world knew that the remarks were accurate only as far as they went; there was more to be said to make a complete and fair picture. Harry, however, didn't give a damn about the unfairness and incompleteness of the home folks' sketch of him. He could have straightened them out, but at the cost of telling them a secret, and the secret had been his too long.

When, back in the Twenties, Harry paid Fairview Falls his first funeral-attending visit he was believed in town to have made somewhere between a half-a-million and a million, besides a New York reputation as a corporation lawyer. He was already divorced from one girl in the Social Register and on the point of marrying another. The legal lights of Fairview Falls were better acquainted with his work in State and United States Supreme Courts. "Even so," said Bess Longden to her husband Charlie, "I think Harry has a nerve showing up at Lewis Bellows' funeral. What was Lewis Bellows to him, or what was he to Lewis Bellows?"

"Well, Pop was timekeeper at the Bellows plant for nearly thirty years," said Charlie.

"Yes, and did Mr. Bellows go to your father's funeral? No, he did not."

The next funeral Harry came home for was Bud Ellis', who went to a comparatively early grave as a result of having nothing to do but eat and drink. "Harry didn't know Bud Ellis," said Bess. "At least not well."

"When they were kids they used to play together, the way you do in a town this size. And Bud's run into Harry in New York a couple times."

"That may be, but I notice Harry didn't come back when Joe Brennan died."

"Harry was in Europe at the time," said Charlie.

"Well, Ed Martin, then. He wasn't in Europe when Ed died," said Bess. "Also, you notice Harry didn't bring his new wife with him."

"I did notice that."

"We never met the first one, and I'll bet we'll never meet this one either."

"That suits me," said Charlie. "I get the impression he isn't going to be married to this one very long."

On the occasion of the burial of Dr. John J. O'Brien, the leading surgeon of Fairview County and owner of Limerick Farms, breeders of champion trotters and pacers, Harry did not stay with the Charlie Longdens. He chose to take a suite at the Fairview Hotel, offering as an excuse the fact that he had a lot of telephoning to do and was actually hiring an extra operator for the hotel switchboard, but in private conversation with Charlie he spoke with candor. "Why should I stay at your house, Charlie? Bess hates my guts. If I tell her I had lunch at the White House last week, she acts as if I made it up or were patronizing you and her. If I talk about shows I've been to or try to make conversation about books she thinks I'm pretending to be an intellectual. You read books, or she does. You go to the theatre."

"Listen, Harry, if you want to stay at the hotel it's okay by me. If you and Bess get on each other's nerves, that's too bad, and on that account it's probably a good idea to stay at the hotel. By the way, I'm glad to see you from time to time, and all that. Success agrees with you. But something I can't help wondering about is why do you always show up at funerals? It's kind of morbid, for one thing, and for another thing, it's always one of the Hill crowd, either people living on the Hill, the old rich families, or people that used to live on the Hill. You want to know my theory about it?"

"Be interesting to hear it, probably wrong though."

"Well, right or wrong, my theory was you have a grudge against these people, the Hill crowd, and now you're rich and famous in your own line, you're taking a great delight in seeing these people dead before you are."

"That's a theory I didn't expect from you, and it's wrong. I'll tell you this much, I hope the day never comes when I'm in a position to tell you why I come back for these funerals."

"How's that again?" said Charlie.

"I'll put it differently. I come back for funerals. There's a reason I come back for funerals. I hope the day never comes when I can tell you the reason. If that sounds mysterious, it isn't. It's just a secret, and you're the only one in the world that even knows there is a secret."

"Well, that's good enough for me, Harry," said Charlie, and he went on to tell his brother what the people of Fairview Falls had been saying about his visits to the town and particularly its cemeteries.

Harry came back to Fairview Falls for the obsequies of old Mrs. Carstairs, who spent most of her time in warmer climates but always made her presence felt in the town; he "buried," as they say in Fairview Falls, his not very close friend W. W. Bell, former governor of the State; and during the war Harry, a one-star general, came up from Washington to pay his respects to the departed Monty Goldsborough, whose family owned lumber mills, paper factories, and a place in the south of France. Each time Harry returned there would be some talk, but it began to be taken for granted that if a big shot died, Harry would be at the funeral.

Last spring he went back to Fairview Falls for the funeral of Mary Packard, and that struck some people an unusual. Mary was by birth a member of the Hill crowd, and she was superintendent of schools, but she was not rich, and her job did not make her the kind of big shot that Harry seemed to admire. The whole town turned out for her funeral and when they were leaving the cemetery Harry said to Charlie, "Will you come back to the hotel and have a drink with me?"

"All right." He had some late-afternoon appointments, but he knew that Harry, who had his own converted transport, was flying west in a couple of hours.

Harry's male secretary and the pilot were in the parlor of the hotel suite, and Harry told them he wanted to be alone with his brother. Harry made a bourbon highball for Charlie and a Scotch for himself. "Possibly you'll be glad to know I've come back to the Falls for my last funeral," said Harry.

"Aren't you coming to mine?" said Charlie.

"Oh, hell, you'll outlive me by twenty years, but what I meant was, no more funerals of Hill people."

"Well, suit yourself about that, Harry, but you're right, I will outlive you, maybe not by twenty years, but by some. You don't look so good. You have enough money, why don't you take a rest, take it easy?"

Harry said nothing for a moment. "You don't remember a conversation we had about ten years ago or more? No, I see you don't. Well, remember my saying I had a secret? Why I came to these funerals? And how I hoped the day'd never come when I'd be able to tell you why I was always coming to these funerals?"

"I remember it almost word for word now," said Charlie.

"Those funerals gave me the only chance I ever had to see Mary Packard."

"Mary Packard?" said Charlie.

"Mary Packard, the only girl I ever loved. My ambition. My conscience. You knew I had ambition, but I'm not so sure you ever knew I had a conscience. Well, Mary was my conscience, what there was of it. I didn't get to be a *Law Review* guy and head of my class to please you, Charlie. It was to make myself look good in Mary's eyes. Same thing when I started practicing. I didn't work so hard for the money and the rest of it, just for the sake of money itself or being a junior partner in the old firm. You see, fellow, I was supposed to come back here and marry Mary Packard. But instead I married Irene, my first wife. Even though I worked hard, the fact is things did come too easy for me all of a sudden, and Irene was pretty impressive. Rich, beautiful, society. Well, you know how long that lasted, but brief as it was, it was long enough to queer me forever with Mary.

"Well, the first funeral I came back to was a kind of showing off. Old Man Bellows! He hardly knew me when he saw me on the street, but I came back to his funeral, and of course Mary was there. Naturally she was there. And then I realized that Mary'd always be at those Hill people's funerals. She belonged there. So I subscribed to the paper, and whenever somebody'd die in that group I'd decide whether or not Mary'd be likely to go to their funeral, and if the answer was yes, I'd go, if I possibly could.

"Every time I came home I saw Mary, never at her house, never alone for more than a few minutes, and every time I saw her I'd ask her to be my wife. She knew why I came home to these funerals. I could have gone to weddings, but she wasn't much for parties. . . . Help yourself, Charlie. I won't have any more." Charlie got up and freshened his drink, and sat down again and lit a cigar.

"During the war you may remember I came up for Monty Goldsborough's funeral, and that was the first time Mary was more than polite. She'd always been polite, but not friendly, not the friendliness she was capable of. She told me I looked handsome in my uniform, younger and older at the same time, she said. And I said, 'Well, Mary, how'd you like to have me around the rest of your life?' and she said, 'That won't be very much longer.' She knew just about how long she had left. Wouldn't let me take care of her. Sent back every check I sent her. Oh, we wrote each other twice a month the last couple of years. That's all."

The brief silence between the brothers was broken by Charlie. "I guess," he said, "nobody ever really knows anybody else."

THE INDUSTRY AND
THE PROFESSOR

A fine black 1947 Cadillac limousine was waiting first in line at the curb when McCrosland came out of the hotel. The doorman and a chauffeur were chatting. McCrosland, blinking in the California sun, stopped at the curb, and the doorman said, "Taxi, sir?"

"No thanks," said McCrosland. "I'm supposed to be—uh, there's a car supposed to be picking me up."

"What is it—a Tanner?" said the doorman.

"It might be. I don't know what a Tanner is. This car is from the Kurtz studio," said McCrosland.

"*Oh,*" said the doorman. "This is your car, right here." He notified the chauffeur, who had been leaning against the marquee post during the doorman's conversation with McCrosland. The chauffeur immediately became courteous and efficient, held the rear door open for McCrosland, and drove him expertly to the Kurtz studio. McCrosland, sitting so far away from the chauffeur, made no attempt at conversation during the drive, and the only statement the chauffeur made was at the entrance to a building inside the studio gates. "I'll be here whenever you want me, sir," he said. "My name's Fenstermacher, or Ed."

"Oh, you don't have to wait," said McCrosland.

"Yes, I do," said Ed. "I'm assigned to you all the time you're here."

"Oh," said McCrosland.

He entered the building and was greeted with a big smile from a man in a policeman's uniform, who was sitting behind a window. "Yes, sir?" said the man.

"My name is McCrosland—"

"Professor McCrosland? Yes, *sir!* We're expecting you. Just have a seat, Professor." The policeman spun the dial three times and mumbled into the mouthpiece. He had hardly returned the apparatus to its cradle before a short young man in a bright-blue suit opened the door beside the policeman's window and introduced himself to McCrosland.

"My name i⌐ Tom Mitchell—no relation to the actor. We often got our mail mixed up when he was on this lot, but we're no relation. In fact, I never even met him when he was here. It's funny, but I just never happened to. Will you come with me, Professor, down to my office, and we can sort of map out a program."

McCrosland followed Mitchell to an office with a hanging sign with the painted words "Special Services—Tom Mitchell." McCrosland took a seat in a very low chair, declined cigar and cigarette, and was silent while Mitchell told an intercom instrument that he was not to be disturbed. A girl's voice cackled back, "O.K."

"Well, did you have a nice trip out? Everything satisfactory at the hotel?" Mitchell asked. "If you want your room changed, we can arrange that."

"I'm very comfortable, thank you."

"Good. Excellent. Um—ah, Mr. Kurtz is all tied up with a producers' meeting today and he's only sorry he wasn't able to take you around himself, but I'm at your service, and I understand you're going there for dinner tonight."

"Yes. I wanted to ask you. Is that black tie?"

"Oh, no. No, no. The ladies are wearing long dresses, but the men aren't dressing. Just an informal little dinner, and I suppose they'll run a picture after. Uh, now—uh, was there anything in particular you were interested in seeing, Professor?"

"I don't think so. It's my first trip to California, and I dropped a line to Irving—"

"Oh, yes. Yes, yes. Irving. Mr. Kurtz's eldest. Oh, *that's* a real talent. You know Irving, too?"

"Not too, Mr. Mitchell. Only. I've never met his father, Mr. Kurtz. Irving was in classes of mine."

"*Oh, I see.* You *taught* him. I see. You teach at Dartmouth. Oh. Mm-*hmm.* Irving was one of your pupils. I—uh, should have thought of that. I don't know why I didn't. You know, I thought you possibly were out here on some kind of a survey, or some such thing. Well, then, you're just—uh, you'd just like to have a quick kind of a résumé."

"No, I simply thought I'd like to see the inside of a studio," said McCrosland. "My vacation, you know. I wrote Irving, and that's how Mr. Kurtz happened to put me up at the hotel and so forth. Just a tourist."

"That's what I meant. I guess résumé isn't the word I should have used in that connection. You're not planning—well, what I'm getting at is you don't plan to write anything, or anything like that."

"Well, no, I suppose not. I teach sociology, but I'd hardly expect to—"

"Of course not—not like some of them come out here for a couple of days and think they could run a studio. I took sociology."

"Is that so?" said McCrosland. "Where?"

"At S.C."

"Oh, yes," said McCrosland. "*Oh, Southern California.* That reminds me, are we anywhere near the U.C.L.A.? The driver said he was at my disposal, so I thought if it wasn't too far I have a friend there."

"Whatever your wishes dictate, Professor." He smiled "You're getting what we call the full-A treatment. I'm not permitted to take you to the executives' private dining room, but outside of that you get the same identical courtesy as ex-President Hoover. Anywhere you want to go, anyone you want to talk to, any questions you want to ask . . ."

"Where's Irving?"

"Irving's up North."

"Alaska?"

"Oh, no. Marin County. On location. Northern part of the state. We could fly you up there tomorrow, if that suits your convenience. Irving's working as assistant director on *Strange Virgin*. Temporary title. You could pick up a nice piece of change if you could dream up another title, by the way. The novel was *Strange Virgin*, but we can't use that."

"No, I guess not. I can see where there'd be some objection to that. I'd like very much to see Irving, but I promised my wife I wouldn't fly, so I guess I'll have to wait till he comes East again."

"Married man, Professor?"

"Yes. Close to twenty years. Why?"

"Well, I make all kinds of arrangements in my job, and those parties at the Kurtz residence—week nights he's off to bed at eleven o'clock on the dot, so if you wanted to see the night life, that's part of my job."

"That include getting me a girl?"

"Oho, that's for sure. Did you have somebody in mind?"

"Well, I've always wanted to meet Mary Bates," said McCrosland.

Mitchell snapped the intercom and said into it, "Get me Mary Bates."

"What?" said McCrosland.

"I just told my secretary to get Mary Bates on the wire."

"It's as simple as that?"

"It is *now*," said Mitchell. "Mr. Kurtz isn't being rude when

he goes to bed early, but he's one of the early risers in this business. His car's always out here when I come to work in the morning and still here when I leave, around six P.M. There isn't a
harder worker in the business than—Excuse me." The intercom
signal light was on. "I'll talk to her," said Mitchell into the instrument. "Mary? I have a friend of Mr. K.'s here, and he's having
dinner there tonight but he figures to get away around eleven-
thirty. . . . But you can break that, sure. I'd appreciate it. We'll
pick you up at your house around eleven-thirty, quarter to
twelve. Goo'bye, now." Mitchell hung up.

"As simple as that?" said McCrosland. "Good Lord, I've
been wanting to meet her for ten years. It's a family joke."

"Well, you got the last laugh. Or will have. It's up to you."

"Well, it's up to her, too, if you mean what I think you
mean," said McCrosland, laughing. "Seriously, you mean I could
sleep with her tonight?"

"Oh, I don't say that. I don't guarantee it. But on the other
hand, I don't know why not."

"Does everybody?"

"Mary? No."

"Well, now, for instance, our Mr. Kurtz? Could he just call
up like that and be reasonably certain that before the night's
over, he'd have slept with Mary Bates?"

"I can give you the answer to that right away. He'd never
call her up."

"Why not? She's a handsome woman, about thirty to the
best of my knowledge and belief, and wasn't it his magic name
that made her break a date, to meet me?"

"I have to explain that. You see, Mr. Kurtz—well, let's take
somebody else. Some other producer, not on this lot. Say—uh,
Jones. I don't know any producer named Jones, but let's say
he's as important in the industry as Mr. Kurtz, or next in importance. Now, Jones would very seldom get mixed up with anybody in between. Jones would have either some absolutely top

star or else kids you never heard of. But not the in-betweens. The in-betweens—they're a headache for a man like Mr. Jones. Maybe they're still young enough to be ambitious and make trouble, or they're old enough to be desperate and make trouble, figuring what have they got to lose. Whereas, with you or I the in-betweener might figure we could help her get one picture. Jones, though, he might have to go for a contract. You notice Mary didn't try to get invited to the Kurtzes' tonight. That's because, in the first place, she couldn't have got invited and, second, because she'd have a lousy time. If they had a party for three hundred people, she'd be invited, but not an intimate affair."

"Interesting. Interesting." McCrosland nodded.

"Well, where would you like to go first, Professor?" said Mitchell.

"Well, I guess I'd like to see them shooting."

"O.K. On Stage Eight—no, that's Boone Crockett. I don't think so, unless you insist."

"Boone Crockett? Say, he's one I kid my wife about. When she kids me about Mary Bates, I can always come back at her with Boone Crockett. Why don't you want to go there?"

"Uh—he's being difficult."

"Temperamental?" said McCrosland.

"No, not yet. He hasn't been temperamental yet. These days, I don't care how big a star is, if he gets temperamental, that cooks him. He might as well start taking television lessons. If a star gets the reputation of being called temperamental, there isn't a producer in town'll touch him. Not a one."

"Oh. I think I know what you're hinting at. Mr. Crockett's got a little hangover."

"No, no, no. Boone's been off the sauce for fourteen months, close to fifteen. He's A.A.—Alcoholics Anonymous."

"Then what *is* the matter? I'm only pursuing this because you told me I could ask any question I wanted to."

"Difficult. He told them to make some changes in the script. He has script approval in his contract. But yesterday he found out they didn't make all the changes, so he acted up. That was yesterday. Today, he's down there on Stage Eight and won't come out of his dressing room. That's difficult. Tomorrow, if he still holds up shooting, he better look out or Bob Swenson'll say he's temperamental. Bob'll give him one warning, and if he doesn't straighten out, Publicity'll tip off one of the columnists, Boone'll be marked temperamental, and he's cooked."

"But what I don't see is if he has the right to approve of the script—"

"Listen, Professor. Crockett's one of our biggest stars, and he gets paid a big bundle fifty-two weeks a year, with over a year to run on his present contract. He has something else in his contract. It stipulates now that if the studio doesn't have a script ready by such-and-such a date, he can make an outside picture—a picture at another studio. But what this studio can do is mark him temperamental and let him die. No other studio'll have him if he's marked temperamental, these days. We have to go on paying him, but what's that? Buttons. When the time comes where we're supposed to have a script ready for him, we can say we don't have one ready, and he's free to go out and try to get an outside picture. But the other studios'll say no, sir, Crockett's temperamental—no part of the son of a bitch. What happens then? He crawls back here, and he knows that *we* know he can't *get* an outside picture. The result? Next picture, he's a good boy. Next picture, he won't even be difficult."

"Does everybody know this?"

"Everybody but Crockett. He thinks it's 1945, when every picture made money, no matter how much of a dog it was. Not now. This is 1949, when you gotta give them the assassination of Lincoln with the original cast. Anyway, Crockett's a Commie."

"He *is?*"

"Well, not a Commie. But he came out verrrrry, verrrrry

strong for Truman. He didn't have to come out that strong. If he wanted to come out for him, all right. That's enough. He didn't have to shoot off his face. I'll bet you'd have a hard time convincing people like Bob Montgomery and George Murphy he isn't a Commie."

"And Jeanette MacDonald?"

"And Jeanette MacDonald. And top producers. Mr. Kurtz won't ever have him in his house again."

"Well, I guess if he's just sulking, I won't see him making a picture," said McCrosland.

"We could go and watch Takso Myckit. She's on Stage Seven. You know, she's the new Swedish importation."

"Is she new? I've seen her name, haven't I?"

"Well, you've seen her name. Lew Kalem has her under personal contract. He brought her over from Sweden two years ago and taught her diction and English and all that. She's here on a loan-out from Lew's studio. Sixty-five."

"Thousand dollars?"

"Uh-huh," said Mitchell. "Her first picture."

"Well, that's a nice, respectable sum for a first picture, isn't it?"

"Well, of course she doesn't get that."

"What *does* she get?"

"Now? I think she gets seven-fifty. It may be five, or maybe it's a thousand. But I think right now it's seven-fifty, depending on what option phase she's in. See, Lew paid her while she was learning diction and English. He'll be there tonight. You'll see him. Mrs. Kurtz is his sister, you know."

"No, I didn't."

"Sure. Then when Takso finishes here, she goes to Warners' on a one-shot deal. I think that's for eighty or eighty-five. The word is when this one's released—the one she's doing here— they'll just forget Bergman, Garbo, all of them."

"But she'll never make the money Garbo made, for instance."

"You mean because Lew has her under contract? But he took the risks. She's making more than she'd ever make in Sweden."

"Very likely," said McCrosland. "You mentioned television. I understand Hollywood's rather worried about that."

"Who worries about television? Radio actors that don't have any more ability than to sit at a table and read a script—*they* worry about television."

"No, I mean the people like Mr. Kurtz."

"Listen, Professor, what can they lose by television? If it's home television on film, are you and your wife going to tune in on a dog-and-pony act, or Boone Crockett and Takso Myckit? Well, who has them under contract? People like Mr. Kurtz. And if it's television in theatres, who owns the theatres? Picture people. And are they going to throw away a billion dollars of movie investments to let television compete in their own theatres? They own the stars, they own the theatres, they own the studios, they own the literary properties. And you're getting the A treatment, so maybe I can get them to show you some television stuff this studio owns right this minute—stuff this studio shot."

Mitchell clicked the intercom, but there was no answer. "God damn it, my secretary's probably taking dictation from the guy I share her with. They let about forty secretaries go, so I have to double up with this one. Anyway, these people are smart apples. They knew about television long ago, and it's in nearly all their old contracts, when people thought it was a joke to talk about. No, these people will land on top. All television did so far, as far as I can see, was give the studios an excuse to get rid of some overpaid cousins. Associate producers that were making a hundred or two hundred thousand a year for nothing. You knock off two hundred Gs off your budget at the beginning—that's a nice start. You get rid of a cousin and maybe take care of your story cost."

"Well, well," said McCrosland. "Mr. Mitchell, could I use your phone?"

"Certainly."

"It's a West Los Angeles number. I have it here."

"Dial O and give the operator the number."

McCrosland did so. "Hello, is this the residence of Professor Titus?"

"Yes," said a woman's voice.

"Martha, this is Ben McCrosland."

"Ben! Where are you? Is Ruth with you?"

"I'm not very far away. In Los Angeles. Ruth is at Columbia getting some credits—on that Master's degree, you remember. I'll tell you when I see you. I was wondering if you had room for me for one night. Tonight."

"Well, I should say we have. Walter's at the lab, but he'll be free this afternoon. Where are you? Can I come and get you?"

"I wish to God you would. I'm at the Kurtz studio."

"I'll be there in no time. I'll meet you at the main gate."

"Thank you, Martha. Thank you." He hung up and turned to Mitchell. "Mr. Mitchell, I don't want to seem ungrateful to you or to Mr. Kurtz. But I don't think I really want to see any more."

"See any more? You haven't seen *anything*."

"Well, yes and no," said McCrosland. "This friend of mine is going to pick me up at the gate, so I won't need the Cadillac. Then I'll ask my friend to take me to the hotel and I'll check out of there. I'll pay my own bill, if you don't mind. And I'll write a note to Mrs. Kurtz and one to Mr. Kurtz telling him how helpful you were, and—"

"But for Christ's sake—"

"Now, don't you worry about a single thing. I can write a very diplomatic letter when I want to," said McCrosland. "I'm sorry I didn't get a chance to see Irving, but I'll write him, too."

"Well, suit yourself. What about Mary Bates?"

"I'm *very* sorry I won't see *her*, but I suppose she'll forgive me."

"Yeah, you'd probably never make your train tomorrow." He leaned back in his chair and tucked his thumb under his chin. "Well, good day, Mr. Mitchell."

"Right," said Mitchell. "Oh, I just remembered—you'll have to be cleared at the main gate. You came in an executive car. I'll phone the gate, and they'll let you out."

"Thank you."

McCrosland left the building and walked to the main gate, where a cop stopped him. "My name is McCrosland, I—"

"O.K.," said the cop.

McCrosland passed through the gate and waited for Martha Titus. At first, the cop paid no attention to him, but McCrosland, standing just outside the gate, became fascinated by the policeman and his equipment. He wore a black shirt, trousers, and cap, and a plaited black leather belt, plaited black leather holster containing a .38 Police Positive revolver, a smaller plaited black leather holster for chain twisters, and, in his hip pocket, a black leather-bound truncheon. The man also wore steel-rimmed spectacles, and, facially, looked more like a night cashier in a cheap restaurant than a cop. He grew restive under McCrosland's prolonged study of him. "Well, what are *you* lookin' at?" he said.

"Hmm?" said McCrosland.

"Nuts," said the cop.

McCrosland turned away and saw a Crosley convertible approaching the gate, and almost immediately he recognized Martha. She was waving and grinning, and she called to him, "I'll turn around."

McCrosland nodded and turned to the cop. "Say, Officer," he said, "if somebody tried to get Margaret O'Brien's autograph, would you shoot him?"

"What are you—a wise guy?" said the cop. He started toward McCrosland. "Let me see some identification." He was moving close, and fast, and McCrosland suddenly ran. Martha Titus, now on her way back, sped up the car and opened the door; McCrosland jumped in, and the cop gave up.

"Ben, what on earth?"

"Tell you when I get my breath," said McCrosland, laughing.

THE BUSYBODY

She first got a glimpse of him in the busybody. She was sitting at the second-story middle window, sewing the new basketball letter on Bruce's sweater. At Bruce's school the boys who won letters were not awarded sweaters unless the team won the league championship and Bruce's team had not even come close, but it was his first letter and that deserved a new sweater, which was to be a surprise for his birthday. Now Bruce was going out for the school baseball team and it would be so nice to have the new sweater to wear at practice, without waiting till the fourteenth of May when his birthday was. She supposed when Ann saw the sweater she would want something costing the same amount. Supposed, nothing; she would want something costing the same amount plus a little more because she was a senior and going to graduate in June, and Bruce was only in first semester of sophomore, he having entered high in the middle of the year. Well, there was an answer to that problem: simply tell Ann, remind her graduation was coming and a word to the wise was sufficient.

It was a little after three when she first had a glimpse of the man. He got off the trolley at the far corner, the only passenger to get off. It was too early for afternoon shoppers to be coming home, and of course hours before the people would be coming home from work. She looked in the busybody automatically when the trolley stopped and she would not have paid any attention to the man but for the fact that for a moment she thought she recognized him. Not recognized him exactly; she knew it was not anybody she was acquainted with, but there was something about his build or his walk as he walked to the curbstone. He was medium height and he wore an ordinary brown hat and ordinary brown topcoat. There was nothing to make anybody give him a second glance, and yet there *was something.*

She rested her hands in her lap and moved a little closer to the busybody. He stood at the street corner. First she thought he might be waiting for another trolley, but that didn't make sense; he had just got off one and the trolleys all went the same direction and the same place. Then for a few minutes he appeared to be waiting for someone; it was as though he knew he was early for the meeting. But nobody came, and then she noticed—after maybe ten minutes—that very slowly, very casually, he was beginning to study the neighborhood. He did it so casually, so innocently, that she would not have noticed it if she had not been watching him without interruption. Inside the drug store near which he was standing, for instance, inside the drug store Mr. Levy or Mr. Jacobs or Jimmy at the soda fountain would not have noticed him. They might have happened to see him, but they would not have noticed that after waiting ten minutes the man had begun to study the neighborhood.

Mrs. Burns never had called the police in her life. It was a messy kind of thing to do and besides she had nothing to go on. A man gets off the trolley at the corner, stands there a while, and then begins, *she thinks,* to study the neighborhood. A man that looked neat and clean, did not even smoke cigarettes—yes, now for the first time he lit a cigarette. Anyway, it was no crime to smoke cigarettes. She smoked so many herself that she kept the pack downstairs in the kitchen to make it harder for herself, but she wished she had one now, for suddenly she understood exactly what he was doing. He was not so much studying the neighborhood as he was looking for one particular house.

He would turn his head toward the west, away from Mrs. Burns, but that was only pretending, faking. When he turned his head toward the east, in her direction, he seemed to spend a second or a fraction of a second longer at it, and she knew exactly what he was doing: from the corner he was trying to locate a house number. Every time he turned toward the east his glance would take in one more house and his glance was always at the same height: the height of the house numbers, which was the same on all the houses across the street.

What had happened was becoming clear to her. He had boarded the trolley downtown somewhere, a stranger. In some way or other he did know what street he wanted to get off at, and he had been waiting to hear the name of the street called out and also had kept his eye out for the street sign, and had been so engrossed in that that he had not made certain of the house he was looking for. "I'll bet a cookie I could tell him," she said. "Twenty-seven twelve." Even as she made her guess he seemed to have concluded his search, for suddenly he left the corner and walked south, very likely to get an eastbound trolley on the next street.

The couple who rented 2712 had been there about a year. The husband worked in the city; a very good position with the Pennsy; not an ordinary electrician's job, but something to do with the electrical department on the railroad proper, because quite often he would go to Wilmington and Baltimore, Lancaster, Harrisburg, Trenton. In fact they had come originally from Lancaster or Harrisburg. Mr. Derfer. His name was Elwood and her name was Bertha. He was probably in his middle thirties and she looked to be at least his age and maybe a year or two older, although she dressed younger. He was in India during the war—Mrs. Burns knew that much—and while he was away she lived with her people in Lancaster o. Harrisburg, whichever it was. Her family were quite well-to-do and Mrs. Hallis in 2710 was under the impression Mrs. Derfer had been married before.

Something had given her that impression. She was not sure whether Mrs. Derfer had been widowed or divorced.

As she remembered back over these things, especially Mrs. Hallis' impression that Mrs. Derfer had been married before, Mrs. Burns admitted that the logical thing was that the strange man was not a burglar, or somebody going around molesting women—although there had been quite a few cases of that a few squares away—but simply and merely Mrs. Derfer's ex-husband. That was the logical thing: he was an ex-husband who had been pushed aside or bought off and was either curious or was seeking revenge. And yet no matter how logical it was, Mrs. Burns did not believe that theory. She hoped and prayed that there was no revenge mixed up in it; it would be awful for the children and the neighborhood to have something happen. But no. This man, she was as sure as she was sure of anything that he did not fit into the picture that way, not as an ex-husband. She just couldn't see them together, at least not as man and wife. She could not even picture this man married to *anybody,* except a long time ago. You could almost always tell which men were married and which men were not, and if this man had been married it was long ago and for a short time. That did fit in with the fact, if it was a fact, that Mrs. Derfer had been married before, and naturally that marriage could not have lasted very long. But this man—no, he had never been married to Mrs. Derfer across the street. A different style of human being altogether, he was and she was.

Mrs. Burns heard the back door close, and for the tiniest fraction of a second she was frightened. "Is that you, Stella?"

"Yes ma'am, 't's me. Why?"

Stella was right in asking why; it was an unusual question. Stella came in every afternoon at this time and did the downstairs and got dinner ready. "Nothing. I didn't know it was that late."

"Quarter four," said Stella. "Well, elevenna four."

"Oh, I'm not criticizing, Stella," she called.

For the rest of the afternoon she put herself to household tasks to keep busy, and the children, the radio, and her husband occupied her thinking until bedtime. Robert was surprised but affable when she made love to him, and when he left the house in the morning there was at least no problem about matching Bruce's present with a slightly better one for Ann, but at 2712 Mr. Derfer, leaving his house, was carrying an overnight bag.

Mrs. Burns ran upstairs to the second-story middle window. At ten o'clock she saw that it was *only* ten o'clock. "I'll have to lie down," she told herself. She did so, without getting any rest. At eleven she got her cigarettes from downstairs. She spent a great deal of time on the telephone, ordering inexpensive things from the department stores and talking to her dressmaker about Ann's graduation dress, rather far ahead of time. After every call she would go to the middle window and look in the busybody and across the street at 2712. At noon the bells in the Catholic church tolled the Angelus. She was so used to that that most days she didn't even hear them, but today she did notice them, especially the last part. She thought of no connection, but she did all at once know that the strange man would not be turning up at 2712 until the afternoon. She knew as well as she knew her own name that he was not in the neighborhood, and the logical thing was that he would not go to the house across the street in the morning, when the delivery people would be ringing the doorbell and neighbors sweeping the sidewalk and all sorts of things.

She stayed at the window until he came, and this time he knew his way. And he was expected. She watched him on the stoop of the Defer woman's house, pushing the doorbell button one long and one short, and the door was opened without anyone's revealing herself. And now for Mrs. Burns the unbearable excitement of the morning was changed to jealousy and shame. She knew she never had seen the man before, never in her life until yesterday. He reminded her of no one but himself.

THIS TIME

They had waited the right length of time. If they had come to him three years earlier with their quote proposition unquote Wilson would have laughed them out of countenance. He would have told them to take their offer to some of those chair-borne guys, those holders of the Distinguished Filing Cross, those terribly eager beavers of the Mayflower bar who were always moaning about how they had been putting in for sea duty. Three years ago he would have said, "Fred, boy, you have come to the wrong man. All I want to do is get out of this suit and start making a buck before I'm too old." That was not quite all he had wanted to do: there was a full commander he wanted to take a crack at, a j.g. that he wanted to take a crack at, four or five civilian acquaintances that he wanted to take a crack at or at any rate bait them into permanent embarrassment. He had wanted to have another child with Gladys, to have a real home of his own, to spend as much time as possible with his boy and girl, to eat and drink what he liked when he felt like it, to play some good tennis while he still was able, to vote everybody out of Washington who had been there for as much as five minutes during the war years, and eventually to achieve the frame of mind which would enable him to encounter an old friend or be introduced to a stranger without instinctively wondering what the other man had done in the war.

Now he was on the train to Washington and ticking off his batting average for the intervening three years: the commander, who had been the exec on Wilson's first carrier, now was a four-striper, lost in the duties and personnel of the regular Navy; the j.g.—Wilson had no idea what had happened to him, and had a moment's difficulty in remembering the kid's first name, which turned out to be Joseph. Wilson had been able to eat and drink all he wanted, made Gladys pregnant almost right away and, much more quickly than he had dared hope, had got over the first strangeness with the older children. He had played a little tennis and squash and campaigned to the extent of telling everyone he knew to vote early and often for Dewey, but almost all his friends were voting for Dewey anyway so he could not take any bows for good intentions or be ashamed of the result. The animosity toward wartime civilians had lasted longer than he secretly had expected it would, but the only outburst of it—a sharp order to his own older brother to shut up about the war—had had no serious lasting consequences. He retained the curiosity about strangers' war service, but he had discovered that he could nearly always tell which men had been in combat. It was a curious discovery: the combat men had an ease of manner which fell just short of a chip on the shoulder, and in those men Wilson eventually recognized what he felt himself. There was a difference, and that was the only way he knew how to put it. It was like something a friend had once said: "I can always tell a Catholic, but I don't know how or why—but I always can."

He had had, in the four months past, two talks with Fred. Only two. Before the first conversation Fred had not given his name to Wilson's secretary ("It's a personal call"). They met in the late afternoon, in the balcony of a West Side automat, and Fred had tried his patience by asking him a lot of routine questions about how the work was going, how were things with Gladys and the children, what he thought of the political situation, what he thought of unification. Fred had seen that the questions were beginning to bore Wilson, and said: "Bill, all the stuff I've been asking you is important. Very important. I'll tell you how important. I don't want you to tell anyone, not even Gladys—don't tell anyone that you saw me or heard from me in any way."

"All right."

"I have your word?"

"Sure," Wilson said. "Of course I realize now you're sounding me out for something. And I think I probably know what. I've heard rumors."

"Well, keep them to yourself. I'm not saying anything."

"Porky Goddard's with you, isn't he?"

"I never heard of him."

"That's the name of the fellow you roomed with for two years, but all right, if it's *that* hush."

"I never heard of him . . . Thanks for being patient, and I'll be in touch with you."

"Where can I get hold of you?"

"You can't."

The second meeting was in an Irish saloon on Eighth Avenue, which Fred had designated not only by name but by actual property number. The meeting was slightly but only slightly more revelatory than the first. "Take my word for it," Fred said. "It's important work."

"It has to be, with all this cloak and dagger."

"Don't kid it, Bill. You may be in it."

"I *may*? *May* I? I'd have to know a damned sight more about it than I do now before I'd say yes."

"If you come in you won't know *much* more than you do now. I'll give you some papers to fill out."

"What? *That* again?"

"Will you come in? *For your country?*"

"Well—all right."

"Good. Here are the papers."

"Okay. Where shall I send them?"

"You don't send them anywhere. Fill them in here. I'll take them with me."

"No seven copies and one for my files?"

"None for your files," said Fred. "I take them all."

"You know I don't belong to the Racquet Club."

"*I* know you don't belong to the Racquet Club. Go on, start writing."

"I just wanted you to be sure. This is like that O. S. S. deal."

"It has nothing to do with O. S. S."

Two months passed before he again heard from Fred.

"Will you make arrangements to come to Washington next Monday?" said Fred.

"I can't. I'm trying a case."

"That'll be taken care of. One of your senior partners is a friend of ours."

"I see."

"You can tell Gladys it's Navy business. Naval Reserve officer and so forth."

"How long will I be there?"

"A month," said Fred.

"I can't do it."

"You've got to do it, Bill. You're in."

"Well—all right. Where shall I go?"

"Take the ten-thirty morning train. I'll meet you."

"I see. You don't want me to go where you are now."

"Where's that?"

"In Washington."

"You don't even know that," said Fred.

"Yes I do. You said *come* to Washington."

"I'll correct that in the future. Meanwhile, take the ten-thirty train Monday. Okay?"

"Okay."

"One suitcase," said Fred. "The smaller the better."

"For that long?"

"It's all you'll need."

"I see."

"No you don't, and don't think about it too much."

Later that day he received, by messenger, a communication on Navy stationery, ordering him to report in Washington on the following Monday, not in uniform. It disturbed Gladys and upset their plans, but she said she had been more or less expecting some such order, or at least was not surprised by it.

"Why aren't you surprised? I am," said Wilson.

"Well, aren't we always hearing about someone going on a junket?"

"This is probably government contract stuff."

"I hope so," said Gladys.

In his arms on Sunday night she spoke only once of what he knew to be in her mind. "Thank God it isn't Quonset all over again."

"Thank God is right. But I'm safely past that age. No Quonset for me this time."

"This time?" she said. "Is it *this time*, Bill?"

"What do you mean?"

" 'No Quonset for me, *this* time,' you said. Is the time now?"

"No, darling. I'm sorry I didn't put it another way. I merely meant that this time, meaning leaving tomorrow, it isn't Quonset."

"No you didn't, but—hold me close."

In the morning she drove him to their station and when he kissed her in farewell she put something in his hand. "I came across this this morning. I hope it's of no use to you." The object was his old silver identification band.

He smiled. "In Washington traffic. Those streetcars go like hell."

"All right," she said. "Hold-out."

"Oh, hell," he said.

"Oh hell is right. *You* can't fool me. Phone me tonight, if you can."

•　　•　　•

Now it was only Newark, and he had thought over a war and a peace since he had boarded the train; the war part in one block of quick reminiscence, the peace part an unformed declaration of love for the four people he loved. Then, while the train was still in the Newark station, he was again thinking of war. A man came into the club car and took a seat across the aisle.

The man was fifty, surely; sixty, possibly. It was hard to tell because he was wearing a beard, freshly trimmed and mostly black. He appeared to be a man of muscular strength but with an illness; he was lightly tanned, but had brown blotches at the temples and across his forehead. He lifted the heavy ash-tray stand with ease, out of the way of his crossed legs, and Wilson noticed the same blotches on the man's hands when he opened his copy of *Time*. But the old man did not read long; he folded the magazine in half and tucked it under his arm and took out a pipe, filled it from a package of Walnut tobacco, and inhaled a large quantity of smoke, which came out of his mouth and nose without his taking the pipe out of his mouth. He seemed to be tired, and if not tired, impatient, with his surroundings, with the slowness of the now moving train, with the world. He was obviously a foreigner; he wore a gold pin in the collar of his striped shirt, and a polka-dot tie, in the English manner. His brown cheviot suit was too heavy for the weather, and he was wearing the vest, which had six buttonholes for buttons, but had another hole between the third and fourth buttons to accommodate the large round fastener at the end of his heavy gold watch chain. He wore brand-new suede shoes. The watch chain told more about the man than the clothes. Wilson was pleased to see that no Phi Beta Kappa key hung from it, which was evidence that the man, unmistakably an intellectual, was not an American. It was an old chain, long out of fashion in this country, and a standard furnishing for this man, as shown by the extra hole cut in the vest. Therefore, the man was not a refugee; if he had been a refugee the watch and chain would have been confiscated. He was certainly a man with a chronic illness, who was being made or at least urged to take care of his health; the tanned skin so indicated. By the time the train reached Trenton, Wilson had put together his observations—the clothes, the watch chain, the new shoes, the Sasieni pipe containing a Philadelphia tobacco, and the man's physical make-up—and made them into a sketch of the man. According to the sketch the man was a foreigner, no longer a young man, who had an illness that was causing him pain or discomfort; a man who had spent most of his life abroad, but his recent years in the United States, long enough to have sampled the domestic brands of tobacco before settling for Walnut, long enough to have needed new shoes, and to be familiar with the procedure of ticket-taking in a Pullman car (he had handed his tickets to the conductors without looking at the men, holding his hand for the tickets to be returned, and asking no questions of the railroaders). Wilson still had not heard the man speak and still was unable to place his nationality. Of one thing Wilson was sure and had been sure almost from the beginning: he thoroughly disliked the man, who was no doubt a gentleman and a superior brain. It was an unreasoning antipathy, encouraged by the beard, the alien character of the man, and his self-sufficiency. Wilson had heard the railroad conductor say to the Pullman conductor, "All the way. Car 114, Seat 4," and the Pullman conductor responded with the same words; consequently Wilson decided to continue to study the man, convinced that he would do something that would advance Wilson's antipathy to antagonism. He did not have to wait long.

Between Trenton and Philadelphia a youngish woman entered the club car, hesitated, and took the seat next to the foreigner. She took out her cigarettes and by the time she had one in her mouth the foreigner had extended his lighter. The woman accepted the light, nodded, and opened her fashion magazine. The man sat far back in his chair and did not even glance at the woman, but there was something about his attitude that convinced Wilson that he was attracted to the woman—as well,

even at his age, he might be. She was wearing a tan gabardine
suit and black silk shirtwaist, with the jacket of the suit draped
over her shoulders. The waist was cut low, and the woman's
bosom was all her own for all to see. She suddenly put the magazine in her lap and drew on the jacket.

"Damned air-condissioning," said the man.

The woman nodded and went back to her magazine. The
man again took out his pipe, filled it, lit it, exhaled long streams
of smoke. At first the woman leaned away from the smoke area,
but in a few minutes, without looking up from her magazine,
she waved her hand in the air, to dispel the smoke. There were
two other vacant chairs in the car to which she could have
moved to get away from the smoke, but she did not move. But
Wilson stood up and said to her: "Would you like to change
places?" At the same time he stared at the foreigner.

"What did you say?" said the foreigner.

"I wasn't talking to you," said Wilson.

"No thank you," said the woman, coolly.

"I didn't hear what you said," said the foreigner.

"What if you didn't?" said Wilson.

"I'm sorry, I am hard of hearing," said the foreigner.

"Oh, nuts," said Wilson, returning to his chair.

The woman closed her magazine and reached out and put
her fingers on the back of the man's hand. "*Alors! Nous allons!*"
she said. They got up and left the car, the man leading, the
woman with her hand resting on his shoulder.

The other occupants of the car—all men—took the episode
in one of two ways: some had not even noticed it or paid any
attention to it, the others smiled faintly at what they considered
a frustrated pickup. The passenger sitting next to Wilson remarked: "Must be the old guy's girl friend."

Wilson was angry, but he quickly recovered: "Uh-huh. I
guess I got a little out of line that time."

"The old goat didn't look as if he could take care of her, but
those Frenchmen. You know," said Wilson's neighbor.

"That's right," said Wilson. *"French."*

"Sure. She spoke French to him. 'Let's go, Pops,'" said the neighbor. "Probably if she'd come in here alone you could have moved in."

Wilson was glad to be able to pass off the situation as a humorous frustration, but he was not interested in the inevitable comments and recollections of his neighbor. He looked at his wristwatch. "Well, maybe I'll have better luck in the diner," he said.

"Good luck," said the neighbor.

Wilson proceeded to the dining car, which was more than half empty. He got a table for two so that he would not be joined by the foreigner and his woman. He wrote out his order and looked out the window in time to see the Pusey & Jones signs that meant Wilmington. Pusey & Jones. E. Pusey Passmore. A man who had had something to do with the Federal Reserve in Wilson's college days. He always remembered the name: E. Pusey Passmore, signed to banknotes. That was all he knew about E. Pusey Passmore, a name he never thought of except on trips to Washington; and all he knew about Pusey & Jones was that they were shipbuilders in Wilmington; and practically all he knew about Wilmington was that the Pusey & Jones yards were there and that a man named Irénée du Pont was married to a woman whose maiden name was Irene du Pont.

He was trying to cool off, to get his mind off the little mess in the club car. The next big station would be Baltimore, as dismal as and very much like the station in Providence, Rhode Island. He remembered having got on the train tight in Washington one night in '41 and waking up and looking out the window and thinking he was in Providence, where he was supposed to get off. He remembered how glad he was to discover he did not have to dress in five minutes and had a night's sleep ahead of him.

He had been wrong in every respect in the little mess in the club car. He was on his way to a vague confidential job in the service of his country, and it was a serious mistake to make oneself memorable. It was *always* a serious mistake to let a woman think he was making overtures unless the woman had first made herself seem available. It was always a tactical error to lose one's temper. He was starting off on the wrong foot, and no mistake about *that.* But he could not continue the severely critical judgment of himself when he thought of the foreigner. He disliked the man more intensely than ever, and the woman's speaking to him in French—good proof that English was not their language —now confirmed for Wilson the underlying reason for his suspicion and animus. The truth was the new job, whatever it was going to be, had already affected his relations with people. The truth was he had immediately suspected the man of being an agent, and all the rest had been confirmation. Well, an agent as obvious as that would not be hard to track down. For all Wilson knew, his neighbor in the club car was doing just that.

He finished his lunch, paid his bill, and returned to the club car. On the way back he passed his club-car neighbor. "Any luck?" said the neighbor.

Wilson smiled. "No luck," he said.

He was the first man out of the car at Washington. He hurried down the platform to the gate and there hesitated. Then he was tapped on the shoulder. "Hello, Bill."

He turned around. "Hello, Fred." They shook hands. "Where do we go from here?"

"In just a minute," said Fred. "I have a car waiting, but first there are two other people on this train. A Mr. Jones and a Miss Smith." He smiled.

Wilson nodded. He knew who they would be.

GRIEF

The man and his wife presented themselves at the hotel desk. "Yes, Mr. Lambert," said the clerk. "We have your reservation, and I have a telegram for you."

Lambert opened the telegram immediately, read it, and handed it to his wife. She read it softly but aloud: " 'Regret to inform you that Conrad passed away shortly after twelve noon. Will meet afternoon train. Heartfelt sympathy to you both from entire school. Signed, J. P. Dunning, Headmaster.' " She returned the telegram to her husband.

"Well, we expected it," said Lambert.

"I don't know," said his wife. "We were told to expect it, but I was hoping we'd get there."

"Well, even if the plane'd been right on time, we wouldn't have got there. We'd still have had to take the afternoon train."

"I know," she said. "I wasn't thinking of the plane being late. I was just thinking—oh, well . . ."

A stout man in a blue suit, with a carnation in his lapel, introduced himself: "I'm Mr. Something, the manager, Mr. Lambert—Mrs. Lambert. Mr. Dunning phoned and asked me to see that you were made comfortable till train time. Would you like to go to your room?"

"Thank you, I guess so," Lambert said. "We haven't very long till train time, have we?"

They compared watches. "No," said the manager. "But you can freshen up. I'll drive you to the train in my car. I wanted to be at the airport when you arrived, but I was kept here."

"Oh, that's all right," said Lambert. "Sal, would you like a drink sent up? I would. I'm sorry I didn't get your name—"

"Casey. C-a-s-e-y."

"Mr. Casey. You don't have to go up with us. Just send up, oh, two bourbons apiece—four bourbons—and ginger ale."

"I certainly will," said Casey. "And meanwhile if there's anything I can do for you in Boston, I'll be only too glad."

"I can't think of anything," said Lambert.

"Well, if you think of anything. And meanwhile I want to express my sympathy. Mr. Dunning told me about the accident. I have two boys of my own. And three daughters."

"Is that so?" said Mrs. Lambert.

"One boy in high school—I guess about the same age as your son," said Casey.

"Well, that depends," said Mrs. Lambert.

"We'll go upstairs now," said Lambert. "You call us whenever you're ready. I hope this isn't putting you to any great inconvenience."

"Oh, no. Mr. Dunning and I are friends. I guess we've been friends for over twenty-five years."

"Is that so?" said Mrs. Lambert.

"All right, let's go on upstairs," said Lambert.

They followed the bellboy with their one suitcase to their room, which actually was part of a suite. There were flowers in the parlor and the bedroom. The bellboy refused a tip and went out just as the drinks came, and payment for the drinks was refused by the waiter, who departed promptly.

"Gosh, I remember this hotel so well," said Lambert.

"But we didn't have a suite, or flowers. Or free drinks."

"No. We had a bottle of bootleg hooch. It was prescription whiskey, I remember. Then in Maine we drank applejack. July—

about the eighth—1929, last time we were here. No, we stayed here on the way back, so it must have been later than that. That's right. I was remembering the first time we were here. The last time was two weeks later, on the way home from Maine. That was a wonderful trip."

"Talking about it doesn't make me forget why we're here now, if that's what you're trying to do." She took a few toilet articles out of their bag, went into the bathroom, and closed the door. When she came out again, she picked her drink off the coffee table and seated herself near the window. She was smoking, sitting in the same position, when he finished his visit to the bathroom.

"Casey seemed like a nice fellow," said Lambert.

"The same kind of charm as an undertaker. I hope he got what I meant."

"When?" said Lambert.

"He said he had a boy in high school about the same age as Con. I said that depends."

"What *did* you mean?" said Lambert.

"I meant if he had a son ten years *older* than Con, his kid wasn't very smart. Or, for all he knew, Con was twenty-three years old and still in prep school. Oh, hell, I was just being sarcastic because I couldn't stand the sight of him. I *know* he got it when I said, 'Is that so?,' when he said he and Dunning were such great friends. I can just *see* him and *Dunning* great chums. Dunning and that Groton manner of his."

"Groton? Dunning went to Boston Latin. Boston Latin, Bowdoin College, and Harvard Graduate School. Dunning didn't go to any Groton."

"Well, you know what I'm talking about. 'Thid' when he means 'third,' " she said.

"Even the taxi drivers talk that way in Boston."

"Oh, I don't care," she said. "Here, do you want this drink? I don't want it."

"I thought you said you *did*."

"I didn't want to make a big issue of it in front of Casey," she said. "All I did was nod my head."

"Shall I order a sandwich or something? How about a cup of coffee and a sandwich?"

"I don't know where *you* get the appetite. Will you, for goodness' sake, stop hovering over me as if I were the little woman. I didn't just *have* a baby."

"I know, Sal," he said. "I'm sorry. I don't know what the hell."

"What time is it?"

"Uh—quarter of three," he said.

They sat in silence until three o'clock, not speaking, not touching their drinks, smoking steadily. She spoke first: "One thing I want to find out, and I'm going to *ask* Dunning. There was supposed to be a strict rule—no firearms. It was in the catalogue, because I read it and I remember wondering why they had to make a rule about it. We weren't sending Con to a reform school, or at least that's what I thought at the time."

"They have that rule in all catalogues."

"Then why didn't they enforce it? The Brown kid must have had his gun all the time. Why didn't they find it? If it was a military school, you'd expect them to have guns, but the last thing you'd expect in this kind of a school is some little gangster hiding a gun."

"It was a twenty-two," he said. "A rifle."

"What does that have to do with it? In fact, it ought to be easier to find a twenty-two than a pistol."

"Sal, you can't call a boy a gangster because he owns a twenty-two," said Lambert. "We won't bring it up, because if we do, then we only cause trouble—"

"Trouble!"

"And Con and this boy must have been friends, and probably Con was accustomed to borrowing the rifle."

"I suppose he borrowed the rifle to shoot himself? The boy that shot him and *killed* him, *he* knew it was against the rules to have a gun. He knew it, or they'd have found the gun. He knew enough to hide it so they wouldn't find it."

"For all we know, Con often borrowed the rifle, and Brown was doing him a great favor. You know how it happened. Brown dropped the rifle and the bullet hit Con."

"What disgusts me is that you believe that. How can a gun go off and hit a boy with one shot that'll kill him? If it was a shotgun—I've heard of that. But not a rifle. Why are you defending this Brown?"

"Because I believe it happened the way Dunning said it happened. Dunning said the boy was handing Con the rifle and dropped it. Nowadays you can kill a deer with a twenty-two— some twenty-twos."

"Oh, good God!"

"He was my son, Sal."

"Yes, but you can have others."

"I wouldn't want another. There was only one Con."

"Then defend him, for God's sake. That's what I'm going to do."

"Defend him from what, Sal? From what? Let's take him home and have him near us as long as *we* live. Let's take him home and defend him from outsiders. I want them to forget him. I want to get everything done here as fast as we can, and take him away as fast as we can. That's all I want now."

"Well, it's not all I want."

The phone rang—Casey announcing he was on his way up. They put their toilet articles back in the bag and were ready for him. He made no unnecessary conversation on the way to the station or at the train platform. They boarded the nineteenth-century coach, and Casey went on his way.

At first, the coach was half filled, but after a few stations they had it to themselves, except for an elderly Negro couple at the other end of the car and a woman in the seat in front of them. Then the elderly couple got off and there were only the Lamberts and the woman, who was of young middle age, wearing a brown cashmere suit and a brown felt hat. On the luggage rack above her was an overnight bag, blue canvas and leather-bound, with the initials "E.B.B." standing out on the binding. They did not get a look at her face until the old couple had got off the train and the woman turned around and said, "I know this isn't a smoker, but do you mind if I smoke?"

Mrs. Lambert shook her head no, and Lambert said, "Not at all. We will, too."

"Thank you," said the woman. She lit a cigarette and held it in her left hand, while with her right hand she shielded her eyes from the sunlight, resting her elbow on the window sill.

"Do you know who I think that is?" said Mrs. Lambert.

"Yes."

"You noticed the initials on the bag?"

"Yes," said Lambert. "Let her alone."

For a moment, Sally Lambert said nothing and did nothing; then she leaned forward and said, "Are you Mrs. Brown?"

The woman turned around and said, "Yes, I am."

"I was sure you were," said Mrs. Lambert.

The woman lost the first look of fear in her eyes and made the effort to smile. "Are you from the school?" she said.

"No, not exactly," said Mrs. Lambert. She settled back in the seat as the woman now frowned questioningly, mystified by Mrs. Lambert's behavior.

"I'm sorry, but have I met you before? How did you know who I was?" Then, for the first time, she studied Lambert, whose unhappy face had pity in it. "Oh, God!" she said.

Mrs. Lambert smiled and nodded.

"Oh, my dear Mrs. Lambert! Mr. Lambert!" said the woman. Her hands went up involuntarily, the right hand extended in supplication.

"Look at her," said Mrs. Lambert. "I think she expects us to shake hands with her."

"Sally, please. No, she doesn't," said Lambert.

THE KIDS

"You wanta see a picture of my father?" said the girl.

"All right," said the man. He half rose, as though politely offering to assist her to find the picture.

"Don't move," she said. "You can remain seated. Don't budge."

He stayed in his corner of the davenport, and she got up and took more steps in walking out of the room than anyone had to— short steps, which made her seem full of cockiness. It was probably the same way she walked when she was out on the sidewalk, on her way to Bergdorf's, but inside the hotel it was not a natural walk. It was a put-on walk, and he was sure it was being put on to show him how sure of herself she was, how accustomed to a suite like this—he gazed about quickly and estimated the price at thirty or forty dollars a day—and how natural this kind of living came to her.

She returned from the bedroom with a ten-by-twelve glossy print, which she placed on the coffee table in front of him, and then she placed herself beside him.

It was a picture of a seagoing tug, with men lined up on the lower deck and a smaller group of men standing beside the pilot-house. "See if you can guess which one's my father," she said.

"Oh, I don't know," he said. "That one." He put a finger on one of the men near the pilothouse.

"No, that's the skipper."

"Well, I figured him for the owner. The 'M' on the smoke-stack."

" 'M'? Why 'M'? Oh, because *I* see, Masters. I only took that name. My name isn't Masters. My name doesn't even begin with an 'M.' It's Slagel."

"Oh."

"Read what it says here at the bottom. 'Genoa, Italy, to New York—4,061 miles.' Do you know what *that* was? That was towing a disabled boat all the way from Genoa, Italy, in wartime, with the submarine wolf pack lying in wait. That's the kind of a man my father was."

"Ship, not boat," he said. "I still don't know which one's your father."

"Make a guess."

"I did and I got it wrong."

"Oh, all right. This one. The only one that doesn't have a smile on his face. Imagine that! I get Mary Sunshine all the time, my friends always commenting on my toothy smile, but the only one in that whole crew that doesn't have a smile on his face—my father."

"Well, maybe the other ones didn't feel like smiling either. They just did it for the photographer."

"Maybe." She turned the picture face down and leaned back. "He was a wonderful man, my father."

"He must of been. The things you say about him. Texas Ranger. Golden Gloves lightweight. Cop. The only thing I don't like about him was he was a cop."

"Well, somebody has to do that kind of work."

"Difference of opinion, that's what makes horse races," he said.

"So they say," she said.

"You know something? Ever since I came here, we been talking. You been talking about your father, I been talking about myself. You stard out asking me what I did in the war. I told you I was in the Marines. Then you stard talking about your father."

"That's right," she said. "It doesn't take much to get me started talking about my father, once I get started."

"Yeah, but can I ask you a question?"

"Certainly."

"Well, with all this talking, you didn't tell me anything about yourself. All about your father, but not yourself. Why is that?"

"Well, what do you want to know? I used to be a starlet in pictures, and then last year they let us all go, all the starlets."

"Before that?"

"I went to Fairfax High," she said. "Hollywood."

"Who did you live with then?"

"How do you mean?"

"Did you live with your mother? Your sister? Your old-maid aunt?"

"My mother. I don't have any sisters or brothers."

"Where was your father then? Out after cattle rustlers?"

"My mother and he were separated, so I lived with her."

"Oh."

"Why do you say *oh* that way?" she asked.

"Well, did you ever hear of the father complex?"

"Sure, but I didn't have it."

"What makes you so sure about that? Did you ever take it into consideration? Did you ever ask yourself if you did?"

"I didn't have to. If I'd have been bothered by it, then maybe I'd have asked myself, but I wasn't bothered by it."

"That's the way you figure it?" he said. "But maybe you had it and liked it. Now, take for instance, there you were, living with your old lady, your mother. By the way, what did she use for money?"

"She was a vendeuse."

"What the hell is that? That's a new one on me. What was it again? A what?"

"A vendeuse. A very high type of saleslady in the best and most exclusive ladies' stores. She made as high as two hundred a week."

"Selling women's clothes she made that much money?"

"She always made good money," said the girl. "She turned down offer after offer to open her own shop."

"Oh, then that was why your father and her separated, because she made more money."

"No. More because he liked to travel and she wanted a home."

"But she ended up without a home, didn't she? He did his traveling, and she had a job. That was no home, was it?"

"We had a nice home till she died. There wasn't anybody I knew had a nicer home."

"But with a father off in Texas chasing cattle rustlers, and the mother at work all day—you see what I mean?"

"What are you trying to do? I don't get it."

"Well, I hate to see you thinking about that father—you know, building him up in your mind while all the time maybe he was a bum."

"Well, he wasn't."

"Well, maybe he wasn't a bum, but it was your mother paid the bills? Why? Because the old man couldn't earn enough. He could get by himself, but he couldn't support his wife and daughter. You know what? Maybe he didn't *want* to support them, you and your mother."

"Well, I know more about it than you do, so you're wasting your time if you're trying to ruin my feelings for him. You're wasting your time."

"He was killed, eh?" said the man. "Did they ever get the guy that killed him?"

"Right there. The other policeman that was in the car with my father killed the man that killed my father."

"Oh, you didn't tell me that before. The one cop gets out of the car and gets killed, and his buddy kills the other guy. They shoot fast down there, daown in Takes-us, don't they?"

"You're a fine one to talk."

"Me? I never shot anybody except a few lousy Japs."

"Am I supposed to believe that?"

"Ask Frankie. You must have a high opinion of Frankie if that's what you think. You think Frankie has people shot?"

"I don't know *what* he does."

"You must have some idea, though, if you think he hired me to go around shooting people. That brings up another subject of conversation. How did you happen to shack up with Frankie?"

"Shack up?"

"You know what the word means, don't you?"

"I know what it means, all right, only I don't think Frank'd like the expression."

"Became sweethearts, then. How'd you happen to do that?"

She thought a moment. "Because he asked me to."

"Well, I wish I'd of seen you first, maybe I'd of asked you. Just think, if I'd of been there Sunday instead of Frankie, it'd been you and me instead of this way."

"What makes you so sure?"

"Well, if all he had to do was ask you, and he never saw you before Sunday."

"Is that why you're so nasty?"

"Is what why I'm so nasty?"

"Because you didn't get me and Frank did."

"When was I nasty? I don't call that nasty, just because I studied you."

He stood up and sauntered toward the window. "Well, the money's right, ain't it? Only I wished to Christ he didn't always keep everybody waiting. He was suppose to be here over an hour ago. 'Go on over and introduce yourself to the new broad, I'll be there at four-thirty.'"

"Is that what he said?"

"What did you think he said? 'Leave your name card at Lady

Masters' apartment'? What I get tired of is sittin' around waiting, but it's better than pushing a lousy hack or hustling a tough buck in a poolroom—all *I* know how to do."

"Is that all you can do?"

"That's all, and I ain't kidding myself otherwise. Why?"

"What if I ask you a question?" she said.

"That's your privilege."

"How'd *you* happen to shack up with Frank?"

"I'll belt you right across the kisser, that's all I'll do to you. Frankie's no queen, and who oughta know it if you don't?"

"Maybe not, but you're the same as I am. A good-looking face to sit with him in the night clubs, and a build. What's the difference if you're supposed to slug people and I'm supposed to be his broad? He buys you with money the same as he does me."

"Oh, that way. Hell. *Hell.*" He laughed at her and commenced to whistle. For a few minutes he moved about the room restlessly, glancing at pictures in the magazines, going from chair to chair. In the course of his wandering he never once looked at her, but she never took her eyes off him. Then quickly he sat beside her and took her in his arms and kissed her.

"I was right, kid, I was right!" he said. "I should of seen you first."

"You see me now," she said.

"Oh, no. What he'd do to the both of us!"

"Well, then sit over there. If he walked in now, he wouldn't have any doubts."

"Yeah." He took a far chair and lit a cigarette, and they stared at each other.

"Turn on the radio or sumpn," he said.

She turned on the radio.

"Get music and we don't have to talk. . . . There," he said. "Crosby. He likes Crosby. He don't like anybody to talk if there's a Crosby record."

"I want to talk, though," she said.

"No."

"What would he do to us?"

"Ah," he said. He flung out his hands. "He'd think up sumpn. He's good at that."

"Are you afraid of him?"

"What am I tryin' to *tell* you I'm afraid of him."

"Let's go away," she said.

"Where to? Anywhere we went somebody'd spot you. And me. What the hell could I do?"

"How old are you?"

"Twenty-six. Twenty-seven, nearly."

"We're young. I'm twenty-three."

"Listen, your old man's better off than we are *right now.*"

She looked away wearily. "Maybe," she said. "And maybe I was better off till you ruined *him* for me."

There was no sound at the door, but they knew it was being opened when the draft lifted the glossy print and dropped it on the floor. "Come on in, King," called the young man.

"Hyuh, kids," said Frank.

THE BIG
GLEAMING COACH

.

At Kissel's Forge, or at least at the Kissel's Forge outlet, since
the village itself was over the hill and out of sight, Banning
turned off the main highway and headed north as he had always
known he would do. He had had an early start, made good
time, and the pleasure of driving this fine car had kept him
from getting tired even after nearly ten hours. He had put more
milage on the car this day than he had in the two weeks since
taking delivery on it. That was natural: a weekend on Long
Island and a weekend in Westchester was all he had driven it;
the rest of the time it had been sitting in the garage, a shame
when you thought of it, what real pleasure it was to drive a car
like this. Twice on the Pennsylvania Turnpike he had had it
over ninety, to see what it would do. Instead of a sense of speed
he got a sense of the latent power in the engine. It handled
beautifully in all other ways, too, from pickup to braking, and
everything else worked to perfection: it was a clear, cold day,
but he was warmly clothed and the top went down at the press
of a button and the windows went up the same way. He mixed
business with pleasure by listening to the radio programs that
were put out by advertising agencies not his own; they were
just as bad as his, and no better; no better than his, and as bad
as that. Operating on a policy level, he prided himself (a) on
knowing what the American public wanted when it wanted it,

and (b) on being ready with something better when the public was ready for it, not only from the merchandising point of view, but taking into consideration the actual product itself. This beautiful automobile, for instance; there was nothing in it or about it that was really new, technologically, as he had reason to know. As a man whose experience with cars went back to the days before the rear-vision mirror became standard equipment he was well aware that it just wasn't good business practice to release the various items of engineering advancement and luxury appointment the minute they came along. Witness the four-wheel brake, witness the balloon tire. Witness the demountable rim! The one-man top! These innovations and others of the same general idea had come along before he knew the difference between a copy chief and an account executive, but he had learned enough since then to be fully cognizant of the incontrovertible fact, namely, that it wasn't sound business practice to shoot the works with all the improvements and refinements you had locked up in the engineering department vaults. A little at a time kept your plants going, if you wanted to look at it from the humanitarian point of view, and provided you with the sales needle for the all-out annual campaign, if you wanted to look at it *that* way.

It was kind of cute the way the human mind worked. Half the day now he had been thinking off and on about stuff like demountable rims and rear-vision mirrors, stuff going back twenty-five years in some cases. He smiled to himself, turning off at the Kissel's Forge outlet. All day or at least half the day he had been thinking about those little symbols, in a manner of speaking, of twenty-some years ago, but would he admit to himself that when he reached Kissel's Forge he was going to turn off and head north in a beeline for the old hometown? He laughed at his obstinacy, and now that the turnoff was made he admitted that that kind of obstinacy was just one more example of what he knew and what his wife often told him (but

what he knew without her ever having to tell him): he was a
kid at heart. He smiled again and drew back his head shyly as
in his mind's ear he could hear someone saying, "Don Banning,
you're just a kid at heart." The voice was not that of Amy, his
wife, or of one of his business associates; more like Janet K., who
came of an old New York family and definitely not café society,
although he sometimes took her to Larue's, which she humor-
ously called Larry's Bar and Grill.

Two nights ago Janet had said: "What's the point of going
all the way to St. Louis by car? You'll be a wreck."

"I think it'll do me good. I fly back and forth over this
country the whole year round but I never get to see it. Last
week, for instance, I was in Chicago twice, Los Angeles once,
Detroit twice. What's the procedure? Met at the airport, whisked
out to one plant or another, spend the day there, lunch in the
executives' dining room, six o'clock comes and believe me, Janet,
I'm ready to go to the California Club or the Detroit A.C. or
wherever it happens to be, have a cocktail or two and go to
bed. Very little time for social engagements. Last week I did
relent a little bit and dined out with a couple fellows and their
wives in L.A. We went to Prince Mike Romanoff's for dinner
but I didn't enjoy it a bit. Wasn't relaxed. Finally I said to my
hostess I wasn't contributing much to the party and she said to
me, 'No you're not, Don Banning.' And she gave me a good
talking to. 'This is the first time you've let us have a look at you
for nearly a year. You know the latch-string's always out for
you at our house and I gave Bud—her husband—explicit instructions that any time you were in Los Angelees you were to be
our guest, but Bud tells me you're trying to be the richest man
in the cemetery.'"

"Oh, really? Who is she, this Clara Barton type?" Janet had
said.

"Oh, why just the wife of a business friend of mine out there.
Fat, good-natured mothery type of person. She's nothing *that*

way to me, in a romantic way. But wait till I tell you the rest. She really let me have it straight from the shoulder. She said, 'You know you've aged five years since I last saw you.' "

"She's crazy," Janet had said.

"That's what she said, though. So I got thinking it over and on the way back to New York I decided that when I had to make this St. Louis trip I'd go by car. I've got this new car, so why not get some use out of it, see some of the country, talk to some people besides other hucksters like myself or fellows in the manufacturing end."

"My thought is when they see that car the common man isn't going to come up and say 'Hi, Bud,' " Janet had said.

"Most likely not, but I always prided myself in my ability to draw people out. One of the greatest experiences I ever had was a year on the Sparksville, Ohio, *Beacon-Times,* reporting."

"Oh, yes. The old hometown. Do you go through there on this Inside America junket?" she had said.

"No, I miss it by around twenty-four miles."

"I should think you'd head right for it. Haven't you any family there?" she had said.

"One sister is all. Her husband and kids. Husband's a lawyer and they have a son at State and a girl in high school."

"What's the matter? Do they owe you money?" she had said.

"Yes, as a matter of fact, they do, or he does. He's owed me five thousand bucks for about ten years and another thousand seven or eight years and last fall he wanted to make it an even ten and I as much as told him to go to hell."

"And naturally that antagonized your sister," she had said.

"I didn't even get a card from her at Christmas."

"Oh, hell, let them have the four thousand. Be a Lord Bountiful. Drive up in your big gleaming coach and distribute the largesse and take a few bows."

"No, Janet, you don't understand about those things. I admire your generous instincts, but you're being generous with my money and I just don't like being patronized by a stuck-up son of a bitch that owes me six thousand bucks already."

"This brother-in-law—I get a kind of a thought wave here, a vibration. Did he always snub you, or at least was he always stuck up?"

"Always. His father was the county judge and my father was a carpenter. That is, he was a carpenter before he became a contractor. This fellow, Jean's husband, he went to Kenyon and I went to Denison for one year."

"I never heard of either one of them, so you're not enlightening me," she had said.

"Well, maybe *you* never heard of Kenyon, but you'd have a hard time making one of the Kenyon boys believe that. They don't believe in Oxford and Cambridge. They believe in Oxford and Kenyon. Or maybe Kenyon and Oxford."

"If I were in your position nothing in the world could *stop* me from driving up to their house and tossing a check for five thousand dollars on their red checkered tablecloth, believe me."

"No, Janet, you don't understand about those things."

"I can understand putting a stuck-up son of a bitch in his place," she had said.

"When am I going to see you again?"

"Call me when you get back. I want to know about your trip."

The landmarks were familiar, of course, more and more so the closer he came to Sparksville. What surprised him was the recognizability of the names on the billboards—clothing stores, shoe stores, the department store, the automobile dealers. He was surprised that so many had survived, although many of them had been second-generation when he shook the dust of Sparksville off his heels. The biggest surprise of that kind was an illuminated sign that read: Quinn's—Steaks—Chops—Dancing Sat.—Two Mi. And in the lower right-hand corner, Curly Quinn, Owner & Prop. The sign was freshly painted, which seemed to indicate that Curly Quinn was still alive. Still, he could be only about fifty-five, sixty. Banning decided that what he would do, he would have something to eat at Curly's, then go on to Sparksville, check in at the Ethan Sparks Hotel, and telephone his sister from there. That way he wouldn't have to eat at her house or spend the night there, and he would be able to tell about her attitude without risking a snub.

He parked under a floodlight at Curly's, ran up the top and locked the car and went inside. The only person in the place was Curly, standing behind the bar and reading a Columbus paper. He took off his glasses as Banning closed the door.

"Hi, Curly," said Banning.

"Howdy," said Curly.

Banning took off his hat the better to be recognized, and put out his hand. "Do you remember me?"

"Well, I do and I don't." Curly did not smile and it was plain that he was not going to smile until he recognized the newcomer for certain. "Yes, I think I do. Banning."

"That's right," said Banning. Curly put out his hand and Banning remembered that the shaking of hands was less prevalent here than in New York.

"Don Banning."

"That's right."

Curly had a cold and he sniffled. "In New York now, I understand."

"Yes. Been there almost twenty-five years."

"Is it twenty-five? Yes, I guess that's about right. I would of thought it was less than that. Let's see. Twenty-five. That'd make it 1923 when you left here." He scratched his head. "Mm-hmm. What'll it be?"

"Got any Scotch?"

"Sure I got Scotch. What kind you want?"

Banning named a brand. "Plain water."

"You want me to mix it for you or you prefer to mix it yourself?" said Curly.

"Go ahead," said Banning. Curly sniffled again and Banning also noticed that his upper plate did not fit very well, causing him to whistle over sibilants. "Have one yourself."

"No, I very rarely take a drink these days. Very rarely."

Banning took a swallow. "Say, Curly, do I owe you any money?"

"I don't know. If you want I'll go take a look. When would that be, about, did you say?"

"Twenty-three or Twenty-four," said Banning. "Early 1924 to put it exactly. February. That's when I left."

"Mm-hmm. I was just thinking, if you left in February '24 that don't necessarily mean you ran up the bill then. You could of been owing it for a month or longer. See, it was Prohibition then and I got a different set of accounts for Prohibition than Repeal. My Repeal accounts I keep in one place and my Prohibition accounts another place. According to law I can't collect Prohibition accounts. I couldn't anyway because of the seven-year law, that outlaws a debt, no matter *how much* you owed me, seventy-five, a hundred dollars, unless the party wants to pay me because they're honest. Don Banning. I remember there was something. It was around twelve or fourteen dollars. I'll go look."

He left the bar and went down a hallway and was gone less than five minutes. When he came back he was carrying an old ledger. "Sixteen-fifty. There it is. Second of January, 1924. D. Banning. Notice the whole bill was twenty-six fifty and I credited you with ten dollars on looks like the fifth or that could be the eighth of April, 1927. You must of sent me ten dollars."

"Yes, I remember now," said Banning.

"You wanta pay the whole thing now? I'll cross it all out if you do, then we can both forget about it."

"Right," said Banning. He handed over a twenty-dollar bill.

"Drink up and have another on the house," said Curly. He made change out of his pocket and laid it on the bar. He poured the Scotch.

"Here on a visit?" said Curly.

"A short one."

"Short beer?"

"No. A short visit. I'm here on a short visit," said Banning.

"Oh, I took you to mean you wanted a short beer," said Curly. For the first time he smiled.

"Many a good time we had in this place," said Banning.

"Yes, I guess so. Now it's your sister's married to Howard Wilkinson the lawyer."

"That's right. Jean. Jean Banning married Howard Wilkinson," said Banning.

"I thought so. They used to come here before they were married but I don't see them much any more. I think they have a boy that comes here in the summer. Anyway it's the same name. Wilkinson. I don't know what his first name is."

"Don. Don Wilkinson," said Banning.

"I guess that's it. I'm not sure."

"I am. He's named after me."

"Oh, is that so? That's nice," said Curly.

"Say, do you remember the night that millionaire from Dayton got lost and stopped here and bought everybody's drinks?"

"When was that?" said Curly.

"About '22 or '3."

"Oh, that far back. I hardly ever remember that far back. If I was to start thinking that far back—I don't remember half the people come here during the wartime. They had close to thirty thousand people in Sparksville during the war, makin' them windshields for airplanes. I served as many as two hundred dinners a night here during the war. They was lined up half-way to town some nights. Take what they get, too. If they didn't

like it they could go back to town and see what they could
get there. No credit, all cash. No checks. No OPA. No nothin'. I
served a three-dollar dinner, nothing wrong with it, everything
fit to eat. Take it or leave it. If I saw local people in the line
I'd give them the preference. I'd take them out of the line. If an
out-of-towner wanted to make a stink about it I'd take him out
of the line too, only I wouldn't put him back. I'd never let him
in the place if I saw him again. Of course I guess quite a few
got in without me noticing. That's why I didn't remember your
millionaire from Cincinnati or Dayton, wherever it was. I don't
remember half those bastards from the wartime. And by the look
of things they'll be back before long. Now they say the air-
plane's out of date, but I don't know, maybe they'll build some
kind of atomic bomb here. We oughta get something. Just so
they don't put up a microbe plant here. I wouldn't want that."

"Well, I have to be going. How much do I owe you?"

"That'll be seventy-five. The other drink was on the house."

"Right, thanks."

"Come in again," said Curly.

Banning changed his mind about checking in at the hotel.
He drove to his sister's house on Broad Street. He parked in
front of the house, and rang the doorbell. A girl of sixteen opened
the door.

"Hello. You must be Helen," said Banning.

"No, just a minute. Who shall I say is here?" said the girl.

"Who is it?" he heard his sister's voice.

"It's somebody for Helen, Mrs. Wilkinson," said the girl.

"It's me, Jean. Don."

"Don?" He now could see his sister coming slowly down the
hallway, drying a dish. The young girl got out of the way.
"Don!" She put down the dish and tea towel and came to him
and they embraced. She called out: "Helen, it's your uncle." He
saw his niece taking off her apron and his brother-in-law coming
down the stairs.

"Hello, Don," said Wilkinson.

"Hello, Howard. Nice to see you."

"Nice to see *you*, come in, take off your things. Have you got a bag there?" said Wilkinson.

"Well what a nice surprise! Nancy, this is my brother, Helen's uncle, Mr. Banning. Nancy is Dot and Ken Towson's daughter. You remember Dot Hoffnagel. Nancy is her *daughter!*"

"Well, what are we all standing here for?" said Helen.

FOR HELP AND PITY

The estate had been a showplace when it was owned by a dishonest but never convicted United States senator, and a showplace it was still, in this day when the rich build small. Trees, mostly cedars, lined both sides of the driveway, which came to an abrupt end at the porch steps, a rather narrow spur connected the driveway and a large courtyard, which occupied the area between the kitchen and the five-car garage, and Forrest slowly drove his Ford into the area and stopped as his front bumper just barely touched the four-foot stone fence that was the eastern limit of the yard. He made a sibilant sound in imitation of a locomotive at the end of a journey and said, "All out for Sister Evie's. Don't forget your belongings, please. Kindly don't forget your belongings."

"Nobody home," said his wife. "The garage is empty."

He looked at the vacant garage and nodded. "So it is."

"Why don't you put this one away?" said Emmy.

"Because remember the last time we were here, and I blithely put our car away and then discovered I'd taken somebody else's space."

"No."

"I told you. I'm sure I did. I put the car in an empty space and the next morning it was out here. Evie's two cars were inside, and Percy Nevers' car, and somebody else that was staying here for the weekend, and Gerhardt's broken-down jalopy."

"Gerhardt?" said Emmy.

"The houseman, yes. Oh, my yes. It didn't take Gerhardt long to peg the poor relations."

"Evie doesn't think that," said Emmy.

"Nevertheless Gerhardt did. So this car was sitting out in the rain. We'd only had it a week then, too, and I was pretty damn sore, but there was no use making an issue of it."

"*I* would have," said Emmy.

"I guess that's why I didn't tell you."

"Evie wouldn't have liked that one bit," said Emmy. "I wonder where everybody is."

"We can soon find out," said Forrest. He got their bags out of the luggage compartment. "Here, will you take this?" He handed her his brown cashmere jacket, and with him carrying the two suitcases they went to the front door. She opened the door and they entered the hall and he set the bags down.

Emmy called out: "Anybody home?"

There was no answer.

She called again: "Hello, anybody home?" The house remained quiet and she said, "We might as well go up."

"I'd rather not and take a wrong room, but anyway I hear somebody," he said. Very soon a maid appeared, a woman in her late fifties.

"Good afternoon, ma'am, sir. Mrs. Allen is playing golf and said to tell you she'd be home at five-fifteen."

"Hello, Mary," said Emmy, with affection.

"Mary."

"Mr. Forrest."

"Are we in the same room as last time?" said Emmy.

"Yes, ma'am. Here, sir, I'll take your bags."

"No, no, no, no, no."

Mary smiled. "Thank you, sir. I don't think I could make it, truth to tell. I was just having a nap."

"I hope we didn't wake you," said Emmy. "Are you alone in the house? Where are Gerhardt and Hilda?"

"Well, that's another story, ma'am, and I'd rather you heard that from Mrs. Allen. Can I get you anything? I'll be up to unpack, but in the meantime."

"We can unpack all right," said Emmy. "Do you want a drink or anything, dear?"

"I can wait till Evie gets home," said Forrest. "Then I think I'll have a cup of tea."

"You finish your nap, Mary," said Emmy.

"Oh, I feel rested now. We did get to bed quite late last night. Don't you unpack, Mrs. Forrest. I'll be up."

"Well, we'll just *sort of* unpack."

"Yes, I'm going to have a shower and change. Are we dressing tonight, Mary?"

"No sir. I think you're either dining at the golf club or the Seaview, one or the other. And I know Mrs. Allen isn't dressing."

In their room Emmy took off her dress and lay, covered with a silk comforter, on a daybed while Forrest took his shower and changed his clothes. He put on a blue polo shirt, white ducks, and loafers. She opened her eyes. "You are a thing of beauty."

"Uh-huh. Joy forever."

"Give me a small kiss," she said.

"Oh, all right. Is this small enough?" He kissed her forehead.

"Just what I wanted." She looked at him. "That's a nice-looking belt. Have I ever seen that before?"

"No. Do you know what this is? It's the cross strap of a Sam Browne belt."

"When did you ever wear a Sam Browne belt?"

"When I was in the field artillery."

"You were never in the field artillery. You mean the Squadron?"

"No, I was never in the *Squadron,* but I was in the field artillery. At Princeton."

"Then why didn't you go in that in the war?"

"Thank you, no. No thank you. Not at my age."

"Stop talking about your age. I'll bet there aren't many of your friends can wear the same belt they wore in college."

"*I* couldn't wear the belly part either. This is the cross strap. Notice I had to let it out. I found it in a trunk when we were moving. You know that stuff we gave to Finland. This was among them. I'd like to have a picture of a Finn in those 1927 clothes. Helsinki must look like The Balt on a rainy Monday, twenty-two years ago. Or more." His chatter was interrupted by a loud crash, metal on metal.

"Two cars," she said.

"I'll go see what it is. You stay here. If it's anything, I'll tell you."

He ran down the stairs and out to the courtyard, where a woman in a golf dress was examining the crushed rear end of his car. A station wagon stood a few feet away.

"Hello, Evie," he said.

"Oh, George, I'm terribly sorry. I sideswiped you." She put up her cheek to be kissed and he kissed it.

"You step on the gas instead of the foot brake?"

"I must have, I guess. I wasn't expecting a car to be here. I just whirled in. Well, call three-two-four, that's the village garage. They'll think there's a constant procession from this house. My lovely Packard's there too. Where's Emmy?"

"Lying down."

"Well, let's go in and call the garage. It isn't much really, is it?"

"It can be fixed."

"I *hope* you're not cross with me, George," she said.

"Why, no. It was an accident."

"But such a stupid accident. Well, let's go on in and I'll call the garage."

In the house she called out: "Hello, there!"

Emmy answered: "Hello. What happened?"

"I just ruined your beautiful car. I'm terribly sorry."

"Are you all right?" Emmy called back.

Evie looked at Forrest. "I'm okay, thanks. Come on down when you're ready."

"I'll be down in a few minutes," Emmy replied.

"It just occurred to me, Evie," said Forrest.

"What?"

"Well, tell them to bring a car we can use over the weekend. You see, my car was parked up against the stone wall, and when you hit it it got a real good sock. I wouldn't want to drive mine till it'd been given a thorough going-over, not just straighten out the wrinkles."

"Okay."

In a little while Forrest and the sisters were having tea on the side porch. "Well, this is what happened last night," said Evie. "I had some people in for dinner and then some others came in after the movies, and—one of those nights. It was hot, and quite a lot of drinking, and someone suggested going to the beach for a swim. But the last thing in the world—I wanted to go for a swim—but the last thing in the world that interested me was seeing that group without any clothes on, or letting them see me, for that matter. Not a moral issue. Just so unattractive. My goodness. Bill Wade. Ugh. They *told him,* you know. The club told him he had to wear a top or do something about that fur coat. And May Dorking. And the others. All practically middle-aged, or more, some of them. Percy still has a good build, at least he's not repulsive."

"*You* have a good figure," said Emmy.

"It's all right, but—well anyway, I said no thank you. So off they went, naturally all calling me sissy, and so Percy and I sat here and played canasta. Percy was spending the night on the way to his sister's. He left this morning, before I was up. Well, anyway, we were playing canasta and the servants'd all gone to bed, when all hell broke loose."

"How do you mean?" said Emmy.

"That whole crowd came back here. Ten people, there must have been at least. They'd had their swim and a lot more to drink, and now they came back here, mind you, and demanded drinks and food, and started the phonograph. I never saw such people. This is my last summer here, you can bank on that."

"What did you do?" said Emmy.

"Well, I knew there was enough noise so nobody in the house could sleep, so I timidly went back and asked Hilda and Gerhardt if they would possibly, out of the kindness of their hearts, get dressed and help serve these people. There was no getting rid of this crowd. I don't know what came over them. Maybe it was the moon, I don't know. In any case, Hilda was willing, but Gerhardt became very insulting. He not only refused, but he said he was giving notice that minute. 'Giving notice,' I said. 'I asked you as a favor to come out and help me, and I'd have rewarded you handsomely, but since you take that attitude you can pack up and leave the first thing in the morning.'"

"How awful!" said Emmy.

"So I came back here and told the people, I said if they wanted drinks, there they were, but I was going to bed. Luckily some of them got some sense in their heads and saw I was upset, so they finally went home. I never put in such a night."

"God, it's a wonder you're not in a straitjacket," said Emmy. "But I think you're wise to leave here. I'll bet you could sell this house for a hotel, or a Catholic school. Somebody—who was it, dear?—somebody we know had a big house and an order of Catholic nuns bought it just like *that*."

"Jim Drummond," said Forrest. He addressed Evie: "What happened to your car, Evie? You didn't tell us that part."

"The car? Oh, my Packard," said Evie. "That was part of the whole mess. One of those people actually took my car to the beach and hit a signpost, and I didn't know a thing about it till the garage called up this morning."

"Good Lord, these people are the worst I ever heard of,"

said Emmy. "You mean somebody just stole your car and didn't tell you they had an accident?"

"Exactly what happened," said Evie. "I've *really* got to leave this place. I wish I didn't even have to stick it out for the rest of the summer."

"Why do you?" said Emmy. "Why don't you come stay with us? You know what we have. Our guest room isn't much bigger than this table, but Evie, you've got to get out of this dreadful place."

"Well, you're sweet, and I might even take you up on it," said Evie. She rose. "I'll go up and change. We're just the three of us tonight, and in view of the servants' leaving—except faithful, wonderful Mary—I thought we'd just go to the club or the Seaview and then maybe to a movie and home early. Does that suit you?"

"Oh, of course. In fact, I could whip up something right here, if you'd rather not risk facing those people at the club. Won't some of them be there? Thursday night?"

"Oh, I won't pay any attention to them. I'll be about a half an hour." Evie patted her sister's shoulder and smiled sadly at Forrest. "Just think, I brought you two together, and you're so happy."

Emmy patted her sister's hand, and Evie left.

Forrest got up and peered inside the house, then seated himself again and leaned forward and spoke quietly. "Go easy on inviting Evie to stay with us, will you, sweetheart?"

"Why?" said Emmy.

"Let's not be—impulsive. We don't want a third person living with us, in such close quarters."

"George, what's come over you?" said Emmy. "Aside from her being my sister, and in trouble—aside from that, we're going to have to ask for a lot of money and I think we ought to offer something in return."

"I know, I know," he whispered. "But let's go easy. Let's not say any more about it unless she does."

"Why? What's the real reason? Is she too attractive? Is that it?"

"No, no, no, no. Evie and I never were anything and never could be anything."

"Oh, that's not true. You could have been, with a little more time."

"All right, maybe we could have been, but we weren't, as you well know, and believe me, now we never will be. So just—"

"She's in trouble, and we—"

"She has a lot of friends that she can visit. What's left of the summer she can take a car and—well, at least she can go around and be welcome from Maine to California. I wish to Christ she was in California."

"That's a *hateful* thing to say."

"Honey, don't say things like that. Please, just leave things the way they are, for the time being. I swear to Christ . . ."

"What do you swear to Christ?"

"I don't know," he said. He stood up and picked up a croquet mallet. "I've said all I can say now."

He went out on the lawn and practised shots until Evie came down and called to him that she was ready. He joined the sisters on the porch. "The garage called and said they wouldn't have time to smooth out the wrinkles on your car, but they'd give it a thorough checkup and have it ready tomorrow. They didn't have a car they could lend you."

"Okay, Evie, thanks," he said.

"You have it fixed in town and I'll pay for it."

They had a quiet dinner at the Seaview, a fair seasonal restaurant. They had a cocktail apiece and beer with their lobster, and Evie had two brandies and then they went to the early movie. They returned to Evie's house, where she said: "If you're tired, Emmy, you go to bed, because I want to talk to George anyway."

"At your service," said Forrest.

"I *am* tired," said Emmy, and went upstairs.

Evie made two highballs and handed one to Forrest and led the way to the porch. She stretched out on a wheeled divan and for a full ten minutes neither of them said a word. It was a blue night and they could hear the surf, like an unending freight train, but there was nothing much to be seen, with the ocean hidden by the dune, and the trees indistinct and unreal.

"Well, I thought you'd be asking me some questions," she said.

He laughed politely. "I thought you'd give the answers first."

"Emmy believed me. Why didn't you?"

"I don't know."

"I *do*. Because Emmy loves me, and you don't."

"I guess that's a fair statement, Evie."

"Why didn't you ever? What was the matter with me? I've often wondered. Lordy, other men were making passes at me and taking me out, even before I got my divorce. At one time I thought you were playing hard to get, but that didn't stop you from making passes at all my friends. I never understood it and don't to this day."

"I don't either."

"And the minute you laid eyes on Emmy—Lordy, you were like a man possessed."

"I was. Still am. I'm a two-time loser, you know, and I fully intended to stay a bachelor the rest of my life. Till I met Emmy. I didn't know it would ever happen to me again. But it did. And thank God it happened to her too, with a perfectly good husband and at least more security than I could offer."

"I wonder why you didn't believe that story. You never succumbed to my charms—" she shifted on the divan "—and you don't believe my fiction."

"I don't know, Evie," he said.

"What happened was, there *was* no party. In fact—"

"Evie, I don't have to know. Emmy believes the story you told."

"In fact there was nobody here except one person."

"Percy."

"No, not Percy," she said. She suddenly sat up, and then sat back again. "You have no feeling for me at all, have you? When I hit your car you never asked me if I was hurt, and that's the first thing Emmy asked me. She asked me if I was all right."

"She's a wonderful girl," he said. "Can I get you another drink?"

"Natch. Natch." She held up her glass and he refilled it and his own. Again they drank in silence, but not so long as the first time. "Well, don't you want to know who the man was that was here?"

"I can't imagine."

"I know you can't. It was Ed Jeffers."

"I don't know him," said Forrest.

"Well, he's a lineman for the telephone company. He comes from Tacoma, Washington, and he never even finished high school. He was in the Seabees during the war, and he calls me— do you know what he calls me? . . . Kicks. K, i, c, k, s. And do you know what I call him? I call *him* Kicks. Everything's for kicks. Kicks is in all his conversation. I call him Kicks and he calls me Kicks. Like those people that dressed alike, the man and girl. In *Life,* I think I saw it. The boy would have a tweed coat and the girl would have a jacket of the same material."

"Oh, yes. I remember."

"I was taking him to his boardinghouse and we hit the traffic thing in the middle of the street."

"Were you hurt?" said Forrest.

"He got a bump on his forehead." She inhaled her cigarette and went on: "I didn't have to take that from a dirty Nazi and his stupid-cow wife. I told them that if they weren't off the property by noon I'd have them thrown off."

He said nothing and presently she stood up. "I'm going for a walk and I don't want to be followed."

"Where are you going?"

"I apologize to no one, and I want that distinctly understood." With a quick step she opened the screen door and walked
toward the dune. Now he could see well in the blue night and
he stood and watched her in her white dress with the gilt belt.
He stood in the same place long after she disappeared over the
dune, until he heard the gentle voice of his wife: "George?
George?"

"Yes?"

"Aren't you coming to bed?" she called. "Evie, send him to
bed."

"Evie isn't here," he said. He heard Emmy moving about in
their room over the porch. She came down to the porch.

"Where'd she go? Did you quarrel with her? Where is she?"

"She wanted to go for a walk by herself," he said.

"Why? What did you say to her?"

"Nothing. She wanted to go for a walk and said she didn't
want to be followed."

"Didn't want to be *followed?* Why did she say *that?*"

"It's all right, she's coming back. I see her. Now you go on
upstairs."

"Where?"

"There. See that white figure on the top of the dune?" he
said. "See, she's coming back. So go on up, Emmy."

She rested her hand on his arm. "Wait a minute," she said.

"I tell you, please, Emmy. Go on upstairs."

"God! She has no clothes on."

"That's her white dress," he said.

"Did you know that? That she had no clothes on? Was she
that way when she left?"

"No. Now for God's sake, my sweet. Be quiet." He put his
arm around her. "Don't let her know we're here."

They watched Evie coming toward them, naked even to the
feet, and then they could make out the set expression and then
they could hear her, more and more, muttering. Her hair would

fall down over her cheeks and she would brush it back of her ears. She came on steadily and passed their corner of the porch and entered the house. And then they heard behind them the sound of weeping, and standing on the porch with them, in a faded blue bathrobe, was Mary the maid, looking to them for help and pity.

ALL I'VE TRIED TO BE

The building was not old as office buildings go. It had two elevators and a mail chute and a directory of tenants that was
ornamental as well as practical. Throughout the building there
were Savage burglary-alarm stations, the kind that set off a signal
at police headquarters if the night watchman failed to make
his stop at each station every hour. After twenty years the building was still no worse than the second tallest in the town, and
had been the best investment the Masons had ever made. The
lodge owned the building, but even without the members' efforts
it would have averaged eighty percent occupancy through the
years. In a larger town, or in a great city, the building would
not have attracted any attention; it was only twelve stories high
and there was nothing about the architecture that would have
frightened Fouilhoux or Hood. Nevertheless Miss Lapham, visit-
ing the building for the first time, was favorably impressed. The
brightwork on the elevator doors and mail chute and directory
had a nice patina and as she waited for one of the elevators she
looked up at the marble ceiling, as one will while waiting for an
elevator, and she was sure that there was not a speck of dust in
the ceiling corners. The man she was going to interview, Mr.
Lewis C. Craymer, ran the building, she knew, and she admired
the way he ran it.

The elevator operator was a girl who bore a very, very slight resemblance to Dorothy Lamour. "Three, please," said Miss Lapham.

"Right," said the girl. She seemed to be counting the time she waited, or possibly was silently going through a song. In any case she suddenly closed the elevator door, as though she had reached the end of a count or a song, and took Miss Lapham to the third floor. "Three out," she said. "If you're looking for Craymer, it's to your right and another right."

"How'd you know I was looking for Craymer?" said Miss Lapham, with a smile.

The girl smiled back. "The other offices on this floor are the dynamite company, and I didn't think you'd be in the market for dynamite."

"You're right, but I might be looking for a job or something."

"They only employ the one woman and she'll be here forever," said the girl. "All the rest are men."

"That ought to be interesting, being the only woman," said Miss Lapham.

"It's plenty interesting where you're *going*," said the girl, closing the elevator door.

Miss Lapham could not be sure whether the girl's manner indicated esprit de corps or disrespect toward Craymer. She went around to his door and knocked. "Come in," a man's voice sang out.

She entered a small reception room—outer office, which was unevenly divided by an old-fashioned oak fence, the kind once dear to country lawyers and justices of the peace. Beyond was a larger office, separated from the smaller by a wood-and-glass partition. The two rooms got the theme of their furniture and decoration from the oak fence. At a quick glance Miss Lapham was almost sure that there was nothing in either room, including the typewriter in the ante room, that was newer than the fence. As she had observed earlier, the building was not remarkably old but *was* remarkably well cared for. But Mr. Craymer's offices were of another day, and so was Mr. Craymer. It was like walking through the Presbyterian Hospital in New York and opening a door at random and discovering an abdominal operation being performed by a bearded man in a Prince Albert.

Mr. Craymer was clean-shaven, except for a small mustache, and he wore an ordinary three-button sack suit, but he wore a heavy gold watch chain, with a collegiate gold charm and an old-time large-size fraternity badge. His gray hair was parted in the middle. A nail-scissors job had been done on his cuffs, but not on his nails, and his stiff collar was cleaner than his shirt by at least one day's wear. He came around from behind his desk to greet her. "This must be Miss Lapham," he said.

"That's right," she said.

"I'm delighted to see you. Have a chair. I've just been getting things, uh . . ." He removed a pile of cardboard folders from a chair and dusted it off with a rumpled handkerchief. The chair was on one side of the desk, which was roll-topped and so crowded with papers that there was scarcely room for the outstandingly modern article, the telephone. "I was just signing some letters," he said. "My secretary only comes in in the morning." He cleared his throat.

"Go right ahead," she said.

He took an extraordinarily long time reading each letter, frowning and clearing his throat and apparently having trouble concentrating on the correspondence. Miss Lapham looked about her. Besides the desk and chairs there was a large plain table, on which were stacks of papers of assorted sizes; several piles of cardboard letter files on the composition floor (there was only one small green rug on the floor, under her feet); wire wastebaskets; a black tufted-leather sofa with a Navajo blanket folded in a corner; an oak filing cabinet with some of the tabs written on and some not; and a small safe with a letter press on top. She noticed also a pencil sharpener screwed into the wall, and quite naked without the covering that is intended to hold the vermicular pencil-peelings; a check protector under the pigeon-hole compartments of the desk; a russet leather shotgun case under the sofa; a man's pair of rubbers, also under the sofa; several rubber-tire ash trays; two unused memo pads for 1947 and 1948, which advertised the neighboring dynamite company; four blackened silver loving cups with crossed tennis rackets on two of them; a battery lamp, suitable for camping, boating, the farm, and countless other uses; and a large silver-plated carafe and tray and three Coca-Cola glasses on the plain-topped table. There were Venetian blinds on the three windows and the window glass was spotlessly clean.

"Mm-hmm," said Mr. Craymer, nodding to his letters. He had been standing; now he sat down in the swivel chair. "This office, we've been so . . . I don't see how we ever get anything . . . I'm sorry, Miss Lapham. Do you smoke?"

"I have some."

"Here. Try a—have you ever tried one of these? They're Fatimas. No gold tips, but finest quality. That's the slogan. . . . Now then, the *Standard* wants some help from me. Is that correct? Did you just start there?"

"I started Monday."

"And you're from?"

"Originally Cleveland, Ohio, but more recently New York."

"Is that so? Well, I imagine a writer can get a lot of experience working on a paper like the *Standard*. I happen to believe in the country doctor, too, you know." He scratched his head behind his ear. "Whenever one of the younger chaps comes to me for advice, I tell them they ought to practice in a small town first, before specializing. Now what was it you wanted to know exactly?"

"Well, part of my job, at least till I learn my way around, I'm supposed to go back in the files and write the thirty-years-ago and twenty-years-ago-today stuff. I guess you've read them."

"I certainly never miss them. I'm in them so often. One or the *other*."

"Well, somebody sent us this photograph and asked why we

didn't run it, but the only trouble was they didn't send the names of the people in the picture. Mr. Pierson said he recognized you, but you were the only one."

"Who's Mr. Pierson?"

"Why, he's the composing-room foreman."

"Oh, Jake Pierson. Jake, of course. The printer. Is that what he is? Composing foreman." Mr. Craymer nodded. "I've seen him going to work, to and fro all these years, and I never knew exactly what he did. Well, let me have a look at the picture."

She handed him the photograph and he immediately smiled. "Oh, my yes. Now I wonder who on earth sent you this. That's me, all right. I can give you the names right off the reel. There's m'self, with the cap in my hand."

"Can you give them to me left to right?"

"Very well. This short fellow, that's Henry Crowell."

"Henry H. Crowell, of the Keystone National?"

"Henry Crowell. Correct. Next to him is Sam Biggers. That's Samuel T. Biggers, the lawyer. Then myself. Lewis C. Craymer. Then Van Vandergrift. He's living in Philadelphia. Theodore P. Vandergrift, retired now, but formerly with Union Carbide. Very well-to-do. *Very* well-to-do. Arthur Schneider. He was killed at I *think* it was Belleau Wood. With the Marines, I know."

"Belleau Wood?" said Miss Lapham.

"Oh, this picture's over thirty years old. This was taken before the first war. You can't put this with your twenty-years-ago. A lot of people would know right away. Then here's dear old Charlie Watkins, my doubles partner for years. You'll see his name on two of those trophies over there. Charlie lives in New York City, and I'm sure if you were in the newspaper game there you've heard of Charlie. Charles W. Watkins. He has a house at 25 East Seventy-ninth Street, New York City, and a large country place at Amagansett, Long Island, where I've visited him many, many times."

"Charles W. Watkins. What does he do?"

"Oh, Wall Street. He's in all kinds of activities in the banking world, and still owns property here in town that I handle for him. Was there a letter with this picture? I wonder who sent it?"

An anonymous letter, that's all."

"Man's or lady's handwriting, would you suppose?"

"I couldn't tell. It was printed. It just said 'I think many of your readers would be interested in this old photograph of prominent local citizens,' or something to that effect. It was a nice note."

"I don't remember the picture at all. I don't remember who took it or why, but of course I know where. It was taken at the old Tennis Club. This was our old team. Charlie played first man and he and I were the first doubles team. We beat all the good teams in this part of the state. In those days they didn't have as many country clubs, golf courses, that is, but every town big and little had a tennis team. Let's see, now, Charlie played at Yale. Henry at Princeton. Sam at Haverford. Van wasn't on the team at Lehigh, but he played a lot. Arthur Schneider at Princeton, not on the team, and I played on the team at Lafayette. I guess there weren't many better club teams in the whole East, when you think of it. How many other towns could boast of so many varsity players? And we had a ladder, you know. You weren't always sure of your place on the team, just because you made it once. We were always challenging each other, taking each other down a peg, so to speak."

"Did you have a name for your team?"

"Why, just the Gibbsville Lawn Tennis Club team. We always traveled by motor, too. The Watkins had a big Locomobile, and the Schneiders had a Lozier. There was room for all of us in one car, and a chauffeur, but not for our duds. After a match there'd always be *some* kind of party. A dance, sometimes, or a dinner party. We'd start out for a place like Scranton, or Fort Penn, in the morning. Have a very light lunch. Chicken sandwich or something on that order, and play our match in the afternoon. Take a cold shower—couldn't always get hot water when you turned on the hot water tap. Then dress and go to some party or other, and usually drive home the same night. Those distances don't seem very great now, but the roads in those days were a different proposition. Latham did you say your name was? No, it was Lathrop was the name of some people I knew then. They were Wilkes-Barre people. Before you were born. How old would you say I was?"

"I could never guess."

"Well, of course you know to some extent."

"Well, if you were twenty-two and out of college in 1916, before the first war. That's thirty-three years ago. You'd have to be fifty-five."

"You hit it right on the head. Fifty-five and play volleyball three times a week. Do you board in town or what?"

"I'm living at the YW."

"Well, if you'd like me to keep an eye out for an apartment, I sometimes hear of them, you know. It isn't my special line, but naturally I hear from time to time. It must get very boring for an attractive young girl, at the YW."

"Well, of course I've only been here less than a week. I only started Monday."

"That's true. You haven't met many people, I suppose."

"Not many."

"I'd like to see you get acquainted with some of the young people. I don't necessarily mean the country club crowd. I resigned there, a few years ago. I like a more active game than golf, and the people there—well, I used to go there and I'd know every single man, woman, and child, but there's a different crowd there now. It isn't what it used to be. Some of us'd rather go to one of the roadhouses, and of course I being a bachelor, I have a small but comfortable bachelor apartment where I do my own entertaining. More like New York than you usually find in a town this size. Nobody bothers me, you know. My little place is over a store that's closed at six o'clock and the people downstairs go home and I might as well be living a thousand miles away, unless I happen to want friends to drop in. What I mean to say is, a man does his work, and then he's entitled to his own private life."

"I agree with you."

"Good. You've been married, I suppose?"

"No."

"I suppose you're like me in that respect."

"What respect is that?"

"Well, I could never tie myself down to one girl. It wouldn't have been fair to the girl I married. For instance, if I were a married man now, I'd go home for dinner and all evening I'd be thinking of an attractive young lady that came and interviewed me."

"Well, I hope you're not going to forget me just because you're *not* married."

"Far from it. Anything but. In fact, I'd like to take you out to dinner this very evening, if you don't mind my terrible old car. I've made a trade on a new one and they're letting me keep this till the new one arrives. I'll sort of hate to part with it, but. . . ."

"Mr. Craymer, did you send this picture to the paper?"

"Did I send the picture? I never saw the damned thing before in all my life. What made you think that?"

"I had to ask you. I just had to ask you, that's all."

"God in heaven. Do you think a gentleman would do a thing like that? I never heard of such a thing in all my life. Why did you ask me that question?"

"I had to. It's been on my mind."

"But do you mean to say that after spending an hour in my company you still had to ask that question?"

"I had to ask you."

"Did someone put you up to it? Is that why? Someone at your office?"

"No, nobody put me up to it."

"I don't understand you, young woman."

The door opened and the elevator girl, dressed in her street clothes, appeared in the outer room. They looked at her and she at them. She said, "Oh," and went out again. Miss Latham stood up: "I didn't realize it was so late."

"I don't understand you," said Craymer. "Look at the picture. Look at it again. Study the kind of people that are my friends, that I grew up with. Then ask yourself, 'How could I ask that question?'"

"I'm sorry, Mr. Craymer. I realize it was a mistake."

"The greatest mistake of your life. My dear young woman— if you don't know people better than that, then you can't expect to get anywhere in writing. You have to know people to write about them. The great masters all knew human nature, and you've just been showing how *little* you know."

"I'll go now, Mr. Craymer," she said gently. "The elevator girl'll still be in your building."

"Oh, the hell with her," he said. "I want you before you go to give me your word of honor—you don't believe I sent that picture to the paper."

"I give you my word of honor. I don't believe you sent it."

"Thank you," he said. "If I thought anybody believed that of me—I wouldn't know *what* to do. All I've ever stood for, all I've ever tried to be. I'm fifty-five years old, and all my life I've believed there were some things you did do and some things you didn't."

"Mr. Craymer, why don't you take me to dinner?"

"You sure you want me to?"

"Quite sure," she said.

He took a deep breath. "Well, of course I will. But you've been very naughty. Very naughty. But I'll take you to dinner."

THE FAVOR

The young man and the girl came out of the fraternity house into the early evening. The young man's reversible was buttoned, all but the top button; he had been waiting for the girl. He slouched his hat on and put his hand under her arm. They had gone only a few steps when there was a rush of sound behind them: the door opening, letting out the voices and the music of the tea-dance. The young man did not look around nor did the girl, but she stopped, and another young man called to her: "Liz!"

"John, wait just one more second," she said to her escort.

"The hell I will," said John, but he stood beside her while the other young man spoke to her.

"I thought you were staying," said the newcomer.

"John wants to leave," said the girl.

The second young man addressed John: "What do you want to leave so early for? Come on, Benton. Come on back and enjoy life."

"I'll enjoy life my own way," said John.

"Liz was having a good time."

"Well, she happens to have a date with me, and we're going to New York."

"Well, will you change your mind if she changes hers? Does she have to go?"

"She doesn't *have* to *anything*, go to New York or go back to the tea dance. You seem to think all you have to do is *ask* her and she has to go back inside."

"Can't we go back for a half an hour?" said the girl. "There's no special time we have to get to New York."

"I knew you'd want to do this if we came to this party. That's why I didn't want to come in the first place."

"Then you shouldn't have said we'd come," said the girl.

"I can see that, all right," said John.

"Just for a half an hour? It won't make that much difference," said the girl. She smiled and the other young man grinned, as though they already had won their point.

"Go ahead. Nice to have seen you," said John. "I guess Lover Boy'll give you carfare." He started to walk away, and the other young man grabbed his left arm and spun him around, but he was expecting that and as he swung around he gained velocity so that his punch in the stomach knocked the other young man to the ground.

"Stop it!" said the girl. "Stop it, both of you! Joe, you go on back or I'll never see you again." The young man got up off the ground.

"I *heard* you were a brawler," said Joe. "Well, all right." He began to take off his coat.

"You heard what I said, and I mean it," said the girl. "If you two fight I'll never see either one of you again. Never as long as I live."

Each of the young men waited a few seconds for the other to make the first move and in that time the moment for the next blow passed.

"It's up to you, Liz," said Joe.

"Oh—if I go with you he'll start a fight, and if I go with him—"

"You *came* with me, but make your decision," said John.

She spoke to Joe: "I'm going to New York."

Joe spoke to John: "We'll meet up again sometime."

"I hope so," said John.

The other young man turned and walked back to the door, brushing off the dried mud and dead grass.

The girl led the way to the car, parked two blocks away in a private driveway. John had a hard time keeping near her side, what with her darting among the Saturday evening townsfolk on the sidewalks. It was plain to see that he was going to be made to suffer.

They got in the car. "Do you want the top up?" he said.

"No thanks," she said.

They drove through the city to the Parkway. The darkness and the cold made the drive seem like the beginning of another day; they had gone to the fraternity house directly from the game, while there was still daylight. And the whole unnecessary nastiness had originated in bright sunlight, between the halves, when they had gone out for a cup of coffee and a frankfurter. Now, on the Parkway, he remembered something he had noticed at the time, but that had seemed insignificant: as they were making their way around the Bowl she would look up at regular intervals, up and to her right, and at one point said, as though to herself: "Portal 16. I've walked far enough. You get the coffee and I'll wait here." In his naïveté he had attached no more importance to the mention of Portal 16 than that she had been measuring her weariness by portals. They had been up late the night before and she had even dropped off to sleep on the trip up from New York. He had turned to her then, when she did not answer a question, and had seen her asleep and small, and she must have felt him smiling on her and happily loving her, for she opened her eyes and smiled at him. That was in the morning. And then in the afternoon the same girl had kept a date at Portal 16, was chatting with this Joe fellow, when John brought her her coffee and frankfurter. The date could not have been made at any time during the day nor during the night before; therefore she had known that she was to meet Joe all that time.

Their speed was controlled by the Parkway traffic and during a slowdown he lit a cigarette. They were almost halfway to New York and they had not spoken. "You been seeing much of this Joe?"

"What did you say?"

"You don't expect me to believe you just saw this Joe fellow by accident?"

"I'm sure I don't know what I expect you to believe."

"Well, you're not going to try and tell me you've never been out with him."

"I never have tried, have I?"

"No, but I seem to recall an understanding that if one of us went out with somebody else we'd tell the other."

"I was going to tell you."

"When? Next year? Five years from now?"

"Hardly that," she said.

"Well, you have plenty of time to tell me now, and you haven't."

"I should think it'd be perfectly obvious that I've been out with him."

"It is now, but it wasn't last night or this morning. Portal 16."

"What about Portal 16?"

"That's where you made a date with him to meet him."

"All right. It was."

"Are you having an affair with him?"

"That I refuse to answer. It isn't so easy to have affairs with me, and you're one person that ought to know it."

"That's the trouble. Maybe I'm the one person that does know it. The only one."

"In that case the next town we come to, turn off and I'll take the train."

"Where to? Back to New Haven?"

"None of your business."

"But it *is* my business."

"There's a sign," she said. "We're coming to the Stamford road. Please turn off there and take me to the station."

"The answer is no."

"Then the next time we slow down I'll get out of the car."

"Don't you try it," he said.

Whatever she said next was lost in the shouts from a car that came within inches of scraping his fender. "Hi-yuh, Johnny! Hi-yuh Liz? Hey, there! See you at Larry's Bar and Grill! Wuddia say, boy!"

"Hi," said John.

The other car then sped forward and began weaving from lane to lane.

"Who was that?" said the girl.

"Medford and Kitty and Robbins and his girl."

"They're drunk."

"They must *be*," he said.

"Taking chances like that. And Meddy Medford was drunk at the game."

"I wish I'd been, then I wouldn't know what I know now. And you're a fine one to talk about taking chances."

"I wouldn't take a chance of killing somebody."

"No? What else are you doing? That's what you're doing with *my* life."

"Oh, don't be so dramatic. You always want to dramatize things. I'm sick of your jealousy every time I look at another man. We're not married. You don't own me."

"You don't have to say any more. I know we're through, but don't try any funny stuff like jumping out of the car. And don't be so sure that Joe guy'll greet you with open arms in case I did let you get out."

"I don't want to create a scene on the highway, but if I did go back to New Haven I'm sure I wouldn't be alone too long."

"Lover Boy. I know his type. Uh-uh." They were at the crest of a long hill and the traffic, now thinner, was slowing down, and at the bottom of the hill strong lights from a trouble car were trained on the approaching cars, compelling John to shield his eyes. As he came nearer the lights, the traffic became single-line, skirting a group consisting of two police cars, the trouble car, and an overturned convertible that was leaning against a tree. Beyond the group John could see the blinking lights of an ambulance headed in his direction.

"That looks like a bad one," he said. "It must have just happened. The ambulance just getting here."

Now they proceeded in second gear until they reached a patrolman who was waving cars on, and there John got a quick look at the smash-up. He stopped.

"Keep going, keep going, you," said the patrolman.

"Officer, I think they're friends of mine."

"Keep going, keep going, I said," said the patrolman.

"But those people are friends of mine."

"You can't do anything for them."

"The *four* of them?" said John.

"Three of them. One's still alive. If you want to stop go ahead past the wrecker and pull over on the grass. But get moving," said the patrolman.

They parked on the grass and John got out and approached a police corporal.

"Yeah? Wudda *you* want?" said the corporal.

"I know these people."

"Yeah? Lemme see your driver's license? That your car? Me see your owner's card."

John handed them over and the corporal wrote down the data, then handed the wallet back to John. "Did you see the accident?"

"No, I didn't. I just got here. The other officer said three of them were killed. Is that right?"

"Yep."

"Which one is alive?"

"If you can call what he is, alive, the driver. What do you wanta do? Go to the hospital with him?"

"Yes."

"What about the girl, in your car, I mean."

"I'll speak to her," said John. He walked to his car. "Meddy's still alive. I said I'd go to the hospital with him. I guess in the ambulance. The cop didn't say so, but I guess that's what I'll do. What do *you* want to do, Liz?"

"Whatever I can."

"Well—I'll be back in a minute. Have you got plenty of cigarettes?"

"I'll go with you," she said.

"No, you better not, sweetheart. I could see them, and I didn't know which was Meddy and which was Robbins, lying there. Will you be all right?"

"Yes," she said.

He looked at her. "I want to kiss you."

"I want you to," she said.

He pressed her hand. "I'll see you in a minute," he said.

"All right, John," she said.

He returned slowly to the wreck and took a position where Meddy, if he ever opened his eyes again, would see him. It was all he could do for Meddy, who had so oddly done so much for *him*.

THAT FIRST HUSBAND

Every year I promise myself that I am not going to do it again; but every year, on a Saturday morning in November, I get into my car and drive the eighty miles to my old college and have another look at the successes. But I have an idea that next year I will keep my promise to myself; this year, I think, was really my last.

We had breakfast at eight o'clock, and Emily insisted on doing the dishes so that they would not be sitting there when we got home. Emily will never leave anything for the cleaning woman if she can help it, and I have never been sure whether it is because she wants Mrs. Rohrbach to think of her as an efficient housewife or for fear that Mrs. Rohrbach will quit if asked to do more than her contractual chores. Probably a little of both, although I lean toward the second reason. Mrs. Rohrbach, I'm afraid, is almost the last woman left in town who will come to clean for us. We have had a parade of cleaning women in and out of our house.

Almost without exception they have been "jewels" through the first week, but Mrs. Rohrbach is the only one who has lasted more than a year, and the least demanding lapidarist would not appraise her very highly. In one remarkable instance the previous week's jewel did not even come back to collect her pay. However, she had not gone away empty-handed; she had worked for us six days, and exactly six bottles of a special bourbon that I got from a friend in Virginia were missing.

We always try to get to the club at about eleven o'clock, and an eight-thirty departure would allow us to make it without pushing. But this year we were unable to leave much before nine. I was sitting on the porch steps, gloves on, muffler in place under my old camel's-hair coat, and smoking a cigarette, when I heard Emily's voice from the second-story window. "Dutch?"

"Yes, dear?" I said.

"Would you mind terribly?"

"What?"

"Just a quick polish? My brogues?" she called down.

I went into the house and she tossed me her shoes from the second-story landing. "Good catch," she said.

"Nothing, really. Old Hill School end. Although I never had to catch two at a time."

"You never had to what, dear?"

I gave her shoes the quickest polish I knew how—a brisk rub with the brush was all they needed, or all we had time for, as it usually takes me a half hour to polish one pair of her shoes. I had a glass of water and another cigarette. "Dutch?"

"Yes?"

"They ready yet? Don't give them the full treatment. We haven't time."

"Just finishing," I said. I took the shoes out to the hall and handed them to Emily, who was sitting on one of the bottom steps. "They're beautiful," she said.

"And so are you, but let's get going now, shall we?"

I have made that trip so many times in the forty years that I have been going to games that I know old shortcuts that are once again main highways. Forty years, and a few to spare. My father took me to at least one game a year before I went to prep school. In school—where I was not a varsity regular—I missed a few years, but I saw nearly every game while I was in college.

And when I got out of college I sometimes sneaked off to see a baseball game as well as the practically compulsory big football game against Harvard or Yale. But my interest in football—not my partisanship, but my interest in the game itself—has taken quite a beating through the years, what with the changes that the rules committee seems to make every time it gets together. Consequently, I do not mind so much being late for the kickoff, but I don't like to miss those two hours at the club.

I have not made much of myself. I know that my judgeship came about through politics. My father had been on the bench, and I have no doubt that some of the votes that came my way were given to me by innocent people who thought they were voting for my father. Obviously I had been in no scandal that would give me a separate identity, but even if I had been, I almost believe that the party and the people would have given me the benefit of the doubt. My family have lived in the same county for two hundred years, and the Otterbein name must be in the county records a million times. Well, that may be a slight exaggeration, but only a slight one. When you think of it, a million times is only five thousand times a year, and in those two hundred years the family has produced lawyers, doctors, ministers, schoolteachers, bankers and even a couple of undertakers whose names would somehow get into the legal records of the county; and when you realize that in any given year there were likely to be four or five Otterbeins signing legal documents, a million may not be an exaggeration at all. And so, while I have no illusions about myself, I am quietly but thoroughly aware of the substantial contributions my people have made to one small section of the United States. The rascals in our family history have been enormously outnumbered, and they have been punished, sometimes by the family itself. I therefore take no guff from anyone, as we say at home; never have, never will.

Close after my feeling for my family and my county comes my attachment for my alma mater, and specifically to the club

It is a college club, but it has always resisted, usually with success, any kind of interference by the college administrations. We own our clubhouse and the land on which it is built, and we are a separate corporation. There have been several attempts to abolish the club and the others that resemble it, but when that has occurred the college administration and faculty are once again reminded that the alumni members are vigilant and loyal and that the feeling for the club endures long after graduation. A member of The Orchard considers himself a member from the time he first shakes hands to the moment when there is no longer life in his fingers. And, incidentally, we have no secret grip. We have a necktie, a hatband and a watch charm, but our ritual is Robert's Rules of Order, and we have no connection with the Greek-letter fraternity whose members founded The Orchard. Our principal secret is that of any club—the discussions and the vote that decide who shall be invited to join. It is interesting to note that in almost every year of our existence the college as a whole has been able to guess accurately the names of the ten or fifteen men who will be invited. We have standards, and they are known: a good family background, a good prep school, a clear complexion, acceptable behavior when drunk, a responsible attitude toward the educational purpose of the college, and the subtlest one of all—a belief that a man who is being considered for an invitation will not, in college or later life, trade on his membership in The Orchard. We have made many mistakes. We have missed out on men who turned out well; we have taken in men who turned out badly. But one of the reasons why I always try to get to the club before the game is that the mistakes who persist in showing up are so much in the minority. The good men predominate, as I suppose they do in other clubs, and our standards are upheld in the superior court of adult life.

On the trip, to what may have been my last football game, we had good luck in the weather; it was bright, clear and crisp. A sell-out and a full attendance were assured, although the one

is not always followed by the other. At one point on the road I
had taken, the cars from the south joined the procession, and a
little later the cars from the north. My own car is inconspicuous
to the point of anonymity, but sometimes our line would be
halted while the adjoining line proceeded past us, and since all
progress was rather slow, we recognized, and were recognized
by, people whom we passed or who were passing us. "Hello,
Dutch . . . Hello, Emily," they would cry. "See you at the club?"
Almost invariably the other cars contained foursomes, but I am
the only living alumnus of my college in our town, and no one
from our town ever went to Yale. The exchange of greetings
with the friends in the other cars had its usual effect, which was
to put Emily and me in the holiday mood while still twice as far
away as Sheridan in Thomas Buchanan Read's famous poem.
Twenty miles away, ten miles away, we would see some friends
and wave to them, and before we had finished chatting about
them there would be another foursome. But about a mile or two
from our destination a large black limousine, and not a hired
one, moved slowly past us, and as I saw the occupants I quickly
looked at Emily to see if she had recognized them too. She had.

"Well, I suppose he has as much right to come to the game
as I have," I said.

"Since when?" she said.

"Well, he's an alumnus, and I'm sure he pays his alumni
dues and all that sort of thing. Anyway, we won't have to see
him. There'll be forty thousand people there today, and he won't
be sitting with our class."

"Thank heaven," she said. "Did you notice who was with
him?"

"No, I was so surprised at seeing him."

"I did. Charley Stockwell."

"Charley Stockwell? With Bob Stone?"

"It was Charley's car. I saw the initials on the door."

"Oh, my."

"Yes; oh, my. The same thing you're thinking. Will Charley bring him to the club?"

"Oh, Charley wouldn't do that."

"Wanta bet?"

Bob Stone, the man whom we were surprised to see, was Emily's first husband, and the twenty-five years since their divorce vanished at the sight of him. All the nastiness was as real again as it had been then. I reached over and pressed her hand, and she returned the pressure. "Let's hope for the best," she said.

"And even the worst—what would that be? We'd have to speak to him, but we don't have to spend any time with him."

There was room to park my old, small car back of the clubhouse, and we made our way up the driveway, through the front door, across the downstairs hall and upstairs to the bar, shaking hands and greeting friends at every step. But Stone was on our minds. "I haven't seen him so far, have you?" she said.

"No, but I have bad news for you. I saw Charley Stockwell downstairs. He didn't see me. Bob's here, you can be sure of that."

In less than five seconds there was a tap on my shoulder. "Hello, Dutch . . . Hello, Emily. How is the former Mrs. Stone?"

I used my cigarette and drink as an excuse to avoid shaking hands. "Hello, Bob," I said, and no more.

"How is the former Mrs. Stone?" he repeated.

"Oh, you meant me?"

"Well, who else could I have meant?"

"Oh, What's-Her-Name? Your second wife."

"She was hardly Mrs. Stone long enough to get used to the name."

"Then I hope she's been able to forget it as completely as I have."

He laughed. "I ought to know better than to tangle with you," he said. . . . . "Dutch, you surprised to see me here?"

"Why should I be?"

"Well, you were the one that kept me out, a hundred years ago. I'm not guessing any more. I have it official."

"Actually I never denied it when you accused me of it. The old rule used to be that you neither confirmed nor denied that. I still adhere to that rule."

"Maybe you do, but some of your clubmates don't."

"Bob, I get paid for listening to lawyers playing tricks with questions. It can be entertaining, but it can also get tiresome. You get nothing out of me."

"Hell, I'm not trying to get anything out of you. The whole thing was kid stuff, and I haven't thought about it in years. I think I've done all right without an Orchard tie."

"I'm glad to hear it."

"I hope you mean that, because I'd like to be friends with you. I can hardly pick up the paper without reading about somebody I know keeling over."

"This would be a good time for us to leave," said Emily.

"Why, Emily? I don't hold any grudge against either one of you. Listen, I stayed away from this place for years because I hated everything about it. Then one day I realized I didn't hate it at all. I was over all that kid stuff. I came here today in the hopes of seeing you, both of you."

"Dutch, let's go away, I can't listen to this. It really turns my stomach."

"Bob, you'll have to excuse us," I said. "Or why don't you go find Charley Stockwell?"

"How do you know I'm with him?"

"I couldn't tell you that; that's one of the club secrets."

"Considering that I came looking for you to invite you to—"

"I don't want to hear any invitation you've dreamed up," said Emily, half turning her back.

"Listen, if you don't think I mean it. My plane is up at the Newark Airport. I wanted you to have dinner with me and I'd have you flown back, or you could spend the night."

"Wait a second, Emily . . . Have dinner with you where?"

"At home. Bloomfield Hills."

"Michigan?"

"Of course."

"Well, there's a Bloomfield in New Jersey too."

"Bloomfield Hills. You could have dinner at my house, and my guy could fly you back to Newark or some field near where you live. If the field is big enough. If not, I could have one of my company cars meet you at Newark and drive you back here, or drive you all the way home. Those details, they're nothing."

"But they're not nothing. I want to hear them all."

"Why?"

"Well, I do. Could you have somebody drive my old jalopy home and have a limousine meet us at Newark?"

"I can do all that. That's nothing."

"What if we spent the night out at your place? We didn't bring anything, not even toothbrushes."

"Are you kidding? I have dinner jackets, shoes, shirts, underwear to fit anybody from a skinny little guy to a two-hundred-and-fifty-pounder. If you want to play golf, any size golf shoes from seven to fourteen-quadruple-E."

"What about Emily?"

"Well, I don't have evening gowns, but skirts and sweaters and shoes."

"Do you serve breakfast in bed?"

"In bed—or on the roof if you like it. And I have a twenty-four-hour staff, don't forget that."

"Horses? What kind of horses?"

"I only have three now. Just ordinary hacks, I suppose you'd call them."

"I was just thinking. A ride first thing in the morning. You have boots and breeches to fit us?"

"Probably smell of camphor, but they could be aired out tonight."

"Fine. We could go for a ride, then come back and have a swim in the pool?"

"The indoor pool, heated this time of year."

"And one of those big, English-country-house breakfasts."

"Be a good idea to have Karl give you a massage if you haven't been doing any riding lately."

"Probably be a good idea. We could be flown back tomorrow afternoon?"

"Stay over till Monday if you like. I have to be in New York on Monday morning. We could all fly back together."

"Dutch, you're asking for trouble. I know this man," said Emily. In the noisy club I could hear her, but Stone could not.

"What did you say, Emily? Am I winning you over?" said Stone, smiling.

"You did that so beautifully once before," she said.

"What?" said Stone.

"I think we'd better say no," said Emily. "Definitely no."

"Oh, you're a spoilsport, Emily," I said.

"She is, you know," said Stone.

"She really is," I said. "I was having such a good time, listening to you running off at the mouth. You stupid slob, do you think for one minute—"

I did not complete my question. He weighed twenty pounds more than I and he was a powerfully built man in good condition. He hit me with an uppercut, and as I was going down he caught me with a left-hand punch that I barely felt. I could not have been asleep very long, but long enough to be taken to an undergraduate's room and laid out on the bed. I opened my eyes and saw my wife.

"You dog," said Emily. "You asked for it."

"That's all the consolation I get from you?"

"You get no consolation from me at all. Why didn't you stop when I told you to?"

"I'll tell you sometime."

"Tell me now. But I think I know."

"All right. Tell me."

"Some misplaced romantic idea of yours. You wanted me to listen to all the things I've missed. Was that it?"

"Not quite. I wanted to hear it all, so that I'd know what you've missed. So that I'll never for one minute forget it."

"That's so much better, you dog." She suddenly began to cry, and she held my poor sore head to her bosom.

We waited until the crowd had left for the stadium, and then we went down and got the car. Emily took the wheel. "I'm going to get a sharp letter from the club trustees. There's a very strict rule against fighting," I said.

"Then I ought to get the letter. I slapped his face good and hard. Been waiting for years!"

About the Author

Son of a doctor and the eldest of eight children, John O'Hara was born in Pottsville, Pennsylvania, January 31, 1905; he died at his home in Princeton, New Jersey, on April 11, 1970.

After graduation from Niagara Prep School, he worked at a great variety of jobs. His career as a reporter was also varied. He worked first for two Pennsylvania papers and then for three in New York, where he covered everything from sports to religion. He also was on the staff of *Newsweek* and *Time,* and, over the years, wrote columns for *Collier's,* the Trenton *Times-Advertiser, Newsday* and *Holiday.*

His first novel was *Appointment in Samarra,* published in 1934, and with its appearance he became, and continued to be throughout his life, a major figure on the American literary scene. He published seventeen novels and eleven volumes of short stories, in addition to plays, essays and sketches, many of which he never got around to collecting for books. Because of his pro-digious energy and productivity, he left behind a considerable body of finished work not yet published in any form.

His novel *Ten North Frederick* (1955) received the National Book Award for 1956, and in 1964 the American Academy of Arts and Letters presented to him the Gold Medal Award of Merit.

DATE DUE

PRINTED IN U.S.A.